A KISS GOODBYE

To Robert Carr, Anna is a mystery and that's the way he'd like her to stay. Over the past thirteen years his last, parting image of Anna, kissing her goodbye before she turned to leave, has been the inspiration for a number of his paintings. Through his work, Anna's face has become famous, whilst the woman herself disappeared long ago. Now a TV documentary has launched a nationwide search for the elusive muse. When she is found, her discovery results in a creative block for Robert – but has far more deadly consequences for Anna herself.

A KISS GOODBYE

A KISS GOODBYE

by

Jane Adams

Magna Large Print Books
Long Preston, North Yorkshire,
BD23 4ND, England.

British Library Cataloguing in Publication Data.

Adams, Jane
    A kiss goodbye.

    A catalogue record of this book is
    available from the British Library

    ISBN   0-7505-2540-1

First published in Great Britain in 2005 by Allison & Busby Ltd.

Copyright © 2005 by Jane Adams

Cover illustration © The Old Tin Dog by arrangement with
Allison & Busby Ltd.

The moral right of the author has been asserted

Published in Large Print 2006 by arrangement with
Allison & Busby Ltd.

Magna Large Print is an imprint of Library Magna Books Ltd.

Printed and bound in Great Britain by
T.J. (International) Ltd., Cornwall, PL28 8RW

Chapter One

Dreamtime, he was always kissing Anna goodbye.

It was never a kiss of welcome, or even between lovers. Not, he remembered irritably, that they had ever been lovers.

No. Always, it was the soft and rather melancholy touch of a kiss goodbye.

In his dream, she would close her eyes; as though about to welcome more than the casual touch of mouths. Then, as she drew back from him, he would see her lips part slightly, the corners upturned in the well-remembered way that seemed unique to Anna. And she would laugh. Warm, easy laughter, which bound him, making him co-conspirator in some joke that he never could quite fathom.

The laughter would reach her eyes. Creasing the corners in a way so many of his women friends seemed never to allow and her eyes would shine, bright with mischief.

He had thought once, 'there's madness in those eyes'. A misty grey kind of madness that made him want to jump on any bandwagon she happened to be driving, see what living was like from the inside.

Then, of course, in his dream, she would walk away from him. Hunching her shoulders against the chill, hands thrust deep into her pockets, just as she had in the waking world. He would drag himself from sleep to find his face slicked with sweat and the salt wetness of tears.

Afterwards, there would be a complete day of disorientation. He would be unable to work, to eat, to concentrate. Would refuse to speak to anyone or attend appointments, or even to return calls.

Then. Then the ... mania. Days, perhaps, if he was very lucky, weeks of intense, creative effort. His best work had been done at these times, work so full of vibrant life that the images seemed ready to draw breath. Even the more bizarre and abstract of his creations seemed to blaze with the promise of it.

His studio was filled with images of Anna. Sketches, drawings, paintings wrought in all dimensions; the finest, most delicate of miniatures to full, life size visions. There was even an Icon. Anna, heavy with gold; hand ground tempera worked on the finest traditional gesso. The support was poplar imported at ridiculous expense from Lombardy. Good publicity, that had been, for him and for Lombardy. He now received regular, and not inconsiderable 'consultation fees' from the Italian tourist bureau.

Then, of course, there had been the books, dealing with this 'Romantic Obsession'. Payments too for the endless stream of reproductions of the latest 'Robert'.

As a matter of principle, Robert never refused to have his work reproduced; wherever, whenever. He scattered Anna's images like so many 'wanted' posters, across the unsuspecting walls of suburbia; the exclusive galleries; even advertising hoardings. Anywhere and everywhere that space – and payment – could be found.

He had done well from his melancholy dreams of Anna. Very well indeed, but now the problems had begun, with a television documentary, provisionally entitled 'The Search For Anna'. It sounded like a very good thing to be a part of.

Or rather, it had.

The problem was, some bright spark of an investigative reporter had been called upon to try and find the 'real' Anna so they could produce her 'This is Your Life' style at the end of the show. Robert had found out about this by accident. His agent had been approached. The journalist professed himself mystified. He had found nothing. Time was running out and his professional reputation was on the line.

Robert's agent, one eye on the need to keep the media sweet, the other on the need to protect the rather curious sensibilities of his biggest money spinner, had called Robert and attempted, discreetly, to extract the relevant information.

'Why do you want to know?' Robert had asked when his agent, Simon Roper, had called.

'Aren't you ever curious, Rob? I mean this girl obviously meant a great deal to you. Don't you want to know what happened to her?'

'No.'

'Oh.'

The agent considered for a moment, and then said. 'Not even a little bit?'

'No.'

'Oh,' he said again.

'So,' Robert asked, 'what's the angle. You didn't even know Anna.'

'Well, media interest and all that. Rob, you've never been one not to welcome a little extra publicity. There are a lot of people out there very much interested to know about the real Anna. You know how it is, Rob.' This last was said in his best 'I'm-only-representing-your-best-interests' wheedle.

'No.' Impatiently, Robert broke the connection, and sat back to ponder the odd mixture of emotions that the conversation had provoked.

The truth was, he had absolutely no wish to 'find' Anna. Even if that were possible. His image of Anna, that idiosyncratic, fragmented pattern which held such sway over his world of dreams; that was the one that mattered, the image which inspired him. That, and the emotions derived from her gentle, unconsidered rejection of him. She had turned and walked away, pulling her coat collar higher against the cold, dirt laden wind of the city street.

For him, that was Anna. Those few recurring moments of intense living; intense feeling. Of sorrowful, dusty, breaths of self pity. He could – did – spend all of his time deriving creative, life-giving, profit-making, satisfaction from those moments so possessively treasured.

To think of Anna as she might be now. Well. It was unthinkable.

His mirror showed him the changes which the years had carved into his own features, and he had lived well. Been careful to maintain the patina of youthfulness. Or at least as much of it as could be purchased easily.

Anna had always been so careless of such things.

For a brief time, he played with the notion of Anna, accepting of the cosmetician's scalpel. Having creases eased from around her eyes; buttocks lifted; implants, to supplement and firm a sagging bosom. He imagined the knife slicing into flesh that he had, in fact, never seen. Sculpting it into something that, while it might well be attractive in its plasticity, would nevertheless not be the Anna he remembered.

He pushed the images away. Then, suddenly irresolute, pried into his mental cinema for more of the same.

Maybe he should go back to working in three dimensions?

He had, briefly, made an insignificant foray into this area. And returned, swiftly, to more familiar ground.

However. The images in his mind of the redesigned Anna, might they be usable? He stepped back; laughed. No. Not Anna. Better to keep to what he knew. There were still so many images, so many thoughts as yet unexplored.

Suddenly, desperately, he felt compelled to start work. The creative urging that usually only followed his dreams of Anna, hitting with total and unexpected force.

There was a half-finished canvas set in readiness. Anna, reclining on a bed, gazing out of the window onto a Matisse-like landscape, almost incoherent in its expressiveness. The female figure was more finely, naturalistically, realised. The flesh, cold toned, picking up the blueness of the walls and bed covers. The coverlet was boldly painted in great strokes of colour that seemed to drip wetly onto a stone floor. He knew that it was beautiful. The strange, jarring mix of styles, one of Robert's trademarks, should, by rights, have an unsettling effect on the viewer. But it did not. Robert was convinced of its effectiveness. It was almost as if his assurance communicated itself to the viewer, evoked an unlooked for but sympathetic response.

Well, it sold, didn't it?

He continued to work, wet into wet, further modelling the flesh into voluptuous roundness. He stepped back; bemused. He had not realised how deeply the thoughts of Anna's physical remodelling had infiltrated. It would, he realised, have to be scraped back and reworked. Not that the effect was displeasing; simply that it was at odds with the more modest proportions of his other nudes.

One must be consistent. Self-expression had become myth-making. Anna's image had to be kept within certain parameters.

The light was fading. He turned on the daylight floods, dimmed them slightly, and began patiently to rework the passage just created.

The phone rang again. Robert glanced at the clock. An hour exactly since his agent had last rung. He reached out, switched on the answer phone; switching off the ringer.

He knew that he would work late that night.

Chapter Two

Morning woke him with the impatient hammering and shouting of his agent at Robert's door and the buzzing of the bell. Reluctantly, he scraped himself out of bed and made his way down through the studio. There was no let up in the level of noise. Dogs barked and a neighbour thrust his head from a nearby window to protest.

'Don't you know what day it is? Some of us have to work all week.'

Robert tugged at the door, stood aside, slammed it closed again and leaned wearily upon it.

'This had better be good.'

'Oh! It is! Or rather it isn't. Look, just wait till we get inside, properly inside.'

'Simon!'

The man had already headed up the stairs. Robert followed. Grumbling.

'Nice. Very nice.' Simon was admiring the unfinished canvas.

Robert followed his gaze, frowned in annoyance at a shadow not crisply enough defined, a slight lack of balance in the tone. Still frowning, he crossed to the painting, began to squeeze paint onto an already overloaded palette, glaze lightly over the still wet colour.

Simon was talking to him or rather, at him. Robert turned as the voice became noticeably louder.

'Sorry. Did you say something?'

Simon stared in complete exasperation.

'I said. Have you seen the Sunday papers?'

It took a moment to sink in. Then, impatiently, 'You know damn well I haven't. You were the one got me out of bed.'

'Well look at them now.'

Robert looked. Headlines, screamed.

'WHERE IS ANNA?'

'ANNA: MYTH OR MYSTERY.'

'DISAPPEARENCE OF A LEGEND.'

Even, 'SEX SYMBOL TAKES VOWS!' claiming that the mysterious Anna had become a nun.

Robert read this one with more than cursory amusement. Then he shrugged, threw the paper down and returned to his painting.

'Now hold on a minute,' Simon ordered. 'I've saved the best till last.' He still clutched one paper in an increasingly print blackened hand.

Sighing, Robert took it, then sat down and began to read properly.

'MURDERED MODEL' read the uncompromising headline. Robert read, laughed in disbelief, and then read again the claims that the reason Anna had so effectively disappeared was that she was dead. There was even a veiled hint that the perpetrator might be Robert himself.

Simon had been making coffee in Robert's cluttered kitchen.

'Don't you ever tidy up in here? Well. What do you think to it?'

Suspicion flared immediately. 'You? Don't mean to tell me you put them up to this?'

'Would I?'

Robert was out of his chair and across the room. Simon retreated hastily. 'Now hold on a minute, Rob. Don't be daft. No, I didn't put anyone up to anything. Fact is, you've got only yourself to blame. If you'd climbed down out of your ivory tower for just long enough to give me the information I'd asked for, we could have told them that Anna was a housewife in Wapping or an international jewel thief and they'd soon have lost interest. It's the mystery that gets to them. When they have the truth you can't trust them to get it right. Leave the media to speculate and well...' He waved an almost negligent hand at the offending papers.

'The best move now, before you have whole fleets of these people trampling down your neighbours' flowerbeds, is to come clean. Tell the real story. No. Don't start to protest, just hear me out. We could turn this whole thing around, make it into the best publicity yet. Now, I've spoken to that

16

Sunday supplement we worked with before. You know, the one that did the piece on the Veresi auction. Very up market. Very, very good price they're prepared to pay for an exclusive.'

He finally paused for breath, aware that Robert had been trying to say something.

Robert cut in. 'I don't know where she is. I've told you time and again, I've never known. Now get out and let me work.'

For a moment, Simon was silenced. Then he persisted. 'Now come on, Rob. I know what you've always said, but you must know. A woman who inspired you this much.' He gestured, waving hands indicating the entire studio. Images of Anna everywhere. 'You can't tell me you don't know. I don't believe it.'

'Believe what you like. I don't know.'

Simon gazed at the man. Then snapped his mouth closed and glared. He tried again. 'But why, Rob? Why don't you know? You don't lose touch with someone as close as you must have been to Anna.'

Robert sighed. How could he explain to this idiot of a man? 'Simon. That's the whole point. Anna was a possibility. A ... an incident. We didn't have a relationship. I liked her, but I hardly knew her. There might have been more but there wasn't. She went away, walked off down the road and never looked back. That was the last I saw of her, Simon,

17

and that was twelve, no, nearly thirteen years ago. Dammit Simon! She wouldn't even pose for me. These pictures, the portraits, the nudes, they're done from memory, from what I thought she might be like. I never even saw her in a swimsuit, never mind naked. That's just it. She was a mystery to me, an enigma. That's all she ever was.'

Simon was gazing at him again in renewed disbelief. Then, his face relaxed, the smile returned. 'Even better. A romantic dream never realised. Unrequited passion. We could take that line, Rob, real tear-jerking stuff.'

'It's been done already,' Robert said dryly. 'Don't you remember that garbage bag of a book, *A Romantic Obsession*, that you persuaded me to lend my name to?'

He rose. Crossed once more to the painting. 'Now, get out of here and let me get on with what I'm good at. I don't want to know where Anna is. I don't want to see whatever it is she's turned into. Now. Get lost.'

Simon wasn't about to be beaten, but he knew Robert well enough to understand that it was time to back off. 'OK. OK. We'll talk later. But we will talk, Rob. You think the media will let go of this one in a hurry you're very much mistaken.'

Robert turned. Pointed towards the door. Simon left.

Chapter Three

For several minutes Sergeant Clyde had watched the young woman. He could see her clearly through the heavy glass doors, clearly enough to see the anxious look – not her face, the opposite pavement was a tad too far away for that; more her general demeanour. She wore a bright red raincoat, belted tightly around a very slender waist, and the stiff breeze blew her dark hair around her face. Twice, she had reached to pull a hank of it back from her eyes, holding it away for a moment, as though teaching it where it should be and hoping it would take notice. In her other hand, she clutched a newspaper.

His first thought had been that she was waiting for someone. His second, following a few minutes' observation, was that she wanted to come in to the police station, but was scared or wary or simply too embarrassed to try. None of these were alien emotions to the desk sergeant. He'd seen them all in varied measures and, it being a quiet afternoon, he occupied himself in wondering whether need would win out over any or all of these.

And then she moved.

'Ah,' he said, 'ah that's right, you come on over.' He'd figured she would, sooner or later. She'd stood there just too long for walking away to be a decision lightly made. Now that she'd made up her mind, she seemed in something of a hurry about it and Clyde frowned at the swiftness and carelessness of her glance before she crossed the road at a practical run.

She paused again before climbing the three steps, her pace slower and, now that she was closer, he could see that the anxious look on her rather pretty face matched that of her earlier stance.

She was older than he'd first thought; not the girl of twenty or so, but a woman perhaps ten years older than that. And there was something familiar about her, as though he'd met her or observed her before, though for the life of him he couldn't place when.

Pushing through the heavy doors she met his gaze and a tiny, nervous smile flicked the corners of her mouth, then widened more emphatically as Clyde put on his friendly face and tweaked a grin in return.

'Can I help you?' He noted that she'd clutched the paper so hard and for so long that the newsprint smeared her hand. It was, he saw, as she lay it on the counter, one of the Sundays, and so already three days old.

'This is me,' she said, indicating an article

on the front page. Clyde recalled seeing it on the newsstand, though this wasn't his Sunday paper. He was vaguely surprised that a woman like this would be reading one of the more garish and gore-ridden tabloids.

He looked more closely at the passage she had indicated. 'Dead Model?' it read and followed with the speculation that the famous Anna, Robert Carr's one and only model, might actually be the late Anna and that Robert might be the one responsible for her being that way.

'I didn't want him to get into trouble,' she said. 'Look, it's such a stupid thing to accuse him of...' She trailed off and Clyde was aware that he had been staring at her. He could see it now, the likeness. It existed in that fleeting smile, in the expression of the eyes, the shape of the nose and chin, though this Anna, in motion and living and standing right in front of him, was both more and less than her painted likeness.

A part of him wanted to be suspicious, to say, quite rightly, that she was the third they'd had that week, but after staring at her a little longer he decided not to bother. He could have passed this Anna or rather, this version of Anna in the street and given her only the kind of second glance any man might give an attractive woman. It was, he thought, as though Robert Carr had captured an essence of Anna in his work. An

21

essence that had also grown beyond the original; that almost eclipsed her.

Clyde cleared his throat self-consciously, aware that these were not thoughts for a Wednesday afternoon desk sergeant to be indulging in. 'I think you'd better take a seat,' he said. 'I'll call someone through to talk to you.'

Chapter Four

'She's the real thing, Rob,' Simon told him. 'I've talked to her and she checks out. Anna Freeman. Who'd have thought it after all this bloody hoo ha?'

Rob said nothing. He didn't know what to say. His silence echoed down the phone line, echoing so loudly that finally he had to speak just to break the tension of it.

'You're telling me she just walked into a police station and announced herself?'

'That's right. Two thirty this afternoon. She'd seen those stupid accusations in the paper on Sunday and finally decided she ought to do something about it.'

'She took her time,' Rob grumbled.

'Yes, well, that may be, but she did it and that's the main thing. I'm persuading her that she'll appear on the TV thing.'

'Persuading her. You mean she's not keen.'

'Well, no. No happier than you are about her being there, but that's hardly the point is it, Rob?' He paused. 'It's funny, you know, seeing the real thing.'

'How does she look?' Rob hadn't intended to ask, but the words slipped past his guard.

Simon hesitated and Rob felt his stomach tighten in anticipation of the worst.

'Fragile,' Simon said at last and Rob realised he'd merely been searching for an appropriate word. Relief relaxed his muscles, then they tightened again as he asked, 'What do you mean by fragile. Is she ill or something?' His imagination immediately crashed into overdrive. Anna, sick, in pain, that sickness and pain reflected in her face, dimming those mocking, dancing eyes and obliterating that wondrous smile.

'No, she's not ill,' Simon told him impatiently. 'Rob, it's just...' he paused again and Rob could almost feel him flicking through his internal thesaurus. 'I'm used to the images you've created. That Anna seems so ... robust. So indestructible. Meeting her in the flesh ... it's like meeting someone off the television and suddenly realising they're much smaller than you expected.'

'She is small,' Rob said. Then again, wondering, 'actually, she's tiny. I'm not a tall man, but she had to stand on tiptoe to kiss me...' He trailed off, remembering that kiss, recalling it with an intensity that took his breath away. All these years he had told himself that the incident, Anna leaving, had been written so indelibly and with such clarity upon his memory that he had stripped it of all further potential. Now, in this instant, he recognised that this was not the case. He had forgotten – how could he have forgotten? – just how small and slightly built Anna had been. Had lost too, until now, the scent of her as her dark brown curls blew across his cheek and left a trace of her perfume. And the warm breath upon his cheek as she had whispered to him 'You take care now'. They were Anna's normal parting words, though now they took upon themselves a new and haunting significance.

Rob glanced around his studio, gaze falling upon the almost finished canvas on the easel and the varied works in progress pinned to walls and strewn across the central table, and he knew he had to use that rediscovered memory, pin the truth of it down before it had a chance to fly away.

'You take care now,' he said before putting down the phone, unconsciously mimicking Anna's final words. Dimly, he heard Simon's voice calling to him as he put the receiver down, failing totally to replace it on its cradle. He had to work on this, work on it now.

He cast the part finished work aside with barely a care for where it landed and snatched a large pad from the map drawers that lined the walls and housed his materials and finished work. He set a board on the easel to support it and began to draw, sketch after sketch, rapidly defined and as rapidly thrown away until, finally, he had it. A second figure in his picture, something in all the years of painting that Rob had always refused to do. But he drew him now, tall and dark and shadowed and ill defined, the charcoal rubbing across the surface as his sleeve caught it and smudging the already sketchy features of the face. Anna beside him, smaller and more fragile than he had ever drawn her, reaching up to kiss his cheek in his first attempt was, by his final drawing, in the act of turning away.

In his mind's eye he could see the finished piece. Larger than the A1 pad he was using now, twice, three times the size and the figures taking only a third of that. The rest would be the street, the wind would be blowing and the figures moving with the wind like the lovers in a Chagall – though the colours would be more muted. The viewer would sense the kiss, rather than see it, Robert decided. It would be there in the memory. In the gesture of the man, leaning slightly forward as though to recapture that moment before it was gone forever. The woman turning from him, hand almost touching as she turned, but her eyes fixed upon the distance, looking past the viewer, out to ... where?

Rob paused in his frenzy and it occurred to him that if he wasn't careful, this could be viewed as an overly sentimental work and also, more importantly, that he had no idea what Anna would be looking for in that far distance or what the Anna that had left him so long ago might already have seen.

Chapter Five

Despite his pleas, Simon had made certain Rob did not see Anna before the night of the television show. Some of it had been shot already: the background, the retrospective covering of Robert Carr's career so far and interviewing the great and the good – and a few close friends Robert hadn't seen for years. The second half of the show was technically unscripted. A free ranging interview with Critic and Television doyenne Edith Parks, though the questions had been previously screened so there were no nasty surprises. And then, the revealing of Anna, who had reluctantly agreed to a five-minute stint at the very end. Both Simon and the television producers wanted to keep this as fresh as possible. They wanted Rob's reaction to meeting his muse and amanuensis in the flesh after all these years.

Frankly, it was the portion Robert was dreading.

He had started work on A Kiss Goodbye, working on the background and broad details of the composition. Even dealing with the representation of the male figure – imbuing it, he felt, with a sense of longing that by turns pleased and appalled him. It was Anna that caused him problems. Ironically, after all these years of painting little else, Rob could no longer see her clearly enough to make the image work. Try as he might, he could not visualise her face. Those scant details supplied by Simon had overlaid the certainty which had previously possessed him and he felt weakened by it. Felt his strength and conviction and ability to convey the truth of what he felt ebbing away from him, draining out through his hands, his brush, his knife every time he attempted to lay paint on canvas.

Vainly, he had tried to convince Simon to let him meet Anna before the night the TV show went out. He had pleaded and cajoled and threatened to all of which Simon made the same reply.

'God's sake, Rob, you were the one so against ever seeing the woman again. Now you're the one making the fuss. You'll be seeing her in a few days so cool down and go

27

back to work.'

That was the problem, Robert had tried to tell him. I can't work, can't sleep, can't eat, don't know what to do with myself. Out loud he had tried to be calm, but he could feel the incipient depression pressing down upon him like a pallet load of chiselled stone, squashing his psyche in that familiar and oh so terrifying way. Finally, even Simon had realised that something was wrong.

'See your doctor,' he advised. 'Go back on the pills.'

Simple as that so far as Simon was concerned. It was two years since Rob had suffered his last bad bout of depression, initiated that time by a viral infection, of all things, which laid him up for almost three weeks. Three weeks of idleness. Of enduring that insistent and confusing inner dialogue that could be quieted only by the unceasing and fanatical push to work. It had taken months before Rob had finally come back to himself.

Two days before the television show, Rob had given in and the doctor, with a reprimand for not coming sooner, had duly prescribed.

Waiting for little white pills to begin to work, Rob self-medicated with whisky and herbal stuff an old girlfriend had left behind – something she used for her PMT, he recalled.

'You're drunk,' Simon accused. 'I thought you'd been to see your GP.'

'I did, he prescribed my happy pills.'

'And should you be taking them with alcohol?' Simon hissed.

Rob shrugged. The producer was heading in their direction. He watched, distracted, as Simon fixed his most professional smile into place and made the introductions.

Rob barely took it in. The female producer was tall and blond and dressed in pinstripe trousers that looked like part of a suit. Her shirt was a bright, fuchsia pink and Rob wanted to tell her that someone with her colouring really didn't go with it. So preoccupied was he by the colour that he found he had shaken her hand and been steered into one of two upholstered chairs on the studio floor, without even registering her name.

He glanced around to see where Simon had gone; spotted him, standing behind the cameras, well out of shot, grinning manically and giving Rob an elaborate thumbs up. Someone began the countdown and Rob barely had time to notice the woman sitting in the other chair before he was on, replying automatically to the questions he dimly remembered from the crib sheet he'd been given and conscious enough, through the soft alcoholic haze, to wonder if he was actually making any sense with his responses.

Edith Parks, magisterial and authoritative, was not, he knew, a worshipper in the cult of Robert.

They stumbled through awkward minutes until: 'Surely,' she was asking him, 'it is the duty of an artist to explore the full range of emotional and cultural responses. It could be argued that your obsession with a single subject prevents your own growth and development. Isn't there a danger that you might grind to a halt, as it were?'

That was more than one question, Robert thought. Not fair. He screwed up his forehead in thought and tried to make sense of at least a part of it, fixed on something about growth as an artist and plunged in. 'Many artists paint themically,' he argued, aware that he sounded rather plaintive but somehow unable to change tone. 'You don't criticise Hockney for his Splash sequence.' Actually, he recalled, he sort of remembered that she had. 'And no one would be churlish enough to have told Chagall that he should stop painting his wife. And Degas' obsession with underage dancers never...' he trailed off, sensing a slight stiffening in his host's rather pointy knees. 'Not that they were all underage, of course, or that the ... social mores were the same then. The opera dancers were recruited as children... Anyway, through the medium of Anna...' yes, he liked that, that would do, '...through the medium of Anna, I have been able to approach the widest range of emotional and cultural responses...' That was it. Echo her words. Can't go far wrong if you throw their own phrases back at them. 'Able to, as you put it, access the full range of emotional and cultural responses that anyone might reasonably require of any artist.'

Did that all make sense? He fancied there were a few too many words in the mix, but Edith Parks was smiling at him. Or at least, she was baring her teeth and curving her lips in what might charitably pass for an approving grimace.

Rob glanced again at Simon, hoping for support or release, and felt the colour drain from beneath his lightly made up face. 'Anna'.

Embarrassed, the colour flooding back into his cheeks so fast he could feel them burn, he was aware that he had spoken her name out loud. Edith was saying something to him, but the roaring in his ears prevented him from hearing her words and only her hand on his arm, jolting him back into the free fall of reality, caused him to realise that he had risen from his seat.

'Sorry,' he apologised. 'I just...'

But she was smiling at him. A real smile, this time, not that deadly, teeth baring grimace but rather the kind of indulgent look with which a fond great aunt might anoint a favoured nephew. Rob swallowed hard and licked lips that had suddenly dried. He caught a glimpse of himself in the monitor and, with a shock, understood that this was what they'd been looking for. His raw, naked reaction on seeing Anna Freeman for the first time in almost a dozen years. They'd set it up and he'd rewarded them.

Robert wanted to run, escape from the cameras and Edith Parks' smile and ... incomprehensibly, from the slight, young woman standing at Simon's side.

A third seat had appeared on the set and Edith was speaking again. 'Robert Carr, may I present your muse, the lovely Anna Freeman.'

Chapter Six

Rob wasn't sure how he'd survived the rest of the show. Dimly, he was aware that he made the appropriate responses. That he kissed her, formally, on both cheeks and smiled reflexively at some joke Edith had made. Most clearly though, he recalled that as he held Anna's slim shoulders and bent to drop the kisses upon her half-turned cheeks, he had felt her trembling like a bird beneath his hands.

Afterwards, there was no escape either. Cars were waiting to whisk them off to some – so far as Rob was concerned – unscheduled reception in a suite at the Carlton Hotel. The choice of the 1930s monument to deco style informed him that Simon must be responsible for this small addition to the nightmare evening. The Carlton had been Simon's venue of choice for everything from business lunches to his own rather extravagant wedding reception.

'What the hell's going on?' Rob demanded, grabbing Simon in the foyer. 'I've done my bit, now I want to get back to work.'

'Calm down, Rob,' Simon smiled. 'Just a few people and a chance to have a proper talk to Anna. After all the times you've hassled me this past week, I'd have thought you'd welcome the opportunity.'

'Oh, sure, have a quiet chat while the sharks circle.' He paused to receive enthusiastic praise from the TV producer – pinstriped jacket now half covering the fuchsia blouse – and to nod at someone else whose name he could not recall but who claimed to have once commissioned him to do something or other. Simon dealt with the names; Rob just produced the goods and Simon knew how much he hated this kind of event. Much as Rob liked the fawning affection of his public, he preferred it at a distance. Being consumed by the full slick oiliness of it was not his idea of a tolerable time, never mind a good one.

'Where's Anna?' Simon asked, looking around.

'In a taxi heading for home, if she's any sense.'

'She'd better not be. I put Marion in charge of getting her here safely.'

'Marion? Oh hell.' Marion was Simon's wife of three years, his PA before that. Rob hadn't much liked her in either role.

'That's enough, thank you, Rob. Now play nice. Ah, there they are. Good, we can go on up, then. I've booked us into the conference room. That should be big enough. It's only an intimate do, after all.'

'Intimate!' Rob glanced at the occupants of the lobby, all seemingly waiting upon Simon's instructions. There must be fifty of them, he thought.

Huffily, he downsized his estimate to twenty and followed Simon's pointing finger to the door. Anna stood just inside looking as if she'd like to bolt. Marion, blonde, tall and exquisitely dressed in deep blue silk, was holding her arm.

'God. This is bloody awful, Simon. She looks terrified.'

Irritated, he elbowed his way through the press – all this space, he thought, and still they herded together like a flock of bloody sheep. 'Good evening, Marion,' he said to

Simon's wife. 'Simon says I've got to play nice, so consider that the final thing I say to you this evening, just to be safe. Anna, come with me and we'll get ourselves a good stiff drink.'

Marion stared down at him, not a bad trick seeing as she was several inches shorter.

'No good looking at me like that, Mar. Until you can look down your nose at me without the heels I shall continue to be unimpressed. Anna?' He held out his arm like an old time gentleman and she laughed, actually laughed, with something like relief and genuine amusement. Her slender hand hooked through his arm, he paraded back across the foyer and called the lift. 'You all right?'

'I guess so. Who are all these people?'

'Um, well there's Simon, my agent and the harpy called Marion you've already met. The TV producer and that harridan that interviewed us, you're acquainted with I assume? The man in the charcoal grey Armani that's two sizes too small once bought a painting from me, I think. Couldn't be bothered to remember his name, I'm afraid, and the woman in that shocking green was once married to... Oh, Lord, I don't remember.' He shrugged. 'Simon invited them, ask him.' The lift arrived and he led her inside. A handful of others followed and Rob found himself pressed close to Anna. He could feel the heat of her body against his right side and smell the same soft floral perfume he remembered from that kiss goodbye.

'Not friends, then,' she asked.

'No. Not so you'd notice. They're people I assume Simon believes I should be seen with. Your perfume. You still wear the same one.'

'What?' She laughed, startled. 'Probably. I alternate these days, though. Sometimes I wear Chanel.'

'Just Chanel? Like Marilyn.'

'Who? Oh Monroe,' she giggled and the years fell away.

'God, I love your laugh.' He turned around to face her, no mean feat in the crowded lift, blanking out those who craned around to stare at him in their turn. He could see only Anna, her laughter and lightness flooding his brain like spiked champagne.

'Rob, everyone's staring at us,' she laughed again, the nervousness gone she was as taken by the moment as he was himself. The lift stopped and the doors slid open releasing their passengers and, as they stepped out, it seemed like the most natural thing in the world for him to take her hand.

'So, are you married?'

'No. Are you?'

He grimaced. 'I did get married,' he said. 'It lasted a year. Fortunately, the pre-nup she signed was watertight, so I didn't lose anything by it.'

Sipping her wine, she spluttered and almost choked. 'God, you always were the shallow one. Is that all it meant to you? That you'd had little enough faith in the relationship to tie it up with a contract before you started?'

He considered. 'Pretty much. I gave it a try; didn't work and before you start to feel sorry for the lady concerned, think Marion.'

She was puzzled. 'You married Marion?'

'No, no, even I'm not that stupid. More of a Marion clone, but toned down. Anyway. I find it strange that you never did.'

'What, marry a Marion? Why?'

'No, you'd never have gone for a Marion. Not even the male version; too much common sense. But, I don't know. I just thought some lucky bastard must have popped the question.'

'Oh, but they did. Two, three times. I just said no.'

'Why? Not good enough for you?'

'Oh, absolutely not.' She tilted her head on one side. 'Is this an interrogation?'

'Yes. I suppose it is.' He studied her. She had changed remarkably little, truth to tell. Small lines at the corners of her eyes, but then the laughter lines had always been there, traced just below the surface of the skin, and so had the tiny dimples at the corners of her mouth. Chin, just that tiny bit too pointed for perfect balance. Grey strands in otherwise dark and luxuriant hair, now doing its damndest to escape from the curious silver and enamel clasp that held it in place.

She wore a plain lilac dress, tailored to her curves and decorated at the shoulder with a silver brooch shaped like a flower. It was a grown up sort of outfit, he thought, recalling the Anna who'd dressed in faded jeans and cheesecloth or skinny strapped tops that she had painted and dyed herself.

'Do you have family here?' he asked, aware that he knew so little about her. 'Brothers, sisters? Have you always been here or did you move away? I mean, I'd have thought we'd have run across one another if...'

'Would we?' she sounded amused. 'Rob, even when I knew you, you were preparing for the big time. We were just a sideline. A rather transient amusement...'

'Nonsense. I had good friends amongst our little crowd.'

'Did you? How often do you see them now, the old crowd? Jenny and Pete and, what was the red-haired guy called, oh yes, Clive.'

'I...' He clamped his mouth shut. In truth, he couldn't remember. 'We drifted apart,' he said. 'Anyway, you can't talk, you've not been near nor by, either.'

'You know that for sure, do you?' She quirked an eyebrow at him, her lips twitching with barely repressed laughter.

'Sure I do, I...' He broke off, wondering if he should admit that how he knew was that the private investigator Simon had hired and then the journalists and the researchers for the show they'd just partaken of had all told him so. That and the irritated phone calls from their one time mutual friends, sick of being interrogated by the umpteenth stranger.

'Where have you been, anyway? What have you been doing?'

'Hmm, no need to ask you those questions, is there? I've been around. I lived in France for a while.'

'Oh? Where?'

'Oh, nowhere you'd know. A small town called Amboise. It's in the Loire valley and it's very lovely. Then I wandered down the west coast of the USA, as you do...'

'As you do. How long did that take you?'

'Oh, six, eight months. That was five years ago. I worked to save the money, went out there, when my money ran out I came back home.'

'And home is?'

'Then, home was still Amboise. I came back to the UK a year ago. That do you?'

'No,' he grinned at her. 'I've only just scratched the surface. You know, it's only recently I realised how little I knew about you.'

'You never bothered to find anything out before,' she informed him. 'I mean I didn't take it personally. It was just the way you were and, anyway, I wasn't so sure I'd have wanted to tell you anything.'

'Oh and why not?'

'Because, dear Rob, you were an insufferable bore.'

Laughter softened her words but Rob was alarmed at how much they still stung. 'Was I?'

He sensed she took pity on him because her reply was soft. 'Sometimes,' she said, 'but looking back, I think we all were. All caught up in the brash certainty of youth and all that. We were invincible.'

'Oh, some of us still are.'

'Really? That's something to be envied.' She sipped her wine, studying him over the rim of her glass. 'Though, thinking about it, you know, I think I'm more invincible than I was back then. Then, it was just an illusion brought on by too much pot and not enough good sense. Now, I know I can survive just about anything. That's a good feeling, don't you think?'

He hesitated, trying to sense the meaning behind the words. 'To be able to say that, you must have experienced … hard times.'

'Who hasn't by the time they get to thirty odd. Oh, but I'm sorry, you draw up contracts so you can avoid those little difficulties.'

'And that's a bad thing?'

She didn't reply directly. Instead, she

40

looked past him and he saw her gaze flick around the room. 'You know everyone is watching us,' she said. 'We are the absolute centre of everyone's attention.'

Rob swivelled round, aware that the hum of conversation ceased as he did so and twenty pairs of eyes switched the direction of their gaze to anywhere but him. 'Just goes to show,' he said, 'we're the most interesting people in the room, that's all.'

Anna didn't respond, she put her now empty glass down on a side table and asked, 'You think they'll call me a taxi from the reception?'

'You're leaving?'

'It's gone midnight. I'm tired and I have an early start in the morning.'

Doing what? he wanted to ask. He clamped his mouth shut. He'd interrogated her enough tonight and for all her good humour he was perceptive enough – just – to sense that she'd had enough. 'I'll walk you down; make sure you get a taxi and ... all that.'

'No need. Really.'

'But ... Anna, when can I see you again?'

'See me?' She shrugged. 'I hadn't really thought further than tonight, to be honest.'

'But I will see you again?'

She studied him again, as though weighing the options. 'OK,' she said. 'Simon gave me your number; I'll give you a call in a day or two.'

'Can't I have yours?'

'No, not yet. I'll think about it.'

'Anna, look. I started a new picture a few days ago.' He laughed, suddenly awkward. 'To be truthful, Anna, I'm having trouble with it. Will you sit for me?'

'Sit for you?' She was evidently puzzled. 'Rob, it seems to me you've done OK without a model for all this time, so why?'

'Because...' How could he explain to her that it had all gone wrong? That the reality of Anna had put a cap on his creativity. Had blocked him as effectively as the mere memory of Anna had proved the well spring.

She was waiting for his response, that half smile playing around the corners of her mouth and her eyes gently curious. He found that in some part of his consciousness he was devouring her. Examining her features, collating and collecting every scrap of information, every nuance of expression and logging it, coldly and cleanly even while the rest of his brain struggled to explain why she must sit for him. Why he must go back and draw from life?

'You drew me a couple of times,' she told him. 'I mean, back then.'

Shocked, he shook his head. 'No. I never did.'

'Uh uh. It was September. Unusually warm, a couple of months before I left. We were by the river on a Sunday afternoon.

Someone had borrowed a rowing boat and Steve and Jez were messing about trying to row it through a load of weed. We all stood on the bank laughing at them, all except you. You sat with your back to a big tree and took pictures with that silly little camera you had and you made a load of sketches.' She shook her head and closed her eyes as though trying to bring the image into sharper focus. 'You weren't very happy with the drawings, I don't think, because you kept tearing them out and chucking them on the ground. When you left, you forgot to take four of them. Two were of me and a couple of Jez and Pete in that bloody boat.'

'I don't remember.' He was astonished, but even as he listened to her talking about it, the memory came back, fresh and strong and warm. Along with his feelings of superiority as he watched his slightly younger companions at play.

'Do you still have them? The drawings?'

She shrugged. 'In store, somewhere,' she said. 'I've not had a proper home for the past few months, so most of my stuff's in store. I've not decided, you see, if I'm staying or just passing through.'

'Have you any idea how much they're worth?'

'Never thought about it. If you want them back, I can fetch them for you.'

'No. They're yours,' he said quickly. Then.

43

'But I would like to see them, sometime.'

She nodded. 'Ok. Now, I really must go. It's late, I'm tired. It's been nice,' she added. 'No, don't come down, you've got other guests even if you can't remember who they are.'

She stood on tip toe, then and kissed him lightly on the cheek. Rob found himself lifting a hand to touch where her lips had touched. He watched, stupidly, as she slipped through the door and was gone.

'Anna,' he moved too late, losing the moment. Foolishly, feeling like someone who has just woken up and found they were snoring in church, Rob looked around. Simon was standing at his elbow.

'Well, that went rather well,' Simon said.

Chapter Seven

Three days and she hadn't phoned, sent a message or even responded to those he transmitted via Simon. Three days during which he had worked on the massive triptych of that final kiss. Oh yes, the project had grown since first inception. It had taken, almost, the form of an altarpiece, the central icon of the lovers' kiss and two panels either side; the male figure standing alone in shadow on the left as the viewer looked at it and the woman, back to the viewer, walking off into some vague, unspecified townscape on the right. Only the central panel retained that original concept. The woman half turning from her partner, her body twisting from him as though peeling back from an earlier embrace. The head of the male figure, still lowered as though expecting more.

In the beginning, Rob had been fearful that this image might appear trite or sentimental, but as work continued, the image became darker, almost menacing. He began to sense things, ill defined and incomplete, but threatening and damaging, hiding in the shadows of his painting. Catching sight of the pictures in an unguarded moment on that third morning, Rob was shaken to the core by the force of the images he had unconsciously conveyed. For the first time in years, he had produced work that did not even nod in the direction of commercialism. No one, Rob thought, would want to live with this. That vertiginous feeling of disquiet and even dread that permeated the work was inescapable.

Rob perched on the edge of his worktable, surveyed his creation and was overwhelmed by it. It was, he realised, a deliberate piece of narrative, but it told a story way beyond that which he had first envisaged. His mind played tricks on him, seeing figures in the shadows that he knew he had not placed there. Saw distance in the painting that went beyond that indicated by the windy street. He mourned for the loss and emptiness that permeated not just the man, but both of the central figures. He had, he felt, embodied what might have been had the world turned more slowly and Rob taken time to think and dream.

And yet, for all its power and all of the commitment he had given to it over the past days, he still knew that Anna's face was wrong; that he could not adjust his vision to adapt to that fey, distracting loveliness he had only half realised before.

It was only eight-thirty in the morning, a good couple of hours before Simon would be in his office and taking calls, so Rob interrupted his breakfast and demanded that he order flowers, reasoning that, on the basis of good manners alone, Anna would have to respond to such a gesture.

'I'd do it myself, but you won't tell me where she is.'

'I can't force her to see you,' Simon retorted. 'Look, Rob, she agreed to come on the TV thing. I'm sure she'll come round to the idea of meeting you again. Just give her a few days.'

'Send the flowers,' Rob demanded. 'Roses. White ones and ... something yellow. Those things that smell nice.'

'Lilies?' Simon guessed.

'Christ, no. Can't stand the bloody things. Freesias, that's the one. Purple and yellow.'

'Freesias,' Simon paused meaningfully. 'Don't you think...'

'Look, I don't bloody know. Ask Marion. She'll be ordering the damn things anyway.' He slammed the receiver down feeling that maybe this wasn't such a brilliant idea after all and went back to staring at the painting.

'What's that?' Puzzled, Rob crossed to the right hand wing of the triptych. He thought he could see something in one of the deeper areas of shadow. Something that had no right to be there. He peered more closely, went and fetched a large hand lens from his desk and peered again.

'Hmm. Eyes playing tricks. I've worked on it too bloody long.'

He straightened, gaze still fixed on that section of the picture where the offending shadow creased and coalesced into something ... something Rob couldn't quite see. He dropped the lens onto his worktable and rubbed his eyes wearily. 'Too much. Much too much.' He drew a deep breath and then a second. Outside, the north-facing windows gave a view onto grey skies and tower blocks. He'd not been out in days, not since the night of the television show. He thought of phoning the local shop. He had an arrangement with them – for which he paid through the nose – that they delivered his day to day supplies. But, having realised this morning when there was neither bread for toast, butter to put on it nor milk or tea, that he was running out of practically everything, Rob decided that a trip to the local supermarket might be a better idea. Besides, he really could do with a break.

He grabbed his coat from the peg near the door, felt in the pocket for his change and debit card, car keys in the other, remembering just as he was about to open the door that he needed shoes, Rob headed out into the world.

Robert Carr could go days and see nothing of the outside world. He could go for days without consulting it in any way, whether by phone or television – owned, but rarely watched. Newspaper – on principle, never delivered. It was, therefore, always in the nature of a shock to be confronted by the noise and rush and smell of the city that existed and thrived all around him whether he chose to take note of it or not.

Rob was not a good driver. He had passed his test in younger, hungrier days, when the need for a licence was driven by the fact it was the only way to get to and from the various part time jobs that financed his path through art college.

These days, it was a pursuit he indulged as

little as possible, accomplished, when absolutely necessary, with a kind of head down bullishness that either intimidated or infuriated other road users – a fact Rob was utterly oblivious to. He was the proverbial driver who had never had an accident but had seen plenty in his rear view ... except that Robert didn't often make use of his rear view.

He wasn't much better with a super-market trolley.

'Hey, watch it!' The woman he had rear-ended turned to shout at him.

'What? Oh,' Rob, examining the situation, stared in surprise to find this middle aged, grey-haired individual in a hairy pink coat, trapped between his wire basket and her own. 'Sorry.'

'Look where you're bleeding going!' She peered at him through thick, pink-rimmed glasses. 'You're that artist fella, ain't you?'

Startled, Rob backed off, pulling the trol-ley away from its large, wool clad prisoner. Free now, she turned full on to face him and leaned forward, across his half filled basket.

'I saw you on the telly,' she accused. Then sniffed. 'I switched off after five minutes.'

'Oh?' Rob felt he should say something. 'Not an art lover then,' he managed, aware as he said the words of how inadequate it sounded.

'Art lover,' she laughed. 'That's a good 'un.

49

Though, give due where it's due. You can at least tell what your stuff's meant to be.' She sniffed again. 'Not like some of 'em.' She nodded emphatically to emphasise her disapproval.

Robert wondered if he should thank her for the observation.

She looked past him, peering around his arm. 'Shift over,' she said. 'There's people trying to get past.'

'Oh, yes, right.' He apologised and squeezed into the smallest space he could, wishing he could be one of those who were passing instead of standing.

'Of course,' she went on, 'I turned back again to see what the lass looked like.'

It took Rob a second or two to realise she was referring to Anna. 'Oh,' he said. 'I see.'

She nodded, encouraging. 'I expect it's hard to do all that from memory,' she said. 'I mean, if you'd not seen her in that long, so you shouldn't feel too bad about it.'

'What ... bad about what?'

She smiled her understanding and actually reached across the trolley to pat him on the hand. Rob flinched and strangled a whimper, but she didn't seem to notice.

'My nephew paints,' she went on and Rob wilted, guessing at what might come next. 'Does it lovely, he does. Dead good likenesses. Works from photos. You ever tried that?'

Numb, Rob nodded, and then shook his head.

'Well, maybe you should try it, love,' she added and roared with laughter.

Rob didn't know what to say.

'Nice meeting you, love.' She finished. 'Nice to know not all celebrities are too stuck up to talk.' Then she did an about face with her trolley and left Rob blinking in the void that she had left behind.

From photographs! God!

He shuddered, then frowned. Actually there was nothing wrong with using references, he reminded himself, and having the odd picture on hand might be just what he required to break through that stupid block he was experiencing.

He glanced behind him to check that she really had gone and she wasn't lying in wait, ready to ambush him again. Then, the woman's comments fully impacted. She had implied that his likeness of Anna was not ... like.

'Hey, are we moving today or not? If you shift over a bit so we can all get by.'

'Sorry,' Rob managed. He moved on again, the remainder of his shopping forgotten. 'What if everyone is thinking that? What if she's right. What if that's why I can't do it any more.'

He had spoken aloud. 'Oh shit.'

A woman with children cast him a

reproving glance.

'Sorry. I'm just...' Thinking aloud. That's what he was doing. OK in his studio; not so OK in the middle of an increasingly crowded shop.

Rob veered off towards the newsstand and gathered every local and national daily he could find. He scanned the magazines and then reminded himself that the TV show only went out three days before and even the weekly publications would not have had time to run anything further than a rehash of the earlier speculation.

The checkout seemed to take forever, the women in front insisting on talking to one another then to the girl at the till and to passing mothers with their small children.

Finally, he made it out to his car and had the shopping piled onto the back seat. He sat in the parking bay and scanned the papers, aware that maybe he'd have already missed the most relevant comments; those printed the day following the TV show. He, as news, was after all three, no nearly four days old.

Damn, damn! No, no look, there I am. What do the bastards say then? Agree with Mrs Grey Hair Hairy Coat, do they. 'My nephew does lovely work' he mimicked. He read the first few lines and then leaned back and closed his eyes.

On a good day, Rob would have taken

little notice of the small and really fairly neutral comments about artistic license and likeness being a difficult thing to realise. About the importance, in these days when any fool with a camera could produce a serviceable portrait, being to recreate the essence of the sitter and not encapsulate every spot and wart and unwanted pimple. Not, the reporter added, that the lovely Anna Freeman had any of the above.

And he was right, Rob told himself, sitting up abruptly and striking the steering wheel hard enough to hurt his fists. Course he bloody is. A photo booth can take a factual picture, for Christ sake. I am an artist. I deal with the heart and soul and the... He broke off as someone passing with two kids and shopping glanced at him through the windscreen.

'Shit, shit.' He dug in his pocket for his keys and slid them into the ignition, taking several deep breaths before fastening his seat belt and pulling out of the parking space without bothering to look both ways. The horn sounding off to his left barely registered.

He did not recall the journey home.

Impatient now, he staggered upstairs with his load of shopping, the newspapers tucked beneath his arm. Halfway up the stairs, he heard the phone ringing in his studio and the answerphone click in.

Bloody Simon, most likely. Well he can

damn well wait. He dumped the shopping on the landing while he found his key and then staggered inside and through to the kitchen, hearing the whirr of tape as it reset itself. Returning to the studio he stared at the machine, a prescient knot in his guts telling him that this wasn't Simon who had left the message.

He pressed the play button. Anna's voice, a little uncertain, relieved, he sensed that he had not been there, thanking him for the flowers.

Chapter Eight

Simon had said nothing for several minutes and the suspense was killing Rob.

'Well? Do you like it or not?'

'I don't know if like is the right word. It's stunning, Rob, but what the hell are you going to do with it?'

'Do with it? What do you mean?'

Simon uncrossed his arms and pushed off from the table upon which his tailored buttocks had been perched. 'Frankly, Rob. It won't sell. It's magnificent, or will be if you bother finishing it, but commercial? No, no I don't think so.'

'I didn't paint it to sell. I painted it

because...' Why had he painted it? Rob was no longer sure. He turned away from Simon and the painting and paced the length of his studio, pausing to gaze out of the windows onto the cityscape spread out below. Everything was still grey, he thought. Grey tower blocks, leaden sky, dreary ribbon of river glimpsed in the distance. Grey rain. Even the red roofs of nearby houses looked grizzled in the flat light. By contrast, his painting was a study in blue and black, the chiaroscuro interrupted only by the stark sources of unnatural light with which he had illuminated it. The faces of the two figures were modelled as though just catching the cobalt gleam of a neon sign and the sullen acid yellow of the streetlamps. The ground beneath their feet was wet where rain had fallen and greased the pavements, light reflected off its surface, emphasised those deeper pools of shadow between the patches of radiance. Anna, leaving, crossed from mottled light into a pool of darkness which hid her face, and only in the central panel had he permitted any kind of glow to fall upon skin.

'Hopper,' Simon said abruptly. 'It reminds me of Hopper. You know, that painting with the ... Nighthawks, that's it. Reminds me of that.'

Rob glanced over his shoulder, noting the lightening of Simon's tone and guessing he had come up with an 'angle'. He wasn't wrong.

'Hopper's big just now. We could use that, play with the retro feel. Rob, how many more of these things do you think you can ... create?'

'You mean, churn out,' Rob growled. 'That's what you almost said, isn't it?'

'Oh, you know me, Rob, bloody Philistine. I didn't mean that.'

'The Philistines were a major artistic culture,' Rob told him, irritated by what he felt was the devaluing of his experience. Not Simon's figure of speech; Rob was honest enough with himself to admit that 'churn them out' was exactly what he normally did. Was the reason he'd probably never actually have to work again if he chose not to. But, this was different. This he had sweated over, suffered for. Endured torment the like of which he'd not experienced since before he'd ever met the lovely Anna.

And it felt good. Felt real. He didn't want the crass commercial sense of someone like Simon to mess with that feeling, to destroy it.

Or, was that really it?

No, Rob thought, that was only part of the story. The other part was that he couldn't see a way to go back to what he'd been doing before. To painting that construct of Anna, made so unreal by his encounter with reality.

'I read the papers,' Rob said unexpectedly.

'Excuse me?'

'I said I read the papers.'

'You never read the papers. Not unless I sit you down in a chair and force you to.'

'And you only ever show me the good ones,' Rob said wryly.

'A lesson learnt through bitter experience.'

Rob scowled at him and then continued. 'I met this woman, today. I was out shopping.'

'Shopping? Since when did you shop?'

'I do have to eat.'

'I thought you ordered in? Had everything delivered?'

'I felt like a change, needed to get outside so I drove to a supermarket.'

'Drove?' Simon looked and sounded almost scared. 'Why not call a taxi? You hate to drive. Fuck it, Rob, the whole world hates it when you drive.'

Rob scowled at him. 'Anyway,' he continued, 'this woman, she recognised me from the TV show. She said she'd only switched on to see ... to see what Anna looked like.'

'And?' he could see the puzzlement on Simon's face. Puzzlement and also a wariness that told Rob that Simon suspected where this was leading.

'And, she reckoned her nephew could do better from a photograph.'

Simon's laugh spluttered. 'She said what?'

'So,' Rob went on, ignoring his agent. 'I

57

bought the papers. I wanted to know if the rest of the world agreed with Mrs Hairy Coat.'

'Hairy...'

Rob waved him into silence. 'Oh, they go on about artistic integrity and how the artist should concern himself with the essence of the person not the literal likeness. All that clap trap, but it means the same thing, doesn't it?'

'Oh, come off it Rob. You want me to take an ad out in the local paper? Your loved ones reproduced in oil. Provide clear photograph. You're talking out of your...'

'Am I? Simon, the fact is I can't ... can't see her any more.'

'I thought you wanted to see her. This morning you were...'

'You damn well know what I mean. I mean, in here,' he tapped his head and then his chest. 'Here. She's not my Anna. Not the one I'd held onto for all these years and ... Simon. I don't know how I'm going to go on.'

Simon was silent. Rob fancied he could hear the mechanism of that adding machine he called a brain, clicking away and calculating their financial loss. Then he shook himself, remembering that Simon had also been a loyal friend in the years before he was even mildly successful, never mind infamous, and that Rob himself was not an easy man to deal with. 'Look,' he said. 'Ignore me. I've

58

just found the whole damn thing unsettling.'

Simon scrutinised him closely. He had resumed his perch on the table edge, flicking the hem of his perfectly cut jacket from beneath him as he sat down. He folded his hands and steepled them in front of his face, fingertips almost touching the long straight nose that gave him such a dramatic profile. A mirror on the end wall caught his reflection and Rob found himself studying it intently, noting the fluidity of the man when he moved, the poised and relaxed air, even though Rob knew the brain was now processing at maximum. He moved so he could see himself in the same reflection. He was dressed in his work clothes. Apart from the addition of a coat and shoes, he'd been dressed like this for his supermarket visit. He fancied he could hear the woman in the hairy coat talking about him to the checkout girl. 'Course it was him, covered in paint and stinking of that oil they use. Linseed, that's it, and turps.' She'd wrinkle her nose then, not liking the smell of turpentine. Would she know what linseed smelt like? Oh, of course she would. Her nephew would use it when he produced his wonderful pictures.

In the mirror, Rob studied their overlapping images. Simon, posed in the one spot in the studio he knew would be free of paint – Rob kept that worktable for layouts and drawings and it was always scrupulously clean. Simon, dressed in that wonderfully tailored suit. Grey wool, white shirt, no tie at the moment, though he'd be sure to have one in his overcoat pocket. Rob himself in his faded jeans and one of the half dozen old shirts he kept for work. He washed them when the paint became too thickly encrusted, rinsing them first in soapy water and turps before consigning them to the machine – a lesson he'd learnt from ruining too much good stuff by mixing them in with the wash. Childlike, he still could not break himself of the habit of wiping his hands down the front of his clothes, though he did now use a rag instead of his shirttails on his brushes. The mirror both joined and separated them, distorting the measure of distance so that Simon, closest to it, seemed to loom in the distance rather than recede and the double image, real Simon and reflected Simon, showed two sides of the whole. For one dizzying, confusing moment, Rob tried to focus on both the right side of Simon, viewed in reality, and left side seen in mirror world and on Rob himself, onlooker in both.

Simon was talking again, but as he still seemed to be nattering about Hopper, Rob tuned him out, figuring that Simon was probably doing what he usually did and trying ideas on for size. Instead, he reached into the top drawer of the map chest behind him and withdrew a sketchbook. A grope in the old syrup tin on top of the chest produced a stub of charcoal. Rob never threw anything away. It was too small to be comfortable in his grasp but he pinched it tight between thumb and finger and, propping the pad against the buckle on his belt, he began to sketch, rapidly, unhesitating.

He had captured and discarded three times before Simon noticed what he was doing and looked directly at him, ruining the symmetry, destroying the vision.

Rob sighed and set the sketchpad down, a sudden leaden weight pressing between his shoulders and a second dragging at the pit of his stomach.

'These are really rather good.' The astonishment in Simon's voice riled Rob.

'Of course they're good. Do you think I'm incapable of doing anything different?'

'No, I've never thought that. You're the one that thought that, remember. Can I keep this?' He selected the second attempt. If showed a double image of Simon, the real and the reflected, and a shadow form beyond that of Robert himself, captured in restless, scribbled strokes that conveyed both energy and irritation.

Rob shrugged. 'Why not? Now, go away. I want to work.'

'OK, I'm off, but I'll call you tomorrow with a reminder. You need time to shower and change your clothes before you go out.'

'Go out? I'm not going anywhere.'

'You're meeting Anna, tomorrow night at Medici's. Seven forty five. I've booked you a table.'

'When did you do that?'

'Anna called me,' Simon told him. 'She said she'd got the flowers and tried to phone to say thanks, but she just got your machine. I assumed you were going through one of your "I'm not answering the bloody phone for anyone" days, so I came over to give you the news. Don't be late for her; you know Medici's will cancel anyone if they don't turn up on time. Like I said, I'll give you a call just to kick you into gear.'

Robert stared at him, the lead weight in his stomach now swinging wildly, threatening to break out through his gut.

'I thought you'd be pleased?' Simon sounded aggrieved.

'I am,' Rob assured him, not sure if that was as true now as it had been that morning. 'It's just...' His gaze strayed back to the half finished painting. Feeling better now, he brushed past Simon and crossed to the massive canvases.

'I'll see myself out,' Simon told him, but Rob, brush in hand, didn't even hear.

Chapter Nine

The phone rang and tore Robert from a deep sleep. He had been dreaming of Anna. She stood on a bridge overlooking a deep, fast flowing river, gazing off at something in the far distance he could not see. His view, beyond her, around her and behind him, when he turned and looked back over his shoulder, was obscured by thick, swirling fog. Sound killing and stiflingly chill, it froze him to the spot unable to speak or to call out to her.

Occasionally, through the thinning mist, fragmenting as an unfelt wind dragged and separated, he could glimpse, or thought he could glimpse, that same river as it had been on that other, long ago day. The day he had talked about with Anna, when she reminded him he had sketched her portrait. But then the image would be gone, veiled once more in that smothering blanket of chill white vapour.

The dream was still with him as he woke, stabbed from sleep by the piercing note of the telephone. For a disoriented moment, he assumed that this too was an aspect of the dream because the voice that replied to his sluggish 'hello' was Anna's.

'Rob. You've got to help me.'

'What? Anna, is that you, what the hell ... do you know what time it is?' His gaze fell upon the luminous hands of his alarm. They informed him, greenly, that it was two-fifteen.

'Rob. I'm scared.'

He sat up and swung his legs over the side of the bed, placing his feet flat on the smooth chill of the wooden floor.

'Anna, what's wrong?'

She was crying. He could hear the tears in her voice and the choking catch in her throat. His own tightened in response. 'Anna, tell me where you are. I'll come and get you.'

'Will you? Please. Will you. I'm at my flat. There's this man.'

'Who? Is he there at the flat?'

'He says he's coming round, Oh Rob, please hurry.'

'Tell me where you are and I'll be right there and, Anna, call the police.'

'No, not the police, it's... Oh Rob, just come over. If he sees I'm not on my own he'll go away.'

He had to remind her again to tell him the address.

Rob stood for an uncertain moment, bare feet planted squarely on the bedroom floor. Should he call the police? Instinct told him that it would be a good idea. They could probably get there sooner than he could and, though Rob was no coward, he'd as soon know what sort and size of man he was defending Anna against. His next instinct was to summon Simon, but, on reaching for the phone, the green hands of the clock caught his attention once again and he paused. It was far too late, early, even. He couldn't justify dragging Simon into this.

Rob didn't bother dressing for bed so there was nothing to remove. He grabbed his work jeans, discarded the night before, rummaged in the drawer for a long sleeved T-shirt and in another for socks, finding, in the half dark, what he hoped was a pair. Found his grey, crew-necked jumper where he'd left it several days before, draped over his bedroom chair, then stumbled through the studio and onto the landing, collecting coat and shoes as he went, pausing only when he'd reached the bottom of the stairs and the outer door to drag them on.

'Taxi or car. Taxi or car. Have to be car. Bugger.' He should have called a cab before leaving home, but that would have wasted precious time. His instincts yelled at him that he should have called the police too. His fears manifested as an insistent crescendo that burrowed into his brain and interrupted his thoughts to the extent that he nearly walked past his own vehicle. Got to get to Anna.

He patted the pockets of his coat, finding

his car keys on the second run through. He fired the engine and remembered to switch on his lights only when a car pipped his horn at him at the end of the street. He pulled out into the early morning traffic without looking either left or right, noticing the cab that swerved to avoid him only when the repeated honking drew a swift and irritated glance. 'See, you moron,' he told himself. 'You could have got a bloody cab. Too late now.'

It was more luck than sense of direction that found Rob in Anna's street. He had known approximately where she meant; the flat being about five miles from his own home and in a converted house a scant half mile from Highgate Cemetery. He abandoned his car, half parked, front wheel wedged against the kerb, the rear end pointing dangerously into the road, then looked around. No sign of anyone in the street and the windows of the houses were almost all dark and curtained. Lights showed at odd windows, concealed but for the narrow crack between drawn curtains or ill fitting blinds, but most people had long since sought their beds. Rob experienced an odd, vertiginous moment; it felt as though he was the only person left alive – or, at any rate, awake. Glancing at his watch, he saw that it lacked only two minutes to three o'clock.

It took him a few minutes to find the right

house. Anna's name was on the bell push for the second floor, but when he pressed it no one answered.

Puzzled, Rob tried again. 'Right house, right flat, so...' He wished he'd had the presence of mind to dial 1471 and recall her number. He could at least have phoned her on his mobile, though the idea that she might have fallen asleep between calling him in panic and his getting here seemed an unlikely one.

He pressed the bell again. Against the general silence, the sound echoed upward and then back down the stairs and Rob could hear it from where he stood. He thought of shouting through the letterbox, but that seemed like a silly thing to do. If she couldn't hear the buzzer, she'd be unlikely to hear him shout. The thought that he should have called the police pressed down upon him once again. What if the man had got in and hurt her?

Impulsively, Rob shoved at the front door.

It opened, swinging inward on well-oiled hinges and, as he stepped inside, Rob noted that the catch had been pressed down, preventing the sneck from re-engaging in the latch. Someone had made certain that the door would not close.

Had Anna left it like that for him? Slowly, quietly, he began to mount the stairs.

The door to Anna's flat had been left ajar.

A narrow band of light showed at the side and foot and illuminated a few inches of the grey cord, landing carpet.

'Anna?' warily, Rob reached a hand and pushed with the very tips of his fingers as though afraid that the door would bite. He almost expected to have Anna jump out at him, laughing at his expense at the joke of dragging him all the way over here on a false pretence. A half memory woke of some similar incident ... but he couldn't quite recall what it was and the next second, all thought of any kind was driven from his mind.

Anna lay in the small space between brown sofa and oval coffee table. She lay, face upwards, with her head towards him. One leg had crashed down onto the table surface. Her arms were thrown outward as though she had tried to grasp something that might break her fall but Rob's gaze was drawn to that brilliant patch of crimson, garishly bright against her white shirt.

'Anna.' He breathed her name, took three or four steps into the room until he was standing over her, staring down into the glassy blue eyes that gazed blindly back. 'Oh, my God!' Breath forced from his lungs as forcibly as if he'd been punched in the stomach and he felt his gut tighten and begin to retch, he forced himself to squat down beside her, telling himself that he should check for a pulse, do something to help her while a second portion of his brain insisted she was dead already and there was nothing he could do.

A small sound caused him to jump to his feet and spin around. A small sound, a mere rustle of movement but, under the present circumstances horribly threatening. Whoever had done this, were they still here?

Rob turned and fled, then yelled in shock. There was a woman on the stairs, standing with her hand clasped at the throat of her pink dressing gown. Rob hurtled past her, almost dragging her with him in his urge to escape, then he was out and running, remembering almost too late that he had his car, he caught the wing of another vehicle as he pulled away, leaving a streak of silver against the blue.

Anna is dead, Anna is dead. That one thought filling his brain as he floored the accelerator and took off without thinking of the direction. Anna was dead and her blood was slick across his palms.

Chapter Ten

DI Vic Marris was a man defined in some measure by the depth and volume of the bags beneath his eyes. They were far too fat for a personage with such a weasel sharp face and gave the impression of rightly belonging to a much larger man.

So too, for that matter, did his suit, once funeral director black, now faded to charcoal; the polish at the seat and knees higher than that on his creased black shoes. Shoulder pads that overshot the shoulders by a couple of inches on either side added to this impression of his wearing someone else's cast offs and raised speculation among his colleagues regarding charity shop rejects and created rumours as to his propensity for rescuing objects from skips.

Observing him, it would have required no real acquaintance to guess that Marris lived alone. Those who spoke kindly of him implied that he was married to the job; those he'd crossed, and these were of considerable number, might have added that no one else would have him.

Marris heard the comments, sorted them, filed them away for future use and then got on with what he was good at; ignoring any-thing that didn't fit with his particular world view and focussing on what he decided was important.

Marris's present focus was on the young woman lying untidily in the centre of an otherwise impeccably tidy room.

'Neighbour identifies her as Anna Free-man. Lives alone. She's been here six, seven months.'

Marris nodded, not moving from his position by the door. Marris liked to look before he moved, collect the pictures in his mind; pictures that he would later collate and file in his usual methodical fashion.

'The neighbour found her?'

His colleague hesitated and Marris fixed him with his baggy, weasel eyes.

'The neighbour called it in. She'd heard someone pressing the buzzer, knew it was for Miss Freeman because she could hear it from above. Then she heard someone go up the stairs. She came out, intending to give Anna Freeman and her visitor an earful for waking decent folk at all hours. Got half way up and this bloke came barging his way down, ran out the front door. Mrs Gillis, that's the neighbour, she came up and looked through the door. Saw that.' He pointed with his notebook towards the body.

'Saw her,' Marris corrected him softly.

'Yeah, right,' his uniformed colleague

71

shifted uncomfortably, 'saw the woman.'

Marris nodded, then moved, just one pace, into the room. He reviewed the scene again, once more noting the tidiness and, more than that, the lack of extraneous objects. He guessed that the flat had been let fully furnished; the leather look sofa, chain and mock mahogany coffee table had that came-with-the-flat look, as did the ginger side-board and the tiny, seat-two-if-you're-lucky Formica-topped table and plastic cafeteria chairs. The carpet was the same grey cord that covered the stairs and landing and the hearthrug, lying rather petulantly in front of the two bar electric fire, was an unremark-able tufted blue and grey.

Marris had stayed in cheap hotels that had more individuality and character.

'You sure she lived here?'

His younger colleague looked confused. 'Yes Guv, I mean, the downstairs neigh-bour...' He trailed off, Maris's weasel eye informing him that the question might have a hidden meaning. 'Sir?'

Marris gestured, a broad, swift movement of the hand that encompassed the entire stage; room, body, bedroom beyond, tiny, cramped kitchen glimpsed through a part open door. 'Tell me what you see.'

'See?'

'That's right, with your eyes. Or better yet, tell me what you don't see.'

The young man gaped, still not getting it.

'No pictures, no photos, no personal possessions. This might as well be a B&B.'

The younger man, PC Geordie Willets, turned towards the woman's voice but Marris didn't move. 'Nice to know someone can use their eyes,' he said. 'The neighbour tell you any more?'

The woman pushed past the uniformed man and came to stand beside Marris. She nodded. She was no more professionally dressed than Marris, clad in jeans, T-shirt and an old sweatshirt celebrating a five-year-old Metallica tour. Red curls brushed the shoulders of a leather bike jacket. 'She reckons she knows who our gentleman caller might be,' said the new arrival, DS Gina Lees.

'Oh?'

'Someone by the name of Robert Carr. He's an artist. She saw him on the telly, so she says.'

A small, almost imperceptible gasp from the younger man, caused Marris to notice him again. 'Well? If you've had a thought you may as well share the bugger.'

'Then this must be Anna. No, I mean *the* Anna. Me and the girlfriend...'

'The girlfriend and I,' Marris intoned.

'Yeah ... well. We saw them on television. He's been painting her from memory for years and they arranged for her to meet him on live TV. You should have seen his face. God, I'd never have known her, dead like that.'

'I doubt any of us would look our best once we're dead,' Marris observed. 'That Anna,' he mused. 'I read about it.'

'Hard to miss it,' the woman observed. 'Any ETA from SOCOs or the police surgeon?'

'No, but this young man's been doing a good job of keeping the scene intact and pristine,' Marris observed wryly. 'Not let me move from my spot, he hasn't.' He turned directly to the uniformed officer, noting that it was true what they said about policeman getting younger. Uniform, anyway. Once you made CID, age seemed to run ahead and produce wrinkles regardless of age. They lay in wait like stingers in front of speeding cars, ready to puncture your ego. 'If we promise to stay put, how about you go down to the car and call control, see if they've got anything on SOCO and the doctor.'

Eager as a puppy, he dug in his coat pocket and produced a mobile. 'I can do that from up here, Guv.'

'You could,' Marris said. 'But you'd rather do it from the car.'

He looked momentarily bemused, then his expression cleared as he recognised the hint for what it was. 'Oh, right sir.' He took off as if Marris was biting at his heels.

Vic Marris chuckled.

'You're a bastard,' Gina told him, shaking her head so the red curls danced.

'So I've been told. You think the old woman got it right about Robert Carr?'

Gina frowned. 'She seemed certain. Of course, it might be associative, you know, she knows who Anna Freeman is, maybe hopes it's the artist lover come calling. She said something else, though. She said she heard someone arguing on the stairs and then Anna's door closing and the argument carrying on. This was a while before she heard someone else, she thinks this Robert Carr, ringing the bell. That's what made her come out. Having been disturbed by the argument, she wasn't feeling that charitable, said he rang the bell enough times to wake the entire house.'

'It didn't though, did it? Wake the entire house.'

'She and Anna were the entire house. The last ones here and they're on notice. The place has been sold to some hot shot developer who plans to turn it into luxury apartments. Everyone else moved on in the past few months.'

'So, Anna Freeman must have been alive to buzz him through the front door?' Marris twitched a questioning eyebrow.

'Not necessarily. The old woman down-stairs lost the front door key a couple of weeks back. She reported it, both to us and to the agent, but no one's given her another one. Presumably, they don't give a damn seeing as the old woman and Anna were due to leave. She and Anna took to leaving the front door on the latch and just locking their own front doors.'

'And anyone could have known that,' Marris nodded. 'And was our artist blood-stained?'

Gina nodded. 'She thinks he had blood on his hands,' she said.

'How very symbolic.' He glanced at his watch. It was almost six a.m.

Chapter Eleven

The medical examiner had arrived. She was one of the handful of local doctors recruited for the role, fitting it in between surgery on hospital commitments. Marris watched as she bent over the body. The table had been moved to give access, its position carefully marked both with tape and photographs. Marris himself kept his post beside the door, watching as SOCO did their thing and the photographer worked his way around the room, guided first by experience and then by Marris's requests.

'Give me one from that angle, will you Clive, yes, that's it. I want a view onto the room from the bedroom door and take a squint out of the window. I noticed one curtain had been pulled aside. My guess is the killer looked out to see who was buzzing the door. Can you see it from there?'

'Just,' the photographer told him. 'But you'd need to press against the glass. I can't get a shot with the camera,' he illustrated, showing Marris how the lens would catch against the glass.

Marris nodded and gestured towards the fingerprint officer. 'See what you can get from there.'

Marris dug his hands deep into the pockets of his waxed overcoat. It looked to be of the same genesis as his suit; the plaid lining grimed and faded and the wax finish scuffed and scarred so severely that it no longer kept off the wet. He wanted a cigarette. His fingers closed around the pack in his right hand pocket. Lighter in the left. He smoked only rarely, some quirk of his nature allowing him to go for days before the craving hit at which point he chain smoked until he felt sick, then quit again for maybe a week or more until the urge returned. It was on him now, niggling like an itch in his lungs.

Marris pushed off from the doorpost and prowled slowly around the room. 'Time of death?' he asked.

'Preliminary findings agree with the neighbour's account,' Dr Gregory informed him, glancing up from her work. 'From temperature readings alone, I'd go for two, three hours. Not much more.'

'Which fits with the neighbour hearing an argument.' He nodded. But it didn't rule out Robert Carr. A single wound, so far as they could tell, thrust beneath the ribs and straight into the heart. The weapon was missing. If the doctor was right about the direction of the stab wound then Anna Freeman would have been dead almost before she knew what had hit her. He watched as the dead woman's hands were bagged. 'No defence wounds.'

'Nothing obvious. Whoever killed her got in close and stabbed before she had time to react.'

'Could it have been a woman?' The question was rhetorical but the doctor shrugged and replied anyway.

'Could have been anyone. The direction of the strike ... none of it calls for unusual strength. Opportunity and accuracy, yes, but that could have been dumb luck.'

'And if I asked you to speculate?' Marris studied her as she sat back on her heels, frowning. She was pretty in an officious sort of way, he supposed. No, attractive, business-like, rather than pretty. Forties, he supposed. Married. He knew he'd dragged her out of bed and her husband had answered the phone. He recalled also that she had teenage kids. Would she go home after this, have breakfast with her family; maybe drive her kids to school before going back into work?

'If you asked me to speculate,' she said slowly, 'and if I were stupid enough to do so at this stage, I'd speculate that her killer was sitting down, there, on the sofa. Anna Freeman was standing. She leaned towards him and he ... or she, struck upwards. If I'm right, then for the victim to have crashed backwards into this position, her killer would have to have been sitting there,' she pointed at the cushion at the far end of the sofa. 'But, of course, that's mere speculation. You'll have to wait for the post-mortem'

Marris nodded. That fitted with his own thoughts.

'We should turn her now,' Gregory said.

Marris gestured assent and watched while the doctor and one of the SOCO gently lifted the body, tilting it sideways so that they could see beneath.

'No sign of a second wound.' They lay her back and the doctor rose, stamping her feet to get the circulation going. 'Move her when you're ready,' she said. 'I don't believe she's been shifted. She's lying where she fell so far as I can see.'

Marris watched as she glanced around, taking in the wider scene. Gregory's focus had been on the woman since she'd first arrived, but now he saw her thoughtful expression as she surveyed her surroundings. Surveyed and interpreted.

'Empty,' she said. 'I make more of an impact on a place when I stay overnight in a hotel.' She shrugged. 'You done with me? I'm due in for morning surgery for eight thirty and I'd quite like to have breakfast before then.'

Marris smiled, thin lips stretching thinner. God, but he needed that cigarette. Maybe he should get some of those patches everyone was talking about. 'Thanks,' he said.

She nodded, collected her gear and took herself away. Marris turned his attention to the other rooms.

Bedroom, bathroom – well, almost. Kitchen ... well, maybe she was into takeaways, there was barely room to make tea, never mind cook a meal. He started with the kitchen, little more than a shoe cupboard with a double hob and a tiny oven. Tabletop fridge taking up precious room on the kitchen counter. Sink, cupboards above. He avoided the fingerprint powder and opened the door with the tip of a gloved finger. Tinned stuff mostly and tea, sugar, flour. Bacon eggs, milk and salad stuff in the fridge. A solitary mug and plate on the draining board. The blue plastic bowl in the sink, cleaned and propped on its side to drain. Sink cleaned and polished. No tea stains, no smell of bleach, just the faint whiff of the lavender liquid he could see standing beside the taps.

Waste bin, empty. It had been lined with a white plastic bag, but that had been removed so that the SOCOs could check beneath and now lay draped over the side. The bin too was clean and, Marris guessed, newly washed. Marris frowned, something registering suddenly. He turned round – almost knocking the mug from the drainer, so crowded was the space – and looked at the tiny fridge. A cardboard box sat on top of it, with a smaller one nestled inside. He recalled what Gina had said about the place having been sold.

'She was getting ready to leave,' he remarked to no one in particular. Boxes, for packing? Did that explain the absence of personal stuff in the living room? Maybe, he conceded, but, as he wandered through into the equally tiny bathroom, not the lack of cosmetics and usual feminine clutter he had noticed the average woman collected.

A bottle of liquid soap – more lavender – had already been fingerprinted, a towel, just the one, on a rail behind the door. Empty shelves greeted him when he opened the mirrored cabinet.

'No toothbrush. No paste. No hairbrush.'

The bedroom. Clothes in the wardrobe,

others in a suitcase on the bed suggested he'd been right. Anna's departure was imminent. A holdall sat on the floor beside the chest of drawers – the only other furniture in the room – and it too was packed with Anna's things.

Marris glanced up as DS Gina Lees appeared in the doorway.

'Packing to leave?' she asked.

'Maybe,' he frowned. There was something not right here but he couldn't place it.

'I've got an address for our artist,' Gina told him. He took the paper she held out towards him.

'Posh address.'

'No lights on and he's not answering the bell, but here's the interesting bit. He left home at around twenty past two this morning, nearly involved in an RTA at the end of his own road.'

'Oh? And how do we know that?'

'The driver of the cab he narrowly avoided hitting thought he might be drunk in charge. Took his index number and called us. When I called in for a PNC report, that was flagged up.'

'Nice to know something works occasionally,' Marris nodded. 'Ok, I think I'll take a drive over there now. I want you to stay here, cast an eye.' He glanced at his watch, an hour until shift change. 'Get some bodies off the day shift to give you a hand.'

'OK,' she said, then, 'you going to tell me what's bothering you?'

Marris thought about it for a moment and then said, 'What's the last thing you pack? I mean, if you're staying somewhere, what goes into your bag the last?'

'Um, I like to be organised. I'll pack everything the night before except the clothes I want to wear and stuff like my toothbrush, hairbrush, make-up...'

Marris watched as she glanced around, searching out the things she had just listed. He waited as she stepped through into the bathroom and then did a quick search of the cases already half packed. The missing items were right at the bottom of the holdall together with the photographs and odd items he might have expected to find on display in the living room. She looked quizzically at Marris.

'Someone picked up the bag,' he suggested, 'walked into the living room then the bathroom, cleared the shelves, came back in here, dragged stuff off the chest of drawers, look, it's not really dusty, but from here, where the light catches, you can see imprints from the hairbrush, makeup bag maybe, other stuff.'

'Then whoever it was started on the wardrobe. And you don't think it was Anna.' She made a flat statement of the words.

'I don't think it was Anna. Ok, I'm off,

anything you find, put on an inventory, where found, what it is and what it's with. We know Anna was planning on leaving, what I want to know is who felt they had to bring her departure forward and why they needed to make it final.'

Chapter Twelve

Marris pushed open the broken door of Robert's studios and stepped inside. Under the circumstances – there being no other known suspect – Robert had to be considered armed and dangerous and an armed response unit had been called to open his door and gain entry into his home.

'All clear,' their commander told Marris as he shepherded his people out and left Marris's team in control. 'The bed's been slept in, but no sign of the occupant.'

Marris thanked him and waited until the sound of footsteps had fallen silent upon the stairs before proceeding into the room.

He had a team of six with him. Three uniform and the balance CID, all stifling yawns and casting speculative glances around the big room that Robert Carr had turned into a studio.

Marris guessed that it had once been a

fabric mill or something similar, the massive windows designed to allow maximum light to flood the room. There were blinds at the windows, but only two were lowered. Behind the blinds, muslin curtains hung from wires. Again, all but two had been pulled back and hooked out of the way. Dimly, he recalled being told that muslin diffused light without fully blocking it but he couldn't recall if the source of that flip of information had anything to do with art or had been on one of those makeover shows he found himself watching when he came in from work. It looked a bit yellow, Marris thought, like it was in need of a good wash.

The wooden floor showed only where it had not been roughly covered with drop cloths. These were paint stained and, here and there, the wood too was marred by blue and green and the odd streak of red where someone had tracked the paint across its surface.

Robert Carr, Marris thought, might be a rich bloke but he was a messy bugger too.

'Guv. Take a look.'

Marris, obediently, looked. Then looked a little closer. The painting was massive – and, though it had been split into three canvases, each occupying their own easel, Marris could see that this was meant to be all part of the same work.

'No surprise in the subject matter,' his

colleague joked.

Marris grunted. In part the man was right. Sketches and works in progress featuring Robert Carr's muse and amanuensis decorated the walls, were propped against tables and, Marris was sure, filled the plan chests which stood against the two shortest walls. But he was also wrong, dead wrong. Even Marris could see that this was different and Vic Marris didn't reckon on having an artistic bone in his lean, sinewy body.

'That looks like a self-portrait, though,' his colleague went on, pointing to the central figure. 'That one too. Funny that, painting yourself twice. Artistic types.' He shrugged. Such creatures could never be comprehended. Strode off purposely to examine the bedroom.

Marris stepped back and looked at the painting again. Around him his team was getting on with their task of looking. Not looking, as yet, for the specific, though Marris trusted they would all know if they found anything relevant to the task in hand. He had no expectation of finding the murder weapon here; as far as they could tell, Robert Carr hadn't returned to the flat after his visit to Anna Freeman. Some clue as to where he might have gone, Marris thought, would make a comfortable beginning.

He studied the painted face of the central figure. The woman looked unfinished, her face half in shadow anyway, though Marris could also see where the paint had been scraped back and the face reworked as though the artist couldn't quite capture the expression he searched for. Even so, Marris could tell that it was Anna, something about the eyes was unchanging and unchanged from image to image.

He backed away and studied some of those other pictures set around the room and confirmed the observation. The 'Annaness' of Anna was in the eyes and, maybe, in the curve of the mouth. He went back to look at the larger work. That was what he couldn't get right in this painting, Marris realised. Robert Carr had scraped back and reworked the mouth, two, maybe three times over if the staining on the canvas was anything to go by.

'Guv?'

Marris turned.

'There's a speed dial list on the phone here. Only three numbers. A takeaway, a shop and someone called Simon.'

The man called Simon had been asleep. Marris glanced at his watch, it was just after five.

'This is Detective Inspector Marris,' he informed Simon cheerfully. 'Who are you?'

'What do you mean, who am I. Who the hell are...?'

'Detective Inspector Marris, sir,' Marris reminded him.

'Is this a joke?'

'No sir, it's far too serious to be a joking matter. I found your number listed on the phone belonging to Mr Robert Carr...'

'Rob?' Instant alert now. 'Something happened to Rob?'

'We're trying to find him, sir. If he's not at his flat, is there anywhere else he's likely to be?'

'You're at the studio? What the hell's going on. No, explain when I get there. I'll be fifteen, no twenty minutes. Stay put.'

The phone went down with a crash and Marris carefully lowered the receiver his end to compensate. 'He's coming over,' he said, the comment addressed to everyone and no one. He sniffed. 'Still don't know who the bugger is, mind you, but I expect we'll soon find out.'

Chapter Thirteen

Simon Roper had arrived with protests and questions on his lips but they were silent now, stilled by the news that Anna Freeman was dead and that Robert Carr had been seen running from her flat.

Handsome sod, Marris thought, scrutinising the tall man perched on the edge of Robert's bed. All that blonde hair and blue-eyed attitude, body like he worked out all day everyday and, even though Marris had disturbed his sleep, the 'smart casual' look Simon Roper had gone for had been selected with a care that was as foreign to Marris as the designer labels he guessed were on the faded jeans, white polo shirt and butter soft leather of the nut brown jacket.

Gina's leather he could forgive; she rode that bloody great Kawasaki, and the surprisingly unsexy jacket and matching trousers were part of the uniform if you rode one of those noisy brutes. Simon Roper's jacket was just pure display. It brought out the puritanical streak in Marris, a feature never far from the surface at any time.

He tried not to hold Roper's fashion sense against him, Marris was aware of his own lack in that department. Instead, he concentrated on the younger man's face and the studied frown – even that looked decorative; symmetrical even – that now creased the broad forehead.

'So,' Marris reiterated, 'you wouldn't know where he's gone?'

'I've told you. He doesn't go out unless someone, usually myself or Marion, organises him. He's not what you'd call spontaneous at the best of times, though...' the frown deepened and Marris prompted.

'Though?'

'Probably nothing. I came over the other day and he'd got himself in a tizz.'

'In a tizz?'

'Yes, you know, it's...'

'I know what the word means, sir,' Marris told him, though the last time he'd heard it used had been from the lips of his very elderly great aunt, a woman also given to use of the phrase hissy fits. 'So, what was this tizz about?'

He noticed that Simon glared at him, then decided to let it pass. 'He'd been to the supermarket and, I don't know, someone recognised him from the television programme. Apparently she'd said something about the paintings not being like the real thing. Rob had taken it to heart rather, gone out and bought everything he could find on the TV show. He was in quite a state when I got here.'

'The critics agree with the supermarket lady, did they?'

'No,' Simon gestured impatiently. 'You have to understand, it's not about creating an exact likeness, I mean, what would be the point?'

'I'd have thought it would demonstrate a certain skill,' Marris suggested.

'Yes, well, there is room in the art world for the photo realists, of course, but personally, and I know Rob always felt the same, to my mind art is more about capturing the essence...' He broke off as though aware he was starting to lecture. 'Look, you're not interested in my views on figurative art, the thing that struck me at the time was, Rob doesn't shop. I don't recall the last time. He'll buy clothes, but even then, well, if he finds something he likes he'll buy three of it just so he doesn't have to go back in a hurry.' He paused and studied Marris. 'You think I'm joking, don't you? Just check his wardrobe and you'll see I mean it. Literally.'

Marris made a mental note he should put that to the test, though far from being a trait to court disapproval, it sounded like solid, commonsense thinking to him and Robert Carr went up a notch in his estimation. Though, Marris qualified, that bit of good sense didn't quite make up for his trailing paint across that magnificent floor. 'But he went shopping this time? Tell me, Mr Roper, if he doesn't shop...'

'Gets it delivered. Next down from me on the speed dial on the phone. I think there's a takeaway on there, too.'

'And he doesn't phone anyone else? Most people have a phone book beside the phone, not just three numbers on speed dial.'

Simon got up and stretched, flexing his back beneath the softly draped skin of his jacket. He went through to the studio and

Marris followed, interested.

'Should be in here,' Simon said, rummaging in the top right drawer of one of the plan chests. 'Yes, here it is.' He produced a tatty looking black bound book and handed it to Marris. It was just under A4 in size and as Marris flipped it open he saw that it was a sketch book rather than an indexed volume for addresses. A sketch book literally filled with names, addresses and numbers, snatches of song lyrics, caricatures – he recognised a younger version of Simon, all spilling curls and big eyes – even reminders to buy bread or call the dry cleaners.

'How the hell does he find anything in here?'

Simon shrugged. He had produced two similar volumes – same size and shape, one even more battered, the other relatively new. 'Rob has a visual memory,' he said. 'You ask him to find a number from ten years ago and he'll like as not be able to tell you what else is drawn on the page and where he was when he wrote it in.'

'You mean he carried these around with him?'

Simon pulled the drawer open further and gestured inside. Marris, peering in, saw that it was jam packed full of identically bound books, each in varying states of disrepair.

'Behold,' Simon said. 'A record of the life of Robert Carr.'

'Jesus!'

'Quite.'

Marris frowned. 'You said he never goes out.'

'I said he doesn't go unless he's organised.'

'OK, but you also said he'd remember where he'd been when he made the entries in the books.'

'Oh, right, see what you mean. Maybe I should have said that Rob doesn't go out now. It used to be different. He used to be different.'

'So, what changed?'

Simon shifted his weight and closed the drawer. 'I think that book is probably the most recent,' he said, pointing at the least mangled of those Marris held.

'I asked what changed.'

'He ... had an illness about three years ago. We kept it out of the media, but he lost confidence after that. When all this started up about finding Anna, it seemed like a good idea. Then things started to get complicated. Well, I started to worry that it was all too much of a strain. I was just relieved when Anna turned up.'

'And now she's dead.'

A look of great pain creased Simon's handsome face. He nodded.

'What kind of illness?'

'Is that relevant?'

'It might be. If, as I think you're trying to

suggest, this was a mental problem, then it might indeed be relevant.'

'Rob had a breakdown, he didn't hurt anyone but himself.'

'Is he a violent man?'

'Rob? God, no! Violence takes commitment, Rob doesn't do commitment.'

It seemed, Marris thought, an odd thing to say. 'He seems to have shown considerable commitment to his subject,' Marris observed.

Simon didn't seem to have an answer to that. He scowled and then looked away.

'Wind changes, you'll stay that way,' Marris told him.

'What?'

Marris ignored the question. Instead, he wandered back to where the three paintings stood together, grouped so that the two outer wings were turned slightly inward. The position, Marris thought, suggested doors about to close, shutting the shadowed couple inside.

'What do you make of this?'

Simon didn't hurry himself, making his point that he wasn't one to be bossed or insulted. He considered for a moment before answering, but Marris figured that was for form's sake, not because he didn't have the answer ready.

'I think it's probably the best and most original thing he's ever done.'

'Original? It still features his favourite subject.' He glanced around the room. 'His only subject, it seems to me.'

Simon shrugged. 'It paid,' he said.

'Past tense?'

'No, it still pays. But I'm starting to foresee a time when it wouldn't. He's had ten good years; time to move on.'

'Would moving on be a motive for murder?'

Simon's look would have withered a man with anything left to wither. As it was, Marris figured he was safe.

'Why would Robert Carr want to kill Anna, Mr Roper?'

Simon sighed. 'Why are you asking me?' he said.

'Because you, apart from a takeaway and a grocers, are the only person on his fast dial and, frankly, I can't see him confiding in the pizza delivery boy.'

The object of their speculation was at that moment standing on the Millennium Bridge and staring down at the river. There was just enough light, dawn light, to make out its surface, the artificial dawn, neon and sodium, fog yellow and that artifice of red and blue, vivid green, that lasted through from day's end to new day. The grey of real light dawn was a relief to him.

He had abandoned his car somewhere

about a half hour before, though he could no longer recall where he'd left it or quite how he'd arrived here. Dimly, he could recall that the top of the London Eye had been visible between the buildings and he'd headed for it, kept walking until he'd arrived at the river. Robert had been navigating by that massive landmark since its first erection and reckoned he could get anywhere around the centre of London by calculating his position in relation to the massive wheel, the overgrown fairground ride both attracting him with its boldness and symmetry and repelling him in the way it tapped some deeper memory he had long since refused to name.

There had been a time, not so long before, when Robert had enjoyed the city, striding out along its streets with that sense of ownership that comes with being resident and that related sense of superiority over all of those needfully pausing to study maps or quiz the street signs.

Robert could recall feeling that. Could bring to mind how it had been to feel that assuredness, that sense of being well, of being in control. But it was long since he had actually felt that way. Though those few in the know told him he had now recovered from what they referred to as his problem, his breakdown, his episode or his illness, depending on their level of comfort when discussing matters of mental weakness, Robert knew that this was far from the truth. He had not yet been able to shake that self-doubt that had delivered itself as part of the package that came with his, albeit brief and voluntary, incarceration in that place. He couldn't bring himself to name it or even to call it a hospital. Recovery centre was the official label. Rehabilitation and recovery. He, unlike the majority of the paying guests, had no need of the rehab – a fact that allowed him some sense of superiority. And, had he recovered? He supposed he must have done in some measure. They had signed him off and allowed him to return home.

Light revealed the horizon to him now, a perceptible change in the grey on grey that hugged the river at its most distant point.

He glanced at his watch, pressing the button that illuminated the face with that same neon blue he told himself he now despised. He had chosen the watch, an inexpensive, black strapped, plain faced, school kid type affair, because of that blue light. It now revealed to him that it was twenty minutes past six.

Rob froze, not because of a reaction to the time, but because for the first time since leaving Anna's flat, he had looked at his hands. He drew a quick, nervous breath. It sobbed in his throat and he looked swiftly around to check no one had heard, the early morning crowd not heavy yet, but already starting to build. No one looked his way. For a brief moment, just to be sure, he rested his hands on the rail and looked down at them, backs and then palms, then thrust them out of sight into his coat pockets.

'Blood,' he whispered. 'I've got her blood on me.'

He began to examine himself, trying to do so without either seeming obvious or taking his hands from his pockets. Impossible task. Slowly, furtively, he slid his left hand out. Rubbing it across the front of his coat confirmed what he had already suspected. It came away still wet and red.

'Oh God. Oh, God, I've got her blood on me!'

He tried to keep the rising hysteria out of his voice when all the while he wanted to run and scream. Did it show? His coat was black, could you see the red against the black?

He looked down again. 'No, no, it's all right, can't see it.'

He bit his tongue, horribly aware that he had spoken this last out loud.

What should he do?

The morning air was cold, too cold to do without his coat and anyway, if he took it off here, people would see, they'd wonder why, all these people wrapped up warm in their jackets and scarves, that woman there in her furry boots. No, that wouldn't do. He'd have to brazen it out, pretend it wasn't there, avoid people. No one would see unless he brushed up close and he got her blood on them.

Rob closed his eyes. The roaring in his ears, blood pumping and surging, became louder and the dark behind his lids suffused with it as though someone shone a bright light through.

He snapped them open, once more drinking in the calm cold grey of the river and the lighter flush on the horizon and the grey stone grey of buildings and gulls and ...

'Simon. Need to talk to Simon.'

Blessing the reflex that meant he was more likely to pick up his mobile than he was his keys, Rob dialled Simon's home number, then cut off before it had a chance to ring. No, Marion might pick up at home, he couldn't talk to Marion. He knew that only Simon ever answered his mobile; Marion refused, on principle. The mobile was a business phone; Marion didn't do business, she wasn't his secretary.

Blessing the woman's stubborn streak, Rob summoned Simon's mobile number. He answered on the second ring.

'It's him?' Simon was shocked.

Answer it.'

Simon had already pressed to accept the

call. He turned ostentatiously away from Inspector Marris. 'Rob, where the devil are you? I know, I know, just calm it down. Tell me where you are and I'll come and get you. Rob, it will be all right, we can sort it out, now tell me where you are.'

He paused to listen and Marris moved around in front of him again, catching his eye and mouthing 'where?'.

Simon shrugged, frowned and shook his head. He was attempting to speak, to break the flow that Marris could hear as an urgent murmur on the other end, but Rob didn't pause for long enough. He shouted over Rob's chatter. 'Rob, Rob, where the devil are you. Just hang on and I'll be there.'

But Marris could tell from his expression that he wasn't getting through. Rob was gibbering, shouting now, loudly enough for Marris, standing a few feet from Simon, to hear the words.

'I've got her blood on me, on my hands, on my coat and it's too cold to take it off. I'm standing here and people are looking at me and I don't know what to do. Simon, I've got her blood all over me.'

The words dissolved, becoming sobs, harsh and dry, and then they too began to fade.

Simon shouted into the phone.

For frozen seconds the two men waited for Rob to reply, then another voice.

'Hello, look, I've called an ambulance, but I can't stop. Your friend's collapsed and there's other people here. He might have been mugged or something.'

'Where's here?' Simon demanded.

'Oh, we're near the London Eye, standing on the Millennium Bridge. You know, the one that wobbled. I can hear the ambulance. I'll put the phone down next to your friend. I'm sure someone will let you know where they're taking him, OK?'

'No, don't...'

A clunk as the phone was placed on something hard told them that the man had done exactly what he said he would.

'Damn it. Fuck!'

Marris looked surprised. The crudity didn't quite fit the smooth exterior, though, he allowed, it was understandable in the circumstances.

'You heard that?' Simon was asking. 'I should have known that's where he'd be. I'd just not thought ... it's been so long.'

'Tell me in the car,' Marris said.

'Where are we going?'

'I'll call in, find out where they're taking him. Bit of luck we'll arrive at the same time as the ambulance.' Marris told him.

Chapter Fourteen

Marris took a few minutes to grab breakfast before heading back to his car, eating a bacon and tomato bap he bought at the hospital canteen and slurping hot liquid that claimed, despite colour and flavour to the contrary, to be tea. Simon, apparently, had an eleven o'clock appointment and would be getting a cab home to change in time for that. For the moment, he was still at Robert Carr's bedside, glaring at the officer on watch and trying, surreptitiously, to free his hand from Rob's bloody grip without it seeming too obvious.

Ninety per cent of Simon believed in Carr's innocence, Marris reckoned, while the other ten was screaming at him that he didn't want a killer for a client and certainly not for a friend. That ten per cent, Marris figured, would be mentally running over their contract and looking for a get out clause.

In the car, he licked the remaining tomato drips from his fingers, wiped his greasy hands on an already grimy handkerchief and set off back to the crime scene. He arrived just after nine. The body was gone, SOCO too – Marris cringed at the overtime he'd have to claim for on that one – and Gina, with three uniformed officers, was involved in the process of picking apart Anna Freeman's tiny world.

'Anything?' Marris asked.

She nodded. 'Found our man, I hear.'

'He found us, in a manner of speaking. He's in hospital, in shock.'

'Got a bigger shock to come, I reckon.'

'You've decided he's guilty then?'

She shrugged. 'Until something happens to make me think otherwise.'

'Nice to see you have an open mind.'

She grinned at him. 'You got an opinion on it, then?'

'I always have an opinion. So, what have you got for me?'

She reached into a box by her feet and removed a clutch of evidence bags. 'What looks like a journal,' she said, presenting him with the first. 'It's not recent, in fact, it's from eleven years ago. I had a quick nose and it talks about Robert Carr, though not at length, seems to cover the summer and into the autumn.'

'Just the one?'

'Um, yes. I thought it was a bit odd, but maybe she wanted to remind herself of that time she knew him, before she met him again, like.'

'Maybe. Which implies there should be others.'

'Um, I don't know. She must have been what, twenty, twenty-one, then. I kept notebooks and diaries and such but it never lasted. I'd make a New Year's resolution every bloody year. Lucky if I could make it to twelfth night.'

'This wasn't a New Year diary,' Marris pointed out.

'True. The neighbour, Mrs Gillis, she reckons Anna told her most of her stuff was in store until she found something permanent.'

'I don't suppose she said where?'

Gina shook her head. 'Nah, course not. What do you want, an easy life? Then there's these, letters and bills. The bills are for this place, but the thing is, they're not in Anna Freeman's name. They're being paid by direct debit, anyway, look.'

Marris looked. 'Ah,' he said.

'Is that a meaningful ah?'

'Could be.'

'You recognise the name.'

'Simon Roper is Rob Carr's agent.'

'Ah.'

'Yes, ah. It's not so strange, I suppose, that he wanted to organise accommodation for the mysterious Anna and I suppose this is more discreet than a hotel, but... What's the date on that other bill, Gina?'

'The one you've got is for gas, and it's dated three days ago. This one, for electric, one month back and there's a telephone bill the same. The period covered is from ... end of January. That's three months ago.'

She frowned. 'When did that television programme go out?'

'Last week. Tuesday night, I think.'

'And the mysterious Anna was found only a few days before that.'

'Oh? Been following this little story, have we?'

'Oh, Greg's into all that arty farty stuff.'

Greg, Gina's part-time partner, Marris was never quite sure if the relationship was off or on, was something in media. Marris didn't enquire too closely for fear that Gina might tell him more than he really wanted to know.

Gina rolled her eyes. 'He thought it was romantic.'

'And you?'

She grinned at him. 'If I try to do romantic, something always goes wrong. It's like, when I try to wear high heels, the buggers always manage to get stuck in a crack, or cripple me feet or give me blisters the size of bladders.'

'A delicate and wondrous image,' Marris observed. He frowned. 'So, either Simon found her before and kept her under wraps or Robert Carr and Simon were in this together.'

'Nah,' Gina shook her head emphatically.

'I actually watched the TV thing. He was genuinely shocked to see her, I'd take bets on it. I mean, he knew she was going to be there, but that look on his face. Nah, he was knocked for six.'

'OK, we'll have another chat to our Simon Roper later. What else do you have?'

'Not a lot. Three photos. Look. This one was with the journal and I'm pretty sure the names written on the back appear in her notes. These two look recent.'

Marris nodded in agreement. Two little girls appeared in both the photos but the second also included a couple that looked enough alike to be their parents, the woman, blonde and smiling, the man, dark and grinning like the world belonged to him. There was an older woman too, a bit brassy, suicide blonde and big jewellery, but with friendly eyes that crinkled when she smiled.

'Do we have next of kin for Anna?' he asked.

She shook her head. 'That's strange,' she said. 'No phone book or address book. I checked her handbag too and there's nothing in there. The other thing that's odd, there's no credit card, no ATM card. Just a bit of cash. I found an envelope in the drawer with £120 inside and there was twenty or so in her purse, but...'

'Odd, yes,' Marris agreed. 'You mentioned letters?'

'Um yes, three. Well, two and a card, well, a notecard thing. My Auntie Val liked notecards, just like this, with flowers on. Used to spray them with her perfume, some godawful violet stuff. I mean, it smelt OK when it was fresh, but by the time it'd been put through the post and handled by a dozen sweaty palms even before our postman got at it...' She sniffed as though recalling the scent and wrinkled her nose.

'And is this missive perfumed?'

'Only by the perfume of years,' she told him grandly. 'Take a look.'

Marris scanned the letters and the notecard. Gina had opened this out so he could see the whole thing inside the evidence bag. It was short and to the point, thanking Anna for a birthday present and hoping she had a pleasant journey back. Marris could understand why Gina had been put in mind of her auntie Val.

The letters were a little more informative. They too appeared to be old. One was dated, from the September of eleven years before. It was only partly comprehensible, written in that sort of shorthand, replete with unfinished and unexplained references such as letters between friends often include.

The second was in a different hand and dated a month later. It commiserated with Anna on not being able to make the wedding of someone called Jenny to Pete and went on to describe in great depth the clothes the bride wore and the misadventures of the reception. The tone was friendly, easy, someone who, again, knew Anna well. The signature was Lyn, with a single 'n'.

The postscript attracted Marris's attention.

'P.S.' it said, 'Joe's found himself another girl. She looks a lot like you, hee hee.'

He picked up the larger photo that Gina had showed him. The names of those in the group of eight people, standing in loose formation beside a river, had been written in pencil on the back. The handwriting differed from both the letters and the card and something told Marris that Anna had written this herself in a controlled, rounded and slightly childish hand. It was as though she'd been practising her 'best handwriting'. He looked for the names on the letters. Steve, the writer of the first, was lying on the grass in front. On his back but with his head turned to face the camera.

Joe was off to the side, slightly detached from the group. He was frowning, as was the surprise face: Robert Carr, front and centre, prepared to be photographed, but seemingly caught off guard as the shutter closed.

Jenny and Pete held hands next to him and Anna stood beside her, dark curls blowing in the breeze and her long white skirt flying out behind the head of the reclining Steve.

'Lyn, with the single "n", must have taken the picture,' Marris decided. They looked so young, so thoughtlessly happy, all except the scowling Joe and the anxious looking Robert Carr.

'It's an odd mix,' he said, 'that one journal, this photo, those letters. The journal I can understand. If I'd been meeting someone I'd not seen in years, I might have wanted to do a bit of remembering first. The photo I get too, but the letters and the notecard...'

'Could be she just found them when she was looking for the journal and brought them back on impulse,' Gina suggested.

'Could be.' He frowned and stared accusingly around the room. 'Nothing more recent?' he questioned, though he knew Gina would have found it and presented it to him had it been there to find.

'Nothing but the bills,' she said. She pursed her lips. 'But I'm looking forward to hearing what Simon Roper has to say about those.'

Chapter Fifteen

Mid afternoon saw DI Vic Marris visiting Simon Roper at his office in St John's Wood.

Simon occupied the ground floor. The reception area was guarded by a woman in her thirties. Her dark hair gleamed, curling forward onto her high-boned cheeks and swinging, as though choreographed, when she inclined her head to listen to Marris's request that she tell Simon Roper he was here.

'Do you have an appointment?' her finger poised above the intercom as though to satisfy him of her intent to deliver the message. Her hazel eyes, coldly expressionless, and tight lips, compressed so that the berry stain deepened unattractively, told him she had no such idea.

Marris waited for her to complete her assessment of him and to come to the same conclusion second time around that he, Marris, was not their type. Sure enough the finger moved away from the intercom. The nails matched the lips, Marris noted. He wondered if they were real.

'Detective Inspector Marris, to see Simon Roper,' he repeated. He'd missed the rank from his initial introduction and was amused to see what a difference its inclusion made.

'Oh,' she said. 'Oh, right. This is about Mr Robert Carr?'

She leaned forward, almost imperceptibly. Marris echoed the gesture. 'Just tell Mr Roper that I'm here,' he said. 'There's a good girl.'

The nostrils pinched and then flared and the lips parted enough for him to see the tips of even and very white teeth. She jabbed her finger at the intercom button.

'There's a policeman here, wants to see you,' she told Simon. 'Yes, that's him.' She released the intercom button and scowled at Marris, the red lips pursed again and the hazel eyes refreezing after that one moment of hopeful warmth.

'So,' Marris said. 'You don't like Robert Carr very much.'

The eyes widened. 'I never said...' She winced and clamped her mouth shut as Simon breezed through from the inner office.

'Come on through,' he invited. 'Sue, hold all calls, please. Yes, come on through.'

The carpet in Simon's office was deep blue, the walls a restful cream. Maple bookshelves stretched the length of one and a large map, of London in the eighteenth century, covered much of a second. A sash window gave a view onto a walled yard, bare

111

apart from a couple of green bins and a half hearted tub of winter pansies beneath the window. A door led through to a further room and Marris opened it to reveal a small kitchen area, a photocopier and other bits of office equipment that Simon didn't want cluttering up his room.

Noticing the policeman's survey of his office, Simon remarked coldly, 'If you're looking for the loo, it's out in the hall under the stairs.'

'I'm a nosy sod,' Marris told him. 'It goes with the job.'

Simon frowned and flopped into the chair behind the desk. He had his back to the window, weak sunlight falling onto the papers on his desk, though blocked by his shadow. Marris wondered how he could work in his own light like that. Maybe he used that fancy lamp, green glass and brass, out of place and antique looking in relation to the rest of the very modern, almost minimalist furnishings of the rest of the room.

Simon was waiting for him to speak. He had changed his clothes since this morning, Marris noted. He was now wearing a grey wool suit and white shirt with a blue silk tie, textured with tiny grey dots. Marris kept silent for a moment longer then, without preamble, he asked, 'How did you know she was the real Anna? What checks did you carry out?'

'Oh, well, personally, I didn't,' Simon told him. 'I hired an agency.' He opened a desk drawer and withdrew a card. 'These people. We've used them before to make discreet inquiries.'

Marris took the card and looked at it. 'Lavinia Harker,' he read. 'Sounds more like an expensive hooker than a PI.'

'Oh, she's not a PI,' Simon objected. 'It's a firm that specialises in security. I've used them from time to time when I've had a nervous client.'

'You mean they provide personalised bouncers,' Marris stated.

'No. I don't mean that, I mean... Oh for God's sake, go and talk to them yourself.'

'Oh, I will,' Marris promised. He was struck by the immediacy with which Simon had been able to produce the card. Most people would have either had it in a rolladex or card file or had to rummage in the drawer for at least a brief time before producing it. There was something of a magician's flourish in Simon's presentation.

'And what evidence did they have of Anna Freeman's reality? I presume they prepared a report for you?'

'A report? Oh, oh yes, of course. Ask my secretary on the way out. She deals with the filing.'

So, Marris thought. He'd had, perhaps, a phone call in confirmation from this agency and then a follow up report that he hadn't got around to reading. 'And the agency gave what evidence?'

'Oh, for God's sake, what does it matter? They were satisfied, we were satisfied.' He took a deep, slow breath to calm himself. 'Sorry,' he apologised. 'I know you're only doing your job. This whole thing has left me rattled, you understand?'

'I've noticed that murder has that effect on people,' Marris observed. 'So, what evidence did they present?'

Simon needed a second long, deep breath. 'She had a passport and driving licence,' he said at last. 'Was able to tell them things about herself that they checked out. I believe they spoke to family and friends and she had personal possessions, a photograph and journal, letters and such. I don't remember.'

'A photograph?'

'Photographs, yes.'

'No, Mr Roper, you said, "a photograph". Something particular?'

Confusion silenced Simon for a moment, then he said. 'I don't know, a group thing, showed Anna and Rob and friends from when he knew her. She proved who she was anyway.'

Marris nodded thoughtfully. He thought about the bills they'd found in Anna's flat. 'When did they find her, Mr Roper?'

'Um, she turned up about ten days before the show went out. Walked into a police station and said, here I am, the woman they're looking for.'

'Dramatic,' Marris observed.

Simon smiled. His first genuine smile since he'd arrived, Marris thought. 'Yes,' he said. 'I suppose it was.'

'So, you and Rob were satisfied.'

'Of course. I told you, she proved who she was and anyway, you think Rob could have been fooled? If it hadn't been the real Anna Freeman, Rob would have said.'

'Did he meet her before the television show?'

'No, we made the decision we wanted to keep everything spontaneous. He wanted to, but I said no. Anna wasn't keen either and, well, frankly, we wanted to get his reaction. You should have seen his face when he caught sight of her.'

'Oh, I plan to see it,' Marris told him. 'I've requested tapes of the show.'

'You have? Oh. Good.'

He fell silent and looked down at his hands, then leaned forward and began to straighten the already ordered papers on his desk. 'I do have a great deal to do, Inspector.'

Marris let the silence sit for a moment longer. 'Did Robert Carr see Anna Freeman after the show?'

'Oh yes, of course. We had a small

reception to celebrate. They got on like a house on fire.'

Marris had always thought that an odd turn of phrase. Why would anyone want a relationship that bore even a passing resemblance to a burning house. 'And after that?'

'Er, no.' Simon ceased fiddling with his papers and sat back. 'She wasn't keen. Rob wanted to, or thought he did. Then he changed his mind, but that's Rob all over. He sent her flowers, she thanked him and agreed to dinner. That was supposed to be tonight.'

He was clearly sobered by the thought and it occurred to Marris that this was the first moment at which the full implications hit home. Anna was dead, stabbed to death in her flat, the flat Simon had probably paid for, and had possibly been done to death by Simon's own client and friend.

'But now she's dead,' Simon said. His face greyed out as though health, vitality, good looks, all paled before the significance of this dreadful fact. Then he moved and coughed and the colour returned to his cheeks and the moment was gone. Marris had no doubt that the moment had been one of sincere grief and shock, but that was all it was. A moment. A stumble on the otherwise smooth track of Simon's daily life, something to be acknowledged, but then passed over until such time as he could deal with it without it impinging on the rest of his existence.

Marris studied the changes of expression that flitted across the younger man's face and then he asked, 'Who'd want to kill this woman?

Simon flinched, then recovered himself. 'Not Rob,' he said and Marris knew he really meant it. 'Rob wouldn't have it in him to kill anyone.'

Chapter Sixteen

Robert Carr, attended by lawyer, sat in interview room two waiting for Marris to speak. The tape ran and the uniformed officer seated by the door shuffled his feet and coughed as though to make sure it had something to record.

Robert Carr sat with his arms resting on the table and his shoulders slumped. He'd not looked at Marris since he'd entered the room. Not turned his head or taken note as his brief had outlined that Mr Carr wanted to cooperate, but also wanted it understood that he was entirely innocent of any crime. That he'd gone to Anna Freeman's flat in answer to a summons from Anna Freeman herself and once there, finding the door

117

open, had gone inside and found her already dead. He'd bent over her to check for a pulse and, in the process, his hands and coat had become contaminated with her blood.

At the word 'contaminated', Marris noted that Robert Carr flinched and opened his mouth, but his lawyer didn't notice, and no words got that far anyway. Marris felt he'd objected to the word, even though the solicitor was using it only in a technical, and therefore coldly accurate, way.

Contaminated, Marris thought. He was with Rob Carr on that one; it sounded wrong. Sounded as though the young woman herself was something to be avoided. Something soiled and unpleasant, instead of someone tragically and in untimely fashion, very dead.

'If my client is guilty of anything,' the solicitor continued, 'then it is of very understandable panic. He found a young woman who mattered to him and who had called to ask his help, dead. Brutally murdered. Which of us would not panic under such circumstances?'

Marris missed a couple of beats, enough to start the PC fidgeting again. 'The old lady from downstairs didn't panic,' he pointed out, keeping his tone neutral and matter of fact. 'In fact, after she'd been back downstairs to phone the emergency services, she stayed with the body until our people arrived.'

'Perhaps,' the solicitor mused, 'she did not have the emotional attachment that my client has to the deceased. Or perhaps she is not possessed of his sensitivity.'

That bit of crassness was enough even to break through Rob's reserve, Marris noted. Robert Carr flinched again and raised his head.

'I ran because I was shit scared,' he said quietly, his voice shaking with the effort of creating meaningful words. 'I swear, I heard someone move and I didn't want to end up like Anna.'

'So you ran.'

'So I ran.'

'But it didn't occur to you that, after you'd reached a safe distance, you should call the police?'

'No, it didn't occur to me, no. I saw the woman on the stairs and I knew she'd phone the police. I thought that would be enough. I mean, I suppose that's what I thought. I don't remember what I thought. I just drove my car until I couldn't think where to go any more, then I got out and looked round. I saw the London Eye and I walked.'

'You just abandoned your car?'

Rob shrugged. 'I don't think I intended to. I don't think I thought anything. I walked away from it then couldn't remember where I'd left it. I walked towards the Eye, that's all

I know.'

'And when did you notice the blood on your hands?'

Rob shuddered, he looked hard at his hands, turning them this way and that as though to be sure, then laying them flat, palms down on the table. 'I was standing on the bridge,' he said. 'I looked at my watch and then I saw ... I saw the blood on my hands. It was on my coat too. Still wet on my coat.'

'Are you going to charge my client?'

Marris thought about it, then thought about it some more. On the table, in a dull, brown file, he had a statement made by the neighbour, Mrs Gillis. It stated that she had heard Anna quarrelling with a man half an hour before Robert Carr arrived. That they had gone quiet and, though she'd not heard the man leave, she'd assumed he had. Then she'd heard the doorbell ringing again and someone going up the stairs.

The someone had been Rob.

What if she'd not heard the other man leave because he'd still been there? Marris thought about the half packed bags.

'This noise you heard. Where was it coming from?'

'I think...' Rob hesitated and closed his eyes. His hands moved as he visualised him-self in the room once more. Marris watched as he turned his head as though hearing that elusive sound again. 'The bedroom,' Rob said. 'It was coming from the bedroom.'

'How do you know it was the bedroom?'

Rob hesitated, closed his eyes again. 'Because I could see the bed,' he said. 'The end of it, through the part open door. It had a blue quilt and there's a chest of drawers just inside the room.'

Marris thought about it. From what he could recall that was correct. Standing where Anna had fallen, it would be possible to see the end of the bed and the chest.

'Was there anything on the chest?' he asked.

Rob was startled by the question. 'I ... I don't recall. Why?'

'And the sound was definitely from the bedroom?'

'Are you charging my client?'

Marris thought about it again. He could charge him, but the evidence, so far, was circumstantial. He could hold him for further questioning, but he was pretty sure that Carr's solicitor would protest on medical grounds. Robert Carr had been discharged on condition he rest; he had, himself, voluntarily come to be interviewed. A word from his solicitor and he could be back in hospital for as long as his solicitor thought it wise. On balance, Marris decided to let things be. 'He's the best suspect I've got,' he said. 'In fact, as I keep telling people, he's the only one

I've got right now. But no, not yet. I'll release him on police bail.' He turned to Rob. 'You understand the conditions of that?'

The solicitor was on his feet pulling Rob upright beside him. 'I'll see that my client has a full and detailed explanation,' he said.

Chapter Seventeen

The offices of Lavinia Harker Associates were on the third floor of a seventies office block. Their floor was shared by a theatrical agent and a catering company, whose advertising blurb, fixed to its opaque glass door, boasted a client list of unnamed celebrities who, despite their desire for anonymity, had been fulsome in their praise for King Catering Corps.

Lavinia Harker had a similar opaque glass door, hers unadorned by anything bar her name, blocked in gold on the upper panel.

Lavinia Harker Associates, Marris read, figuring that the associates were either too numerous to mention by name, too unimportant or, more likely, completely fictitious.

Two young women typed furiously in the cramped reception area. In contrast to Simon Roper's front of house presenter, neither had silken bob cuts so the hair moved as one single entity nor did they have the berry coloured lips and matching nails.

One of them at least knew how to smile, though.

'Can I help you?'

Marris smiled back, or at least, he thinned his lips in what he hoped was an approximation.

'I'm looking for Lavinia Harker.' He held out his identification.

'Ooh,' she said, addressing her remark to the other woman. 'He's a policeman.'

Two pairs of eyes, one large and blue the other meltingly brown, regarded him with wonder and curiosity and informed him that, unless these two were clients of the theatrical merchants next door, police officers were not expected visitors at Lavinia Harker Associates.

Brown eyes, he guessed she was no more than nineteen, was on the phone to someone. 'Miss Harker says to go on through,' she said. 'And I'm to ask would you like a cup of coffee. I make it fresh, not that machine stuff.'

So, Miss Harker was expecting the meeting to last long enough to brew coffee. Anna's name, in fact the news of the murder, had not yet made it to the media, so far as he knew. It had earned a brief mention on the lunchtime bulletins, but was still being described as an incident, new-speak for murder, of course. The street name had been mentioned, but that was all. But, Marris thought, more likely Simon Roper had called ahead and made certain he was anticipated.

'Coffee would be nice, thank you,' he told brown eyes. She got up at once and fled through to the little room at the side which he could see was equipped, quite well equipped in fact, as a tiny kitchen. Blue eyes fluttered as though she too would like to be doing something for this visiting dignitary. She made the best of it by hopping to her feet and opening the office door.

Marris thanked her, noting that she too looked no more than nineteen or twenty, and squeezed past carefully into the other room.

Lavinia Harker got to her feet and sashayed over, hand outstretched. 'Thanks Cheryl, that's fine. Come and sit down, Inspector Marris.'

Marris quirked an eyebrow. He'd not given his name and neither had the girls. 'Mr Roper called you, I take it.'

She nodded. 'And I'm grateful that he did. Is she really dead?'

'I'm afraid so, yes.'

Lavinia Harker held his gaze for a moment as though she might discover some doubt there. She shook her head. 'But who? Simon says you suspect Robert Carr.'

'He was seen at the flat at the time of her death. He admits to being there.'

'But not to killing her. Surely.'

'Did you ever meet Mr Carr?'

'No, never, there was no reason to. Simon is also very protective of him. Though I suppose he's reason to be.'

'I gather he's Roper's cash cow,' Marris said.

Her moue of disgust was not entirely convincing. 'Crudely put,' she said, 'but you're right, of course. In his position, I'd be protective, too.'

Marris studied her. Not as young as he'd thought at first glance. Late forties, he'd guess now, but well preserved. No, he corrected himself. Well looked after, good skin, a minimum of make-up – either that or very skilful application. Hair that had been professionally dyed so it had some tonal range to it and a figure that showed work, though whether the work was gym-based or came courtesy of a scalpel Marris didn't want to speculate.

She wore a calf length skirt that fitted close to the hips and a short sleeved top. The suit jacket hung on the back of her chair.

He wondered if the Miss of her title was real or just convenient.

'You vetted Anna Freeman.'

She frowned and a slight knock at the door

delayed her reply. Brown eyes entered with a tray of coffee and biscuits. The biscuits, Marris guessed, were her own idea.

When she'd gone, Marris asked, 'Are they the associates?'

Lavinia Harker laughed. She had a nice laugh, he thought. Warm and not too restrained.

'No, they're fresh out of college, bright enough to be capable but not so bright as to be easily bored. I get them, train them up, keep them six months and send them on their way.'

'Sort of work experience?'

She nodded. 'Several companies in the building do the same. The so-called secretarial college one floor up takes their money and churns them out like so much mince. I pay better than most, but it's still cheap,' she said candidly. 'But I do at least make sure they're employable when they leave.'

'Isn't it tiresome, having to train them up each time?'

'Data input, word processing, reception skills, it doesn't take a lot of teaching. The college gives them the basics, I just show them how it really works. Anyway, you're not here to ask me about my girls.' She smiled, raising the coffee cup to her lips, 'Or are you?' The smile was mischievous. She sipped, watching him over the rim of her cup.

Marris stretched his mouth into that

semblance of a smile. 'You vetted Anna Freeman,' he stated for the second time.

She nodded slowly. 'I suppose I did.'

'Suppose?'

She frowned as though weighing the details and finding them wanting. He guessed from her expression this wasn't the first time.

'I earn my money by being good at what I do, being careful, keeping a low profile and giving top priority to client confidentiality. Usually, when I'm asked to do a job like this, I have to find the person, check them out, verify their identity and then report back, often without the ... person in question being aware of it.'

'What kind of work do you cover?'

She shrugged. 'Often, it's to do with legacies,' she said. 'It's amazing how often folk want to repair the family rift with a postmortem gift. This tendency to be generous to the prodigal doesn't always go down too well with other family members, as you might well imagine. But, anyway, the work I do is varied. These days, I have agents to do the foot slogging, but I can still hack it when I have to.'

Marris nodded. He could believe it. 'And Anna?'

She shook her head. 'I was told that this woman would come to me with relevant ID, all I had to do was check it out, see that she was the same person as it said on the passport. No background checks, just a brief conversation. She was in my office for less than an hour.'

'And your verdict?'

'For what it was worth, and actually, it was worth more than my hourly rate, I verified that the woman and the passport picture seemed to be the same, that the driver's licence checked out, though it was an old one and she admitted that the address wasn't up to date. She had a few personal items, pictures, a notebook ... sort of diary, I suppose. A couple of drawings she claimed Rob Carr had done and the signature seemed genuine. Simon certainly seemed happy about it. I talked to her, but in all honesty, Inspector Marris, all I could and did say in my report was that she appeared to be the real Anna Freeman.'

'You had doubts?'

'I had no certainties.' She paused. 'Drink your coffee. Honey will be mortified if you don't.'

'Honey?'

'Baker. Her parents must have hated her. Mine did, giving me a name like Lavinia. It was always Lavvy in school.'

'Kids can be cruel. You said she brought some personal items with her.' He tasted the coffee, added a little sugar. The craving for a cigarette was back, catching him off guard.

He checked his pockets, pack and lighter were still there, so far he'd resisted today, but he knew he couldn't last.

Lavinia Harker was rummaging in her filing cabinet. She came back with a hanging file which she lay, open, on her desk.

'I photocopied the pictures and the letters, a couple of pages of the diary. And the driver's licence and the ID page on the passport.' She shrugged. 'If they'll help, take them.'

Marris shuffled through the papers. The letters and the large photograph he recognised from the flat. Pages from the notebook squared with what he'd seen of it too. 'Is this a copy of your report?'

'Yes, you want that too?'

'I'll take it if you don't mind. Just now it's impossible to know what will prove useful and what won't.'

He felt, rather than saw, her nod agreement. 'Like that in my job too,' she said.

'And you did no preliminary work on this?' She was frowning when he looked at her, the mouth pursed and eyes creased. She shook her head.

'No, bloody wish I had.' She shrugged. 'To be truthful, it was a bit of easy money and, frankly, if Simon and Robert Carr didn't give any more concern for truth than this I didn't see why I should bust a gut. I did my job, they got their publicity. Job done. I

129

covered my backside by stating my concerns in the report.'

'Did Robert Carr know you were checking on Anna?'

She shrugged again. 'I assumed so. I didn't ask. Simon didn't say, but wouldn't you have wanted to know?'

'I suppose he just presumed he'd recognise her anyway,' Marris said thoughtfully. 'He'd spent years painting her, after all.'

'Wonder what he'll do now she's gone?'

Last time I saw him he was busy falling apart, Marris thought.

Chapter Eighteen

By five fifteen Gina Lees was stuck in traffic in Kingston-upon-Thames. She was also lost in a section of one way systems she didn't remember from the last time she'd been there, though, when she came to think about it, that had been several years before.

Jenny and Pete Walters, the Jenny and Pete holding hands in the photograph, were married now apparently, and had two kids and a rather large dog. She finally reached their home, a nice looking house on a new development just outside Kingston, which, she realised to her chagrin, she could have reached without exploring the town centre itself.

Gina Lees was not best pleased.

She'd taken time to go home, shower and change; the biker jacket, scraggy jeans and Metallica T-shirt might be fine for an early morning call out but, she figured, a decent pair of trousers and an ironed shirt might be more appropriate for this visit. She took a second or two with the rear view mirror to check her hair and redo her lipstick; she had a bad habit of gnawing the stuff off when she was stressed, and sitting in slow moving, almost stationary traffic qualified as stress for Gina. She half wished she'd come on the bike, but that would have meant full leathers and a helmet and, glancing along the length of the street at the identical faux mullioned windows, she decided this would not have been a good idea. She caught at least three pairs of eyes checking up on this stranger who was probably selling something in their cul de sac. The lamppost nearest to her car had a prominent 'Neighbourhood Watch' sign attached to it with a metal band. It was neither defaced nor, evidenced by the line of rust that had gathered along the top edge of the band, had it been disturbed since installation. She supposed that the watchers from the windows were probably loyal members of the watch crew.

The Walters' house was separated from the

pavement by two small patches of close mown lawn and a token flowerbed beneath a jutting window. The flowers flopped forward as though exhausted by their effort to reach the light blocked by the over-hanging window. The bay, itself, in common with most of the others in the street, was dressed with lace nets. Gina had an almost passionate dislike of nets.

The bell was answered on the second ring.

'Yes,' the man, still dressed from work in a suit and tie, was in no mood for idle visitors.

'Mr Peter Walters?'

'That's right.'

'I'm DS Lees,' she explained, holding her card so he could see it in the light from the hall.

'DS?'

'Detective Sergeant,' she explained.

'Oh, of course. A police officer. Well, if it's about the neighbourhood watch, I've already told a dozen people. I don't have time and neither does my wife and while I applaud their actions it really isn't...'

'It's not about the neighbourhood watch,' she said quietly. 'It's about Anna Freeman.'

'Anna?' Irritation transmuted to bewilder-ment. 'What about Anna?'

'I'm sorry to tell you this, but I'm afraid ... Anna was found dead early this morn-ing.' It sounded rather stark, put like that, but she knew there was no real way of softening the blow.

His face blanked, then he laughed nervously. 'Rubbish, Anna can't be dead. She was on the television only a few nights ago.' He examined Gina's face, looking for confirmation that this couldn't possibly be so, found none.

'I'm sorry,' she repeated. 'Could I come in?' She smiled reassuringly. 'Then perhaps the neighbours could stop speculating about what I'm trying to sell.'

The family had been eating, gathered in a box of a dining room. Long curtains hid what Gina assumed would be patio doors. Two small children, one in a high chair, looked up with interest as she came in with their father. Jenny Walters began to ask 'Who was it?' then froze mid sentence as her husband introduced 'Sergeant Lees. She's come about Anna. Jenny, something dreadful...' he paused, looked at the children. 'Um, maybe we should go through to the other room.'

Gina wondered if either of the kids were even capable of understanding what she was going to say, but then she knew very little about kids and had no major wish to discover more. 'I'd like to talk to your wife as well,' she said and watched as they exchanged a nervous glance.

'Um, they've nearly done. I'll ask Jim and Ellen next door if they'll have them for a few minutes, though it'll soon be bath and bed time so I hope it won't take long?' She bit her lip as though suddenly worried that her final remark might be misconstrued, make her sound as if she didn't care. 'Is it serious?'

'Anna's dead,' her husband told her.

'Oh, my God... How? Has there been an accident?'

Gina shook her head. 'I'm afraid it wasn't an accident,' she said. She watched as Jenny's eyes widened and the implications sank in.

The older of the two children regarded her mother with silent interest. The little one bashed her spoon on her high chair tray.

'Dead, dead, dead,' she chanted in perfect time until her mother reached and snatched the spoon away.

Half an hour later they were sitting in the smart but equally cramped living room drinking filter coffee. The children were next door.

Gina leaned back into the depths of plum velour, watching as the Walters discussed the copy of the photograph she had found in Anna's flat.

'Do you remember it being taken?'

Jenny looked up briefly and nodded before returning her gaze to that image of their decade old selves. 'We all look so young,' she said. 'Where did you get this?'

'It was found in Anna Freeman's flat. Do you keep in touch with any of the people in the picture?'

The couple exchanged another glance.

'Christmas cards, that sort of thing,' Pete replied. 'I think Lyn must have taken these pictures, is that right?'

Jenny nodded. 'She was into photography then, had a darkroom set up in the cupboard under her mother's stairs. Mandy, her mum, used to complain it stank the place out.'

'But you have addresses for the others?'

Again that exchanged glance. Gina had noted this with couples who'd been together for a while; this inability to express thought without looking to the other to make sure you'd got it right.

'Should have,' Jenny said. 'Except Clive, he's working abroad, but I've got his mother's phone number somewhere. You remember, Pete, I dug it out for Simon when he called.'

'Simon called you? When was that?'

'Oh? I assumed that's who'd given you our address?'

Actually, no. That came from Robert Carr.' Or, rather, it had come from one of the little black sketchbooks Marris had taken from his drawer. The address, together with a rather cruel, but, Gina now saw, very accurate caricature of Pete, with prominent ears and

135

slightly crooked nose, drawn beside it.

'Oh, all right.' Pete explained, 'No, Simon called a couple of months back, asked if we had any idea at all where she might be. I have to tell you, we were a bit short with him. We'd already had some reporters round, camping on our doorstep and then some private investigator type.'

'He didn't exactly camp,' Jenny reproved. 'He phoned a couple of times and he called here once. We told him the same as we'd told Simon, he'd do better to try Joe Sykes. Joe and Anna were an item for a while before she left. I know they kept in touch for a while. Simon wanted to know if she'd left anything behind that might give him a clue as to where she'd gone. I told him even if she did, we have enough trouble keeping track of the Lego and the jigsaw bits, never mind something left behind ten years back.'

She paused, shaking her head. 'Who'd want to kill Anna? She was a lovely girl.'

From the corner of her eye, Gina caught Pete shift uncomfortably in his seat.

'What was she like?' Gina encouraged. Anything you can tell us, however trivial, it might help.'

They were back to sharing glances again, Gina noted with a little irritation. God, woman, think for yourself, you know you can.

'She was beautiful,' Jenny said. 'She

136

laughed a lot, joked a lot, was ... I don't know, a free spirit I suppose.'

And that means...? Gina wondered. She asked, 'When she left, was it a surprise to anyone?'

'No,' Pete this time. 'She always said she wanted to travel, originally meant to go at the start of summer but Joe persuaded her to stay. She had a job somewhere in France. We got cards for a while, then it all petered out the way these things do.'

'And the last time you saw her?'

'As we told Simon, we've been married seven years. She came to the wedding.'

And she seemed?'

'Same as ever. I remember joking with her about Rob's work, it was just getting well known then. She got stroppy and told me to keep quiet about it, so I did.'

He sounded ruffled by the memory and Jenny's hand coming to rest on her husband's arm told Gina that she'd touched a nerve.

'Did you see her on the television show?'

'Sure, we watched,' Jenny told her. 'I sent a note via Simon with our new phone number in case she wanted to get in touch.' Her face crumpled suddenly as it hit home that now Anna never would. 'Oh, God, this is just too awful.'

Gina waited until the brief storm began to subside.

'Does Rob know?' Pete asked. 'He must be devastated.'

'He knows,' Gina assured him.

'Well, tell him, we're here for him if he needs us. I mean, I never much liked the man but...'

'You didn't like him?' Gina could see that the momentary honesty had been instantly regretted.

'I mean ... I didn't actually dislike him, just...' He sighed. 'He could be a difficult man, distant, a bit aloof. He was older than the rest of us by about five or six years. It doesn't sound much, but there's a big difference between twenty and twenty-five, I suppose.'

Gina nodded. She turned at the sound of tapping on the window. The next door neighbour stood outside with the younger of the children in his arms. She was dressed for bed in pyjamas and a bright pink dressing gown. She was fast asleep.

Jenny excused herself. Gina could hear her fussing over her child and chatting to the neighbour, then the creak of the stairs as she carried her to bed.

'Were you in love with Anna?'

She hadn't been certain before, but his head jerked towards her, eyes full of guilt and accusation. 'No, of course not. I'm in love with Jen, always have been.'

She decided to let it go. For now. 'You

mentioned addresses, phone numbers. If I could bother you for those, then I'll be on my way.'

He nodded briefly and got up, crossing to an over-large sideboard that dominated one end of the room. For a few minutes the silence was broken only by the scratching of his pen as he copied the information she required. 'Here,' he said. 'Now, if you don't mind, I'd better go round and collect Megan, she'll be ready for bed too. Routine is important to children, you know.'

'I'm sure it is,' Gina told him. 'Thank your wife for me, won't you. If I need any thing else, I'll try to come back at a better time.'

The sudden frigidity of his expression informed her better than words that such a visit would not be welcome anytime.

Heading for the car, she thought about those utility bills in Anna's flat. Simon was already paying her bills when he was still ringing round ostensibly trying to track her down.

Something very dodgy was going down here. Gina glanced at her watch, seven fifteen. She looked at the addresses Pete Walters had given her and wondered if there was still time at the end of this already very long day to pay a visit to Joe Sykes.

Chapter Nineteen

Rob had almost forgotten about the man in his studio. It was only when he caught the movement at the edge of his field of vision and heard the footstep on the wooden floor that he remembered.

'You're still here? Sorry, I ... I was involved. I shut the world out that way.'

'Must be nice to be able to do that.'

Rob looked for a double meaning, an edge of sarcasm on Marris's words but found none. 'It's not nice,' he said. 'It's survival.'

The other man nodded slowly and fished in his pockets again, half withdrawing the pack of cigarettes and then dropping them back into the capacious space. The coat must once have been expensive, Rob thought, the plaid lining giving away the brand, though it was so stained and faded it looked almost as though the man inside had been camping out in the coat since the first day of ownership. The studio was warm, but he'd shown no sign or inclination to take it off. Rob wondered if it had developed into some sort of second skin, remove it and he's vulnerable. An almost overwhelming urge to see Marris without his camouflage came over him and he wondered if he turned the heating up it would have the desired effect.

'That painting,' Marris was pointing at the triptych. 'What's that all about then?'

'About? Art doesn't have to be about anything.'

Marris came closer, head on one side. He has such a thin neck, Rob thought. How can he support a head like that on such a thin neck?

The rounded head, narrow and balding at the crown, tilted back the other way and Rob had this sudden urge to reach out his hands, catch it when the neck snapped and it fell. He shifted position trying to shake the idea, find something else to focus on, fell into the trap of noticing the off-centre bald patch on the right hand top of Marris's head.

'It seems to me you're telling a story here,' Marris said. 'You and the young woman, a woman that both is and isn't Anna. You meet, she kisses you, she goes away, but it seems to me that even while you're kissing her she's ... somewhere else.' He looked at Rob for approval of his narrative, jerking that head back upright on that stick neck with such a suddenness that Rob's hands wanted to reach out again.

He managed to divert them, reaching instead for his brush, then realising that to apply paint to the picture he'd have to get closer to Marris, closer and on eye level with that damned bald patch. How can anyone have an off-centre bald patch? And worse still, an off-centre comb over.

'Shave it,' he said, the words falling out of his mouth before he could trip them up and distract them.

Marris raised an eyebrow.

'Nothing,' Rob said. 'Nothing.'

'Gina thinks the same,' Marris told him. 'That I should have a number one all over and be done with it. Crew cut as they used to call it, but I think if I did I'd look more like a skinhead. Might get myself arrested and that would be embarrassing.'

He smiled at his own joke, the thin lips stretching sideways without curving. Rob imagined those ugly grey aliens you saw in films with their big eyes and slit mouths must smile that way. He swallowed hard, trying to focus. Marris had big eyes too. Big, dark, too big for the thin musteline features. Predator's eyes.

'Well,' Marris was saying. 'How close did I get?'

Rob was baffled, then he realised Marris was talking about the painting.

He put the brush down and backed away, pausing when his buttocks came in contact with his layout table. He lifted his weight so he could perch, uncomfortable that Marris came to rest beside him.

'Eleven years ago,' he began. 'I said good-bye to Anna in a street like that. It was November and the wind was blowing litter into the air. It wasn't dark, just at that time when the world greys out and you know night is coming but it's not quite here. I watched her walk up the street and all the time, right until she turned the corner, I was fighting the urge to run after her, to call her name, to say, "Anna, don't leave me here". But I never did.'

'Did you love her?'

Did he love her? It was a question he had asked himself so often. 'There've been times I thought I was in love,' he said. 'I even got married once. It lasted a year. Her name was Veronica, but she told everyone it was Veronique. She was pretty and talented and told me all the things I wanted to hear about myself so I asked her if she'd marry me and she said yes.' He paused remembering that even as he'd been asking the question... 'Even while I was asking the question, I was planning the wording for the pre-nup. I went home and wrote it out. Same night I proposed to her. She signed, I married her. She left me. I was generous.'

'Shows a certain lack of faith,' Marris observed.

Rob shrugged. 'She still calls herself Mrs Carr, trades on my name. I don't care enough to object.'

'What does she do?'

'Oh, she's an actress, still pretty, still talented, getting too old for the girly roles she used to get lots of.' Rob smiled at the thought. 'I can't see her content to play character roles,' he said. 'Too scared of the wrinkles.' He shrugged. 'I hear she's thinking of marrying again. I hope he has the sense to write a pre-nup.'

'And Anna, would you have expected her to sign?'

Rob laughed, the thought of Anna saying yes, never mind signing up to anything, was too absurd. 'Anna would never have married me,' he said. 'She might, had I been more fortunate than any man deserves, agreed to move in. She'd have stayed 'til something else came along, then off she'd have gone, turned up again, maybe, days or months later and not expected me to mind.'

'And would you have minded?'

'I'd have minded but I'd have put up with it.'

'Are you sure of that?'

Rob considered. It wasn't a new question but somehow, now that it had been removed forever from the realms of possibility, it seemed all the more profound. Was he sure? Would he have been able to cope with her being there, then not? Or, was the question even simpler. Could he have coped with living with Anna, with anyone at all? When

Veronica had moved into his space, it had almost destroyed him. He would wake in the morning to find some stranger in his bed that wanted breakfast before he started work. Someone who expected routine, wanted him to be there when she came home or come to see her perform in that stupid modernist thing she'd been in when he'd first married her.

Had he coped better with that, he might have considered that dealing with the vagaries of Anna would have been possible.

'Love isn't the same as possession,' he said and found that he meant it, that his mind seemed to clear and his thoughts solidify for a brief moment, instead of racing endlessly and meaninglessly in his head.

'And did you love her?'

Rob felt there was only one honest reply that he could give. 'I still don't know,' he said.

Marris prowled while Rob went back to work. Rob half heard him, but took little note. It was only when he nudged Rob's arm and handed him a cup of tea that Rob registered him again. Glancing at the clock, he saw that it was almost eight. The scent of food wafted from the kitchen.

'You've been cooking? In my kitchen?'

'I asked, you grunted, I got on with it. It's only bacon and eggs and I made toast and opened a tin of beans. Plenty of tea. Put

145

your brushes down and wash your hands.'

Rob blinked, then followed him into the kitchen and sat down as directed. Got up again and scrubbed his hands at the kitchen tap.

'You cook for all your suspects, do you?'

'Only the interesting ones. For your information, the last time I ate was last night. You have food, I have questions, fair trade?'

Last night, Rob thought realising that went for him as well. 'Just one question before we eat,' he said. 'I need to know. Do you think I killed her?'

He watched Marris pause, a laden fork halfway to his mouth. 'If I felt certain you'd done it you'd be locked up in a police cell. The truthful answer is, I don't know. But hear me, Robert Carr. If you're innocent, I'll lock up whoever did kill her. If you're guilty; I'll put you inside and not think twice.'

Chapter Twenty

Joe Sykes had changed little since the picture had been taken. Pete and Jenny Walters, pictured as students, he in jeans and skinny T-shirt fitted close to a skinny body; she in a short skirt and cropped strappy top, long hair in twin braids, were still recognisable as

146

the people they had been. But the effort of change, of life and settling down, had written itself on their clothes, their hair, their plum-coloured chairs and their self-statement now marked them as successful in particular and distinctive terms. It said, we work hard, we do well at our work, we reap the rewards and we have two children to complete the scene.

Gina doubted they'd even though of those elements as marking proof of life when that picture had been taken.

Joe Sykes on the other hand still wore his dark hair curling in his neck and the same surly, I-know-I'm-still-good-looking-even-when-I-scowl expression on his tanned face. Gina would have sworn the jacket he wore was the same too. He'd been the only one in the picture wearing a coat, the warmth of the day evident as much in the lack of clothing the others wore as in the sun sparkling and flaring off the river backdrop. The jacket, she decided, was of value as a statement rather than a simple item of clothing.

He'd not been home when Gina arrived at Mill Cottage – no sign of a mill so far as she could see, in fact, no sign of anything much. The tiny house, one of two, reached by a long winding lane not marked on the map, was impossible to find until she managed to get instructions from a dog walker.

The windows were dark, no chink of light

from inside. Peering at her watch and wishing it had illuminated hands, Gina had been about to call it best and go home when a voice out of the darkness startled her enough to leave the floor.

Damn him, he must have seen her and walked along the grass verge. She'd have heard his steps along the road.

'I asked who you were looking for,' he said again.

'Mr Sykes?'

He nodded.

'I'm Detective Sergeant Lees. I wondered if you could spare me a minute or two.'

He looked her over, his eyes evidently more used to the dark than hers, then nodded briefly. 'Best come in then.'

Unlocking the door, he reached in to switch on the light, then stood aside and gestured for her to enter. Gina recalled seeing some documentary or other on body language. She had a vague feeling that to insist someone preceded you through a door was some kind of power play but she was, by this time, too tired to care.

'Well, what can I do for you?' He glanced briefly at her identification, then shrugged out of the backpack she'd not noticed before and let it slide to the floor. His jacket followed, thrown carelessly on a chair.

'You ride a motor bike?'

He glanced at the jacket. 'No, not any

more. Did do once upon a time.'

'Oh? What?'

He paused in the act of filling the kettle. 'You came out here to ask me that?'

'No, just curious.'

'I had a Thunderbird. Triumph. You know, from the time this country made motor bikes.' He placed the kettle on the hob. 'I've got no time for rice burners, too much plastic. Seen one you seen them all.'

'Oh, I don't know.'

His eyes narrowed and then he laughed. A lady biker,' he said. 'Well, well. And what's your ride?'

'A rice burner. 1100cc Kawasaki.'

He looked her up and down again, reappraising. Gina was used to people doing that when they knew what she rode. She was tall, five ten in stocking feet, well over six in heels, but there was nothing heavy about her. She'd tried once explaining that it was about balance as much as strength, about being able to put your feet on the floor so you could keep the beast upright rather than brute strength, but people rarely got it.

Joe Sykes did. He nodded in what might be approval. 'Still a rice burner though. Anyway, what brings you here, lady biker?'

'Anna Freeman.'

'Anna Freeman.' He laughed. 'Suddenly she's flavour of the month.'

'Not for everyone. Someone stabbed her

to death last night.'

Gina would not usually have been so brutal. Marris trusted her too often for her liking to be the harbinger of such tidings because she knew how to play it, but there was something about Joe Sykes that made her want to shock him to get a reaction. She knew as soon as she said it she had judged it wrong.

His expression of mild amusement, slipped from his face along with the colour. 'No,' he said. 'No, no, you've got that wrong. You must have got that wrong.'

Oh great, Gina reproved. She chooses now to make the wrong play.

'Sit down,' she said softly. 'Here,' she took his arm and led him to a chair. 'I'm sorry. I shouldn't have broken it to you like that. Is there someone you'd like me to call?'

He shook his head and allowed her to sit him down. 'You for real?'

'I'm sorry. I'm afraid so.'

'Christ! Who?' His expression changed again. 'That bastard, he did it, didn't he. He did for her?'

'Who?' Gina asked him, though she could guess.

'That bastard Rob Carr or whatever he calls himself now. Just plain Robert Cartwright when I knew him.'

The name change was news to Gina. 'Why would he want her dead?'

'How the hell should I know? He's a crazy bastard, isn't that enough?'

'Crazy,' she asked mildly. 'In what way, Joe?'

He was recovering now, the colour returning to his lips and cheeks. 'She left because of him, you know that? He wouldn't leave her alone, no matter what she said to make him. He was always there, hanging around, watching her.'

'She went out with you, didn't she?'

He nodded. 'Seven months and five days. Then it was all, "I need some space, Joe, need to go away for a while". She said it wasn't me. You know, what people always say when they want to let someone down gently?' She nodded and he laughed harshly, 'But I knew it was him. She went away because of him and now, now she's come back, he's gone and killed her.'

'You're not making sense, Joe. Really.'

The kettle on the hob began to squeal. 'I'll get it,' she offered.

'No. I'm not helpless.' He brushed past, angry. The moment of weakness had to be erased from his mind and from hers.

'Tell me about Rob, Anna and the others.'

'What's to tell? We were – they were – little more than kids. Rob and me, we were a bit older. Twenty-four, twenty-five. Anna was nineteen when I met her. She turned twenty when we started going together and I

151

thought, this is it, this is the woman I want. She was ... I loved her, right?'

Gina nodded. 'Were you the jealous type?'

He laughed again but there was no humour in it. 'I tried not to be,' he said. 'Anna was a flirt, I guess.'

'Guess we all are at that age.'

'I was learning to put up with it. She never meant anything by it, just being Anna. She talked about going away, but I said, no, wait for a bit. I thought she'd change her mind.'

'You never thought about going with her?'

'Yeah, I thought about it. When it came down to it though, she didn't want me along, didn't want anyone, she said. Wanted to be a free agent. Only compensation is that it hurt him as much as it bloody hurt me.'

Gina withdrew the copy of the picture from her bag. 'Have you seen this before?'

He glanced at it. 'Sure, the picture's mine.' He stirred the tea and then swung round, the spoon in his hand. Waved it at her. 'And I want it back, you tell that bastard, he'd better get that stuff back to me.'

Gina was confused. 'Robert Carr has your things?'

'No, that other one, his agent. I told him, that stuff was only on loan. He promised me he'd have it copied and get it back. I tried phoning him, all I get is some bloody woman telling me he's out or in a meeting.'

'Simon Roper?'

He nodded, dropped the teapot lid noisily into place.

'How come he has your things?'

He frowned, dragged a tea cosy over the pot. 'He started calling us up couple of months back. Got onto Pete and Jenny.' He jabbed at the two figures in the photocopy. 'Those two. They put him onto me, said if anyone had anything of Anna's it'd be me. If anyone had heard from her, it'd be me. I mean, like she'd give me a call. But anyway, he kept on the bloody phone, day after day. Had I got anything that might give him a clue to where she'd gone. In the end I agreed to lend him some stuff just to make him go away. He wanted to come down here but I told him to piss off. I'd send him a few bits.'

'Did you send him everything?'

'Like hell.' He paused, looked Gina in the eye. 'She's really dead?'

'I'm sorry. Yes.'

'Bloody hell.' He turned away, angry with himself and with her, Gina guessed, for being the bearer of bad news. 'Aren't you supposed to be asking me where I was last night?'

'I was getting to that.' She couldn't keep the smile out of her voice. 'Where were you last night?'

'What time?'

'You tell me. Your movements from six

153

p.m. till six a.m. should cover it.'

'You know closer than that,' he was facing her again now, the intensity of dark eyes boring into her.

'I know closer than that,' she confirmed.

He nodded. 'So, I'm a suspect?'

'Right now, it'd be fair to say anyone could be a suspect. It's early days.' She tried to keep her tone neutral, not sure what he would read from or into her words.

He weighed her up carefully before giving his reply. 'I finished work at six, hung around chatting to a mate until quarter past, then drove home. Went out about eight, walked down to the Dog, in the village, that's the pub. There till closing time, it's quiz night, I'm on the team. Went back to a pal's for coffee. Talked till midnight, came home. Slept. Up at seven thirty, work for half past eight. Anything else?'

'Names of the friends you were with on the quiz team and the one you had coffee with last night. I have to check, you know that. And your work details. What do you do, Mr Sykes?'

He nodded. He looked satisfied as though she'd told him something, but Gina wasn't certain what. 'I drive a fork lift,' he said. 'Place called Hendry's back in Kingston. It's a warehouse, supplies one of the big catalogue companies.'

'You like your job?'

'It's a job.'

'Mr Sykes, did you keep anything else of Anna's? I got the impression that you did.'

He was standing with his back against the cooker, arms folded, staring down at her. She wished she'd been wearing heels. His movement as he pushed away from his support was sudden enough to have her jumping back. He seemed not to have noticed, but Gina was sure she saw the hint of a smile.

He crossed the room and went to a large cupboard built into an alcove. From there he extracted a cardboard box. He dumped it on the sofa and sat down beside it.

'This,' he said, 'and this.' A second notebook, similar to the one in the flat, was dropped onto the cushion together with a letter and a postcard, a keyring with a key and another letter. He rummaged some more and produced a second photograph, the mate to the one she'd seen and copied. The difference was, there was no Joe in this picture, his place had been taken by a short-haired woman in a printed dress.

'Lyn?' she asked.

He looked surprised, but nodded. 'She took that one. She printed them. I asked for copies.'

'I'm going to need to borrow these.'

'I didn't say that. I said I'd show you.'

'And I need to show my boss.' She took a

couple of evidence bags from her bag and opened one up, gestured that he should put the book inside.

He sighed, but did what she wanted, placing the other items in the second bag. 'Definitely still a suspect then?' he asked.

'Like I said, anyone is until we eliminate them.'

'Including him?'

She knew he meant Robert Carr. 'Including him.'

'Some compensation then.' His eyes flashed dangerously, then the fire went out again. 'Look, I'd like you to go, OK?'

She nodded and got to her feet before adding, 'Did you see the television show?'

'Why would I want to do that?'

'See Anna again after all this time.'

He shook his head emphatically. 'I prefer to keep my memories of her as they are,' he said. 'My Anna was back then, not part of some damned media circus.'

Chapter Twenty-One

Gina drove far enough up the lane to be out of sight of the house, then pulled over onto the verge, hoping there wasn't a hidden ditch waiting for her to fall into.

'I was just about to call you,' Marris told her. 'Any joy?'

Briefly, they brought one another up to speed. 'So,' Gina asked, 'what now?'

'Well, I know you're hoping for me to tell you to get home to bed...'

'That would be nice.'

'Nice but not about to happen. How long will it take you to get to our Mr Roper's place?' He gave her the address and she calculated.

'No way I can be there before ten, half past, maybe.'

'I'll meet you there. I don't know exactly what he's playing at, Gina, but I figure it's time we found out.'

Simon Roper didn't seem all that surprised to see them. He made some small complaint about the hour, but that was all.

Marris said nothing until Simon had led them through to the living room and invited them to sit.

The room was calm and quiet, no television, just music playing softly in the background. Mahler, Marris thought, though he couldn't be sure, the volume was too low for him to tell. He wished Simon would either turn it up or off, the faint melody nagged at his consciousness, impinging without ever making sense.

'We've had an interesting day, Mr Roper,'

Marris told him.

Simon inclined his head, indication that he should tell him. So Marris did and while he told his tale, Simon's gaze did not once leave his face, the fixedness of it as much an avoidance strategy as if he'd looked at the floor the whole time. Marris said, 'It wasn't Anna Freeman in that flat, was it?'

'No,' Simon replied softly. 'No, you're right, it wasn't. She was supposed to collect the rest of her money and leave on Friday. That would have been it.'

'And you think you'd have got away with it?' Gina asked him.

'I don't think; I *knew*. I knew, because that's ultimately what everyone wanted. Anna in her place. People in general don't like too much reality.'

'You think that's why someone killed her? She wasn't in the right place?'

Simon didn't reply. He got up and poured himself a drink from the cabinet in the corner of the room.

'How did you do it?' Marris asked softly. And how did you convince Robert Carr to go along with it?'

'Rob?' Surprised, Simon turned back to face him. 'Rob didn't know. Rob, bless him, has his head too far up his own artistic backside for it even to cross his mind that I might...'

'Betray his trust?' Gina offered.

'It wasn't like that.'

'Then sit down, Mr Roper, and tell us how it was. Or would you rather I charge you first?'

'With what?

'You've obstructed a murder investigation, Mr Roper. We believed we were looking for the killer of Anna Freeman; you've now set us another problem. Was the killer after Anna or was his intended victim this other young woman?'

'Maria Warner,' he said. 'Her name was Maria Warner. She was an actress.'

He came back and sat down on the small sofa beside Gina. Eyes down now, cradling his glass in his hand and gazing down at the thickly carpeted floor.

'How did you do it?' Marris asked. 'How did you coach this young woman, where did the information come from?'

Simon laughed bitterly. 'Oh, that was easy. You see, I've known Rob since not long after Anna left and there were plenty of little things he let slip. I have this mind that tells me, all things are useful sooner or later, so I kept notes. I never planned this, but when I had to do it, most of what I needed I already had.'

'Had to do it?' Gina was outraged.

Marris held up a hand and gestured silence. 'Then you contacted Rob's old friends,' he said. 'And Joc Sykes came up trumps.'

159

Simon nodded. 'And I added a couple of sketches I'd got. Discards, things Rob started and then chucked away. I ... pick them up. He never notices what's there and what's not once he's done with it. I knew Lavinia Harker would want something personal, identifiable, if she was to give her approval to Anna, as it was she wasn't sure. I told her it was a rush job and to put her doubts in her report so she was covered, but it didn't matter. Rob thought she'd been checked out and I knew he'd be unlikely to push. I spent two months coaching her, getting her cover story right. I told her, you only have to be on show that one night, then you can disappear again, just like Anna.'

'And if the real Anna had turned up and challenged you?'

'So much the better. There was enough publicity about my Anna being on the show. I thought it might flush the real one out of hiding. If it did, Maria would still have been paid, no worries for any one.'

'But Rob? You couldn't fool Robert Carr?'

Simon shrugged. 'It was Rob that made me certain I could pull this off,' Simon explained. 'I began to see that he'd never really known Anna. He'd admired her, studied her, the way Rob always studies women. But know her? No, he didn't go that far. Rob would see what he wanted to see and he did exactly that.'

'I thought you were meant to be his friend?' Gina challenged. 'What you did was deceitful at the very least.'

'You could see it that way,' Simon admitted.

'What about the friends?' Marris interrupted. 'They must, out of pure curiosity, have watched the programme. Didn't any of them suspect?'

Simon hesitated. 'Lyn Chapel,' he said. 'She phoned me, wanted to know what I was playing at. What Rob was playing at going along with it? Joe Sykes twigged too, well out of all of them I suppose he would. I asked them both to hold off doing anything for a week or two and then I'd explain why. I told them it'd be worth their while. I got the impression that Joe would go along with that, but Lyn seemed ... reluctant. Actually,' he confessed, 'she told me to stuff whatever it was I was offering, but in the end she agreed to meet with me and give me a few days' grace. I thought, if she let me explain why, tell her about the pressure Rob had been under, she'd be sympathetic. From what she said on the phone, she felt that if Rob let himself be fooled, that was his lookout anyway.'

'And did the meeting go to plan?'

'I had to cancel. I rearranged for this weekend, but then Joe Sykes called me up and I knew it would all be out in the open anyway. Now it's just down to damage limitation.'

'And what did Joe Sykes tell you?'

'That he'd sold his story. He wanted to boast, I guess. He was drunk and annoyed and wanted to tell me that it would all break this Sunday. He wouldn't tell me which paper had taken the story, just hinted they'd paid him more to spill than I ever could to keep quiet. He told them he'd got proof that she wasn't the real thing and that they were very interested in the stuff he lent to me.'

'He'd provided your provenance and now he wanted more,' Marris clucked his tongue as though despairing the duplicity of man. 'Simon, you're not stupid, surely you realised this wouldn't work long term. Someone would talk, maybe this young woman you hired to play the part.' He paused and looked meaningfully at Simon. 'Maybe she threatened you; maybe she wanted more than you were prepared to pay.'

Simon Roper was not accustomed to being accused of murder and it took a moment to register. A horrified look twisted at his mouth and the words almost wouldn't come. 'You can't be even remotely serious. My God! You're accusing me of...' He got up and opened the hall door.

'Where are you going, Mr Roper?'

'To my study, to call my lawyer.'

'At this time of night?' Marris clucked his

tongue again, this time at his watch. He sighed. 'All right, Mr Roper, we'll do it your way, though I didn't really want to make it such a late night, seeing what an early start we had this morning. Tell your lawyer to meet you at the nick. I'll get you processed, then we can all get off home and I'll come back to talk to you in the morning, say, around ten. That do you?'

Again Simon did not immediately register what he meant. Then he half closed the door. 'You'd charge me and leave me in a police cell?'

'I'd caution you, take you in for questioning. I can do that on suspicion, Mr Roper. I wouldn't actually charge you yet, you see, that would come later, after we'd had a formal chat and you'd confessed and signed a statement. But, frankly, Mr Roper, I started at five this morning with a dead body and it's way past time I was in bed, so, like I say, I'd get you settled in for the night and then come back and finish in the morning. We'd have plenty of time, you see. It's getting on for midnight now, by the time we'd got you booked in it would be one, one thirty. I can keep you for a full twenty-four hours without bringing a formal charge.' He let the full weight of his words sink in. 'Or,' he paused, 'we could continue with our talk here, comfortably and you could go and lie down in your own bed when it's over. I

163

doubt you'll sleep much, but at least you can stay awake in comfort, get up and watch the early morning telly, make yourself a cup of tea.' He paused again, waiting.

Simon shut the door with a sharp click and sat back down.

'Now,' Marris said. 'Where were we? Oh yes, you were telling me about your little deception.' He frowned. 'You know, you and Robert Carr were onto a good thing and, so far as I can tell, it was all above board. Why risk it with a scam like this? Anna must have family?'

Simon shook his head. 'None we could trace and believe me we tried. Her parents died when she was a teenager, I think in some accident or other. She had a stepbrother, older than her. He lives in the US, I think. He was never close and didn't answer any of our appeals, so we figured ... I figured he was pretty safe. I was ready with a cover story anyway, if it all went pear-shaped I'd say I'd never met Anna, so how was I to know. Lavinia had already made her doubts known, she'd be fine. Rob could always say he didn't want a confrontation on live TV but that we'd got our lawyers involved straight after and no, we didn't know who the impostor was and she'd done a runner anyway.'

Marris laughed, the thin lips drawing back to reveal fang like canines. 'My Lord, what a web you wove for yourself. I hope you kept notes.' He looked more closely at Simon's face. 'You did, didn't you? You kept crib sheets, make sure you could keep your story straight whatever happened. My Lord, Mr Roper, you missed your calling! Ever considered a career in politics?'

'It isn't funny,' Simon writhed uncomfortably beneath his scrutiny.

Abruptly, Marris's laughter ceased and he leaned forward, his gaze hardened and fixed on Simon's face. 'No, Mr Roper, it isn't funny and I'm still not clear why you did it anyway.'

Simon tried to break free of those black in black eyes, the irises as dark as the pupils in the soft light of the living room. The only escape was to close his eyes. He shut them tight.

'There seemed no other way,' he said. 'Oh, I know, that sounds weak and downright stupid, but the bad publicity, the wild claims, they were upsetting Rob and so I thought, contingency plan. Always have a fall back opposition. That's all she was meant to be, Maria, a safety net. I thought, it'll all be a five minute wonder anyway. Just give them what they want on the night and it'll be forgotten by the end of the week.'

'That sounds remarkably naïve,' Marris observed.

'No kidding. But you've got to believe I did what I did to protect Rob. I was acting in his best interests. Or thought I was.'

'Pity it didn't turn out that way. Now, I need everything you have on the real Anna Freeman and on this other young woman, Maria Warner. We need to see if we can figure out who the killer was after, Miss Warner or Anna Freeman, because if it was Anna Freeman, and she's still out there, he could try again if he finds he's hit the wrong girl.'

'What I still don't get,' Gina had been silent for a while but now she turned back to an earlier question, 'is that Robert Carr suspected nothing. I just can't believe that.'

'People see what they want to see, by and large,' Simon said wearily. 'It was in Rob's interest to go along with it and, I think he really liked Maria. She said a lot of things the night they met that must have reinforced the idea that she was Anna, talked about events they could both recall … but, I don't know. I think he had begun to realise. I mean not to put it into words, but … he said he couldn't see her any more. That her image didn't fit.' He sighed heavily and rubbed his eyes wearily with the heels of his hands. 'I told myself, at least it's got him creating again and not just going through the motions. That it was all worth it for that anyway. I'll admit, when I saw that painting I was nonplussed but … it'll sell, I've no doubt of that. Despite all of this.'

'Or because of it?' Gina asked.

'All of which is unimportant just now,' Marris reminded them. 'A young woman is dead and, though her name might not have been Anna Freeman, she's still someone's child.'

Chapter Twenty-Two

Rob woke, alone as usual. He had slept deeply after a restless start, and opened his eyes to find bright sunlight streaming in through his window. For a blessed, blissful minute or two, he lay there, relaxed and peaceful, until the memory returned, forceful and vengeful from having been ignored while he slept.

'Anna.'

He closed his eyes and turned his head from the light, then opened them again, staring at the grey wall. It didn't matter, eyes wide open or tight shut, the image of her, lying on the floor, broken and tangled, swam before him, projected onto that screen no one else could see but which impinged on every moment of his waking mind unless he could find some other thing to block it out.

Reluctantly, he rolled out of bed and showered, tried to eat. He had this strange memory of having spent time last night entertaining Inspector Marris; this odd impression that Marris had cooked for him, eaten with him, mother-henned until he forced down eggs and bacon. Examining his kitchen for evidence that this had really occurred, Rob found only contradictory data. The kitchen itself was clean and tidied, eggs and a pack of bacon were missing from the fridge, but only one set of crockery and a single knife and fork lay on the draining board.

He tried to recall. Did they wash the pots and pans after their meal? Did he, Rob, then get himself something else later? Had he dreamed the whole thing?

He wondered how he could broach the subject with Marris without seeming completely insane. He could hardly ask straight out. 'Excuse me, but did we have supper together last night? I had the strangest feeling...' It sounded like some rather lame chat up line.

He poured himself more tea and then, elbows on the table, rested his head in his hands. Was it happening again? Was he heading for another episode?

No, he couldn't deal with that, not on top of everything else. Since, at least, he wasn't under arrest, he had to do something positive with the day.

Leaving his breakfast things where they

were he went through to the studio and rummaged in the top drawer of his plan chest for his black books only to remember that Marris had them, that Marris was using them to track down his friends and associates and anyone that might know who'd killed Anna.

Rob wondered if he was really allowed to do that, take stuff from someone who hadn't actually been charged with an offence. For that matter, was he allowed to break the lock on a door? Someone, Simon presumably, had fixed a new one and his solicitor had given him the new key, but it still felt like an invasion. He went to the phone and reached for the receiver. Grey fingerprint powder showed the marks of his fingers and thumb. Rob studied the marks. Did he really hold the receiver like that? Fingertips only, no sign of a palm print you might expect. Most people, Rob had noted, cradled the receiver in their palm, holding it secure, sometimes pressing it between their shoulder and chin to set their other hand free.

Not Rob, it seemed. The imprint of three digits had been marked by the silver grey powder.

He laid his fingers against the pattern, lifted the receiver. Yes, that felt right, that felt like the way he did it. Was it really so strange?

He had the powder on his hand now. Lowering the receiver, he felt it between his fingers and thumb. Expecting it to be gritty, he was astonished to find it grease fine, almost smooth as talcum. Absently, forgetting in fact that he'd been going to use the phone to give Marris a piece of his mind and demand his books back, Rob wiped the powder against his trouser leg, then went in search of his coat.

Minutes later he was out on the street trying, and failing, to find his car. Belatedly, he remembered that he'd driven it to Anna's flat. Then where? He could recall the sense of panic as he'd driven away and then parking the car ... but that was it. He'd been able to see the London Eye when he got out, and could visualise the street in his mind's eye. Try as he might, though, he couldn't turn his image in the direction of the street sign.

Rob sighed, chances were it had been towed anyway and he didn't really have the time or inclination to find where it had been taken to. Maybe the police had it? Maybe Marris had it along with his books?

'Damn,' Rob had been meaning to phone Marris when he'd got distracted by the bloody powder. What should he do now?

Standing on the corner of his street, Rob thought about it. Should he phone Simon?

No, he called Simon for every bloody thing. This was something he could work out alone.

He took out his wallet and, searching through, found a business card for a taxi company that took Visa. Simon, knowing he'd rarely got cash on him, had given this to him, told him he could call this firm if he found himself stuck somewhere.

Did he have his mobile with him?

Relieved, Rob found that he did. He dialled the number carefully, spoke to someone, explaining that he had quite a way to go, then waited patiently for the few minutes it took for the cab to arrive. He wondered how much this trip would cost, bearing in mind that he'd also need a taxi back, then with an effort put the question from his mind. He'd not had to worry about that kind of thing for several years now, but he still did. There was still this thought always at the back of his mind that sooner or later the bottom would fall out of his world and dump him, unceremoniously, back where he'd started from. Rob had no idea how he would cope with that.

Lyn stared at him. 'Bloody hell,' she said 'It's you. What the hell are you doing here?'

'I came to see you.'

She peered over his shoulder at the waiting cab. 'In a taxi?'

'I forgot where I'd left my car.'

'That figures. Well, unless you want him to wait, you'd better pay the man and come inside.'

Lyn hadn't changed, Rob thought as he

followed her inside. The paint on the faded blue door was cracked and peeling off in long strands, though by contrast, bright tubs of flowers stood guard on either side and the front hedge was clipped and tidy. He'd been here before, but not for several years. In fact, hadn't it been her housewarming party?

Inside, the front door opening straight into the front room, the house reflected that duality in Lyn's personality too. Three walls were magnolia plain, the fourth an exuberant fuchsia, a colour that caused Rob to wince in pain. The same shade had been used for the soft furnishings, but, thankfully, only in the silk cushions thrown in a heap on the two-seater sofa. Lyn took the chair and pointed him at the settee. 'Sit,' she commanded. Rob sat, turning so that the offending cushions were behind his back and out of his field of view.

Lyn stretched out her long legs – bare feet as usual, painted toenails – and sat back, hands clasped across her still taut abdomen. He'd swear she wore her hair in the same way, short and wavy but still managing to get in her way. She lifted a hand now to brush an imaginary strand back from her eyes.

'So,' she said again. 'Why are you here? I heard the news this morning, of course. I'm puzzled as hell, but I'm willing to hold fire while you fill me in. I must say, though, I'm surprised to get the Rob Carr in person. I thought you always communicated through that man of yours. Simon whatsit.'

'Roper,' Rob filled in. 'Simon Roper.' He was glad he could supply that bit of information because, frankly, the rest of the conversation had him baffled.

'News?' he asked. 'What do you mean news?'

'That woman being killed. It was on the morning bulletin. Apparently happened late the night before? You must have known?' She leaned forward to examine him, the cool grey eyes boring into him.

'Anna was on the news?' It clicked into place now, sort of. Of course. It would be on the news, wouldn't it?

Lyn snorted, amused, angry, Rob never had been able to read her non-verbal forms of communication even when he'd seen her regularly. What hope did he have now?

'Anna!' the sound again, followed by a brief guffaw.

Rob was incredulous. 'Anna's dead,' he exclaimed. 'And you think that's funny?'

'No, I don't think it's bloody funny. I think it's tragic that some bint of a girl got herself killed because of some game you and that Simon fella are playing.'

Rob shook his head, even more bewildered. 'What game? Lyn, you're not making sense, I don't have a clue what you're talking about.'

She narrowed her eyes, squinting at him, lips pursed as though he were some fascinating but slightly disgusting bug that had just landed on her salad. 'By God, you don't know, do you? Well, I'll be damned.'

She sat back and continued to examine him, this time with astonished concern rather than ill-concealed distaste. 'I'll make us a pot of tea,' she said. 'This is going to take Assam, I think. Something strong.'

Rob watched her sail out through the door, wondering if he should follow. He had forgotten quite how acerbic and shocking Lyn could be; how, even when they'd all known each other in Anna's time and she'd been barely out of her teens, she'd still seemed more like someone of his great aunt's generation in her manner and demeanour. He'd always assumed she was a lesbian, until a mutual acquaintance had put him straight. No, Lyn liked men, dated off and on, but she'd yet to find one she didn't intimidate. Rob figured she must still be looking.

He wasn't sure he liked Assam tea.

'Lyn?' He got up and went through the door she had vanished through. It led to a second room and then through that into a galley kitchen. Lyn looked far too big for the tiny space. Tall and broad-shouldered, though narrow-hipped, she managed to dominate just about every space she entered.

He'd have made a bet she'd even make his studio look small and cramped.

'Lyn, I...' He'd been about to tell her he didn't like Assam tea, but she was already ladling it into a fat brown pot. The open cupboard behind her displayed a complete collection of tea, both black and green and herbal. 'I see you have one for every occasion,' he said. She smiled. The first time since he'd arrived. It softened her face, distracted from her rather square jaw and put emphasis on her really rather lovely eyes. 'You should smile more,' he told her, the words coming out, as usual, before he could catch them.

She chuckled. 'Still no self-control in the mouth department,' she said. 'Though, I have to say, you did all right on the television the other night, defended yourself quite nicely against that old cow Edith Parks.'

Rob wondered if he should thank her, but anything he might have said was drowned out by the piercing squeal of coming to the boil. She turned away to lift the kettle from the stove, tugging the whistle from the spout and waving the steam away from the pot as she poured boiling water on the black tea.

'There, that should do us.' She filled a second pot with the rest of the water, arranged mugs and sugar on the tray. 'I suppose you'll want milk,' she said, 'though, in my opinion, it's better without.' She added a jug to the tray, handed Rob a biscuit tin and then ushered him, using the tray as a prod, back through to the front living room.

'Now sit back down,' she instructed, 'and let's see if we can sort out this tangle.'

For the next few minutes, Rob listened, not daring to interrupt the flow, as Lyn told him how Simon had been calling round to old friends in the hope of obtaining Anna memorabilia. Of how Lyn had directed him to Joe Sykes and how she'd really thought nothing of it at the time, seeing it as logical that they'd want background for the television programme.

'Then,' she said. 'I watched the show and I knew it was all a scam. I must admit, I was surprised at you at the time. I mean, how could you lend yourself to such a deception?'

'Deception?'

She tutted, exasperated. 'Rob, I'm beginning to realise you were taken in by that girl.' She studied him again, hard-eyed once more. 'God almighty,' she said. 'You've made yourself believe that she was the real thing.'

Rob, getting impatient now, clunked his mug down onto the tray. 'Lyn, I don't know what you mean. Truly, you've lost me. True, we had trouble finding her and I didn't believe it was a good idea, but finally, she turned up, walked into a police station about a week before the broadcast and...'

'She wasn't Anna,' Lyn said firmly. 'Rob, get a grip and listen to me. That girl might have looked like her, acted like her, walked like her, but that wasn't Anna. Rob, you just wanted it so much you allowed yourself to be fooled and now, probably because you and that Simon expected everyone to be fooled, the girl is dead.'

Rob's legs felt as thought they belonged to someone else. The effort it took just to place one foot in front of the other exhausted him, reminded him of those dreams in which you try to run, but gravity, thick as treacle, holds fast to your feet, your ankles, your knees and, however much you strive and sweat and struggle to escape, you're running backwards in slow motion, dragged inevitably and irrevocably towards that very place you don't want to be.

It was like that now, walking down towards the river, to that place he had talked about with Anna ... if she had been Anna. But how could she have those memories and not be Anna?

He sat down gratefully, resting his back against the trunk of the twisted willow, thankful that this at least was still here, still as solid and as firmly rooted as he recollected.

That night, after the television show, she had talked to him, chatted about that day when he'd made those drawings, and, now she mentioned it, he could recall the action of making them. Closing his eyes, he could see the sun on the water, Jez in the boat, hear the laughter. Jenny and Peter were getting serious about one another by then and ... he opened his eyes again, allowing the film to run: Jen and Pete kissing, lying on a blanket on the grass, oblivious. Lyn tutting at them, then smiling, exchanging a glance with Anna. Anna with her arms wrapped around her knees, shouting at Jez, 'Ship the oars, there's a clump of ... too late. Oh look, he's caught a crab. Jez, Don't stand up you idiot!'

Lyn howling with laughter as he swayed and stumbled in the boat, trying to reach the lost oar. People standing on the bridge, pointing.

Jenny and Pete, sitting up to offer encouragement. 'Sit down, old man,' Peter shouted. He was going through that phase, old man this, old boy that, annoyed the hell out of everyone and lasted until Lyn dunked him in the river. Jenny, with her hands over her mouth squeaking about whether or not Jez could swim. 'Course he can,' Anna telling her. 'He was in the team.'

Joe, where was Joe. Ah yes, gone to fetch ice cream. He came back across the bridge with cornets stuck in a box lid so he could carry them all. Pausing to watch the fun and frowning, then looking at Anna with that hunger in his eyes. A hunger Rob shared.

And he, Rob, sitting beneath the tree, sketchpad on his lap, pencils sticking out of his shoe where he'd wedged them, in order of hardness, between his trainer and his sock.

Rob watching, always watching. Anna's face, luminous, lightly tanned, the breeze lifting her dark hair so it caught the light and showed red against a bright blue sky. Anna looking up as Joe bent down to give her the ice cream. Smiling up at him. Lyn grabbing hers as he passed, pretending to skim the lid out of her reach. Jen and Pete, momentarily distracted from the action in the boat and Rob, watching, always watching. Joe blocking his view of Anna as he sat down beside her. That momentary jerk of his head in Rob's direction and that half smile that said, I have what you want.

Rob closed his eyes again and, in his memory, looked down at the sketches torn from the pad and weighted with a stone. The top one was of Jez in the boat, the second, he could see the edge of it beneath, he knew portrayed Jenny and Peter, wrapped up in their own world, and there was one of Lyn, the Amazon, tall and straight and broad shouldered. An athlete in cropped trousers and a vest top, body sculpted in tanned muscle. He had drawn Lyn many times, Rob now recalled, though he no longer had, to his knowledge, a single picture of her.

Back in the present, Rob took a deep breath and reached for the phone in his pocket. The day was bright, but it was still early spring and the air was chill, the ground beneath him and the trunk of the willow still damp from a winter of steady rain.

'Phone Simon,' Lyn had challenged. 'Demand to know if she was really Anna or not, but I'll guarantee that girl wasn't ours.'

He had left her house before she could goad him further but had not dared to call his agent.

'Look,' she had told him. 'Look at these.' She had boxes full of pictures she had taken back then, processed herself. Rob had no idea she had taken so many, though, looking back, Lyn usually seemed to have her camera with her ready to record any event, major, minor or anywhere in between on black and white film or on the slides she'd amuse them with on drunken evenings back at Jenny and Pete's first flat. Jen had an old projector she'd salvaged from somewhere and they'd flash the pictures up on a bit of white wall. Lyn had a talent for catching people unaware and unprepared. An uncanny knack for the absurd...

And the pictures of Anna. Anna, it seemed, had modelled for her. Often. Anna as Rob had never seen her. Serious and reflective gazing out into some mid distance; playful and laughing, eyes shining with fun. Anna, lying on her side, chatting comfortably to the photographer, unselfconsciously naked. Rob had never seen her, imagined her like that. Always, in his paintings, even his most explicit images, there had been that sense of reserve, of uncertainty. The Anna of his dreams might have laughed up at him, then kissed him gently as she said farewell, the Anna of his imagination held herself aloof. She might be out there, on display, but always separate from both artist and public. That Giaconda mystery he wanted to evoke in his work had been Rob's trademark; his habit. His acknowledgment of the fact that he didn't really know the girl. Didn't know her at all.

Thinking about her now, this dead woman who had looked like Anna, Rob was appalled at how easily he had allowed himself to believe. He fancied, with hindsight, that he had seen those subtle differences. The eyes, not quite so widely spaced. The chin, just a little less pointed and the laughter he had told himself he loved so much. Wasn't that just a fraction too loud, too coarse? Too...

Rob groaned. The truth was, the Anna of his visions, the Anna he had painted, had been subtly modified so often, remodelled as and when it suited his work that he doubted he now remembered anything with such hoped for precision. In the final analysis he had, as the critics suggested, attempted to recreate, to capture the essence of Anna. That which was greater and more precious than the mere sum of its measured parts.

Sitting there, beneath the willow, rapidly chilling and stiffening in the damp and cold, Rob found himself weeping for the Anna Lyn had known and he had not. For the young woman who had been so relaxed and intimate with her photographic interrogator that she had allowed her right into her very soul.

Slowly, Rob hauled himself to his feet. He punched in Simon's number and waited for the call to connect, almost willing Simon to be absent, to have left his phone at home, to see Rob's number come up and refuse to reply.

Simon answered on the second ring.

'Rob! Where the hell are you? I've been to the studio.'

'I'm not there.'

'No, I gathered that. Rob, are you all right?'

Rob took a deep breath – he seemed to be making a habit of deep breaths this morning. He released it slowly and then he said. 'Simon, I have to know the truth. That wasn't Anna, was it? Not that night in the TV studio nor lying dead on the floor. That wasn't Anna.'

The silence, no attempt to either bluster

or reassure, told him the answer.

'Why?' Rob asked.

'I don't know any more. I got myself in a hole, Rob. I thought ... I thought it would be better if we squashed the rumours. I'd seen this girl, an actress, though she'd only done bit parts so far. She was practically unknown and with makeup, coaching, a change of hair colour...' he trailed off. Rob broke the call and stared down at the phone as though it were responsible for the whole damn mess. The he switched it off and put it back in his pocket. Slowly began to trudge back to Lyn's house on the other side of the bridge.

Chapter Twenty-Three

The morning briefing had been little more of a resumé of events, but late in the afternoon Marris called his troops back together again.

Gina had endured the task of breaking the news to Maria Warner's mother, a task no one relished. Marris himself had interviewed Maria's agent. He now felt they had a slightly better picture of the young woman who'd played her role so well it might have got her killed.

'According to her agent, one Paul Mascin, the job didn't come through him. Someone approached her direct. That fits with what Simon Roper told us. It seems he found her by trawling through the stage magazines and casting directories. She told her agent she was taking some time out and he accepted that. She wasn't much in demand and he just figured she was short of money and had taken a job somewhere. The mother saw her irregularly anyway, that right Gina?'

Gina nodded. 'She didn't much approve of Maria's career choice,' she said, 'but, in any case, Maria hadn't lived with her mother for a while. Incidentally, the other photos in the flat were of Maria's mother, sister, brother-in-law and their kids. According to the mother, it wasn't unusual for her to,' she riffled through her notebook for the quote, "drop off the edge of the world for weeks at a time and come crawling back when she needed a sub". From the sound of things the money loaned rarely got paid back. I don't think there was any real animosity between mother and daughter; just your basic apathy.'

'Friends? Background stuff?' someone asked.

Gina glanced over at the questioner. PC Geordie Willet, she noticed. 'There's a list of contacts being printed up, you'll get it in the morning briefing. It's a bit on the vague side though, collated from what the mum knew and what the agent told Inspector Marris.'

'That's the task for tomorrow,' Marris added. 'I'll allocate specifically in the morning, but remember this, I want you to stick like randy dogs to the vicar's leg to anyone that can tell you about Maria Warner. We know as little about this young woman as we do about the mythical Anna.'

'Mythical, Guv,' someone laughed. 'We chasing ghosts then. Ain't that what that TV show does?'

Marris didn't ask what show that might be; he'd enquire later of Gina. Discreetly. 'She might as well be a bloody ghost for all the tracks she's left.'

'What about this Maria's father?'

'Long gone, no forwarding address. At least none the mum would give me, though I expect he'll come crawling out of the woodwork when the story breaks.'

Marris nodded in gloomy agreement. The story released this morning had been that a woman believed to be Anna Freeman had been murdered in her flat, but Marris was painfully aware that it would be his task at the press call, scheduled for the following morning, to further deepen the mystery.

'Maria Warner was younger than Anna,' he said. 'Only twenty-four. Her agent described her as something of a blank canvas and looking through her portfolio,' he paused and pointed at a bound volume lying on the desk, 'you'll see what he means.' He snatched it from the desk and allowed it to fall open. 'Maria played a school kid ten years younger than her actual age. That was her biggest role so far, apparently. Some kids' drama I'd never heard of. This one, Maria playing someone Anna's age. This character's blond, but you can see how she pulled it off with the Anna disguise. Anna had the same kind of face. Pretty, changeable, not too obvious. Not drop dead gorgeous so's everyone would notice her.'

'She dyed her hair,' Gina continued, 'Probably imitated Anna's make-up, but updated it. We have to assume she saw better pictures than this one,' she held up the group shot taken by the river. 'We know that Simon provided her with some background, but...'

'Surely that wouldn't have been enough?' PC Willets again. 'She had to fool people that had known her well and even ten years on, they'd notice the small stuff. Did Simon Roper know her back then?'

'No, and it's a good point,' Marris applauded. 'Roper provided the notebook, the pictures, the background he'd gleaned from Robert Carr, but someone else would have had to provide the polish. My guess is that one of Anna's old friends was in on it and did the coaching.'

'It seems so elaborate though, and we know this all started two, three months ago.'

Willets shook his head. 'Seems a massive chore just for the sake of a TV show.'

'And the free publicity that went with the TV show,' Gina said. 'I'm prepared to believe that Roper did this as a fall back. That he hoped right up until the last minute that the real Anna would turn up.'

'So, why didn't she? 'You'd have to be living in a hole not to have heard they were looking.'

'And that's another pertinent question,' Marris said. 'Where the hell is the real Anna Freeman? Is some of that adverse publicity nearer the mark than Roper and Carr would have us believe?' He frowned. 'In any case, my guess is that Maria Warner would have wanted the story to come out sooner rather than later and I'm not certain Simon Roper was prepared for that. He seems to have convinced himself she was doing it for the money, I'm not so sure. You can imagine the publicity there would have been once the story broke. Maria Warner, the stand-in for the famous Anna Freeman. To a young and, we understand, ambitious young woman wanting more than the odd bit part, this must have seemed like a gift. Like bloody fairyland. She wouldn't have gone off quietly and kept stum.'

'You think she was killed to keep her quiet, Guv?'

'I think that's one possibility, but what we

need to know first and foremost is who our murderer thought they were disposing of. Did he want Anna dead or was Maria the real target?'

'So,' the question came from the back of the room. 'Who've we got in the frame so far? The Roper bloke and the artist. Anyone else?'

'The ex-boyfriend, Joe Sykes. He's got previous for GBH, but it was some time back. Did six months. Got into an argument and attacked a fella with a knife. They were both pissed at the time, but it's something else to check out. He does have an alibi for the night in question though and, so far, it seems solid.'

'The other friends, anything there?'

'Clean,' Marris said. 'Peter Walters has points on his licence for doing fifty in a thirty zone. He was caught on camera, as they say. Lyn Chapel was cautioned for a public order offence, but it never came near a court. She's a peacenik,' he added.

'Guv, no one says that any more,' Gina reproved.

'Except me.' Marris told her. 'Anyway, that was eight, no nine years ago in her final year of University. She trained as an artist and photographer, so you'd have thought she'd have got on with Robert Carr, but apparently there was friction.'

'Oh?' This was new to Gina.

'I read it in Anna's journal. Incidentally, we now have two of Anna's journals, both indirectly courtesy of Joe Sykes. Presumably he didn't need them for his story. According to Simon Roper,' he explained, 'Sykes has sold a story to one of the Sundays about this being a scam and the real Anna still being missing presumed.'

'Is she presumed?' Willets again.

'Right now she's not anything but an enigma,' Marris told him. 'I've had both journals photocopied. You can pick up a pack in the a.m.' he paused. 'Questions? Right, think of some ready for the morning. Now, get off home.'

Gina waited and watched as the rest of the crew wandered out in ones and twos. Wearily, she turned down an invite to the pub. No one invited Marris. Marris didn't do pubs or after work association for that matter. What, Gina wondered, did Marris do?

'What's on your mind?' he asked, reaching into his pocket again, half withdrawing that crumpled pack of ciggies and fondling it before dropping it back again.

She shrugged. 'I reckon she's dead.'

'Who? Anna? Natural causes or otherwise?'

Gina shrugged. 'Wouldn't like to say, but she's dead all right and has been since she said goodbye to our artist friend.'

189

Chapter Twenty-Four

At eight thirty on the Saturday morning, seated in a sports hall that had been commandeered for the purpose, a less than soigné Inspector Marris – waxed raincoat removed for the occasion but black suit still much in evidence – dropped his bombshell.

'Our investigations have revealed that the victim was not Anna Freeman,' he paused for effect, a collective intake of breath followed by an equally communal murmur of anticipation. 'The young woman found dead at 41B Alden Rd and who was calling herself Anna Freeman was in fact a twenty-four-year-old actress by the name of Maria Warner. There's a press pack available giving some background, though at the moment our information detailing the young woman's movements for the past month or so in particular is best described as sketchy. We would appeal, now, for anyone who knew Miss Warner and particularly anyone who'd had contact with her in the weeks prior to the television show, or the days since then, to please come forward. You may believe you have nothing relevant to tell us, but you may, in reality, be in possession of the vital clue, that tiny scrap of information that will help us fit the facts into the wider scheme.'

'Are we to understand, then, Inspector, that this young woman, this Maria Warner, appeared in Anna Freeman's place? That she was interviewed by Edith Parks?'

'You may presume that,' Marris inclined his head.

'Was Rob Carr in on it?'

'Must have been,' someone else shouted. 'No one could be that thick.'

Marris decided that was enough for the moment. He rapped on the table and waited for silence. 'You understand I have nothing further to add this morning. The tragedy is that a young woman is dead. The further anxiety is that the killer will now realise that his victim was not Anna Freeman. I would appeal for Miss Freeman, or anyone who knows her whereabouts, to come forward, urgently. Thank you, ladies, gentlemen.' He got up and left the makeshift stage. They'd organized press packs – the press officer had been up since the early hours working with Marris, deciding what should go in and what should not. He wanted maximum sympathy generated for Maria Warner, this young woman with, clearly, a bright talent if she could fool Rob Carr and the rest, destroyed before she had a chance to use her skills legitimately. And they had another woman missing in the shape of Anna Freeman;

Marris wanted the utmost concern created for her. He wanted her found and an end to this nonsense and petty mystery.

Though he had to admit that Gina may have the right of it. He wasn't sure that a living Anna Freeman would ever be found.

Glancing down the length of the hall he could see the press officer handing out the dossier. It included a list of the roles Maria Warner had played, a brief biography. The picture of Anna and her friends taken by the river. Extracts from the journals. Marris had not been sure about this, but on balance he felt he'd done the right thing. The journal entries he'd included were bland and inoffensive, one describing her excitement about a party she was going to and another analysing her worries about how she'd done in her exams. They were the kind of entries you might expect to find in any book written by a teen or someone in their early twenties, a mix of angst and joy and ordinariness. The impression gained was that this was an ordinary, fun loving girl becoming woman and he hoped it would strike a chord. He knew that all of this would find its way into the evening editions and probably into the Sundays. He wanted Anna, wherever she was, if she still was, flushed out of hiding, both for her own sake and also because Marris thought she, and they, owed it to Maria Warner.

The girl had died because she'd taken a job, that was all it amounted to. Unless, of course, Maria had courted trouble in her own right.

So far, Marris could see nothing in her life that suggested that, but this was early days and he told himself to keep an open mind. Maria Warner could be a drug smuggling serial killer for all he knew.

Pausing before he got into his car – also black and more legitimately shiny than his suit had any right to be – he recalled his first impression of Maria. That first sight of her on the apartment floor. Stabbed once, then cast aside and left where she fell. Presumably lying there while whoever had done the deed packed her stuff, stepping round and over her to reach pictures from the shelves and books from the table. Marris puzzled as to why they had started to do this and then left things where they were. It would have taken no effort to take what they'd packed away. And why leave the notebook and pictures behind?

In a way, he thought, sliding into the driver's seat, the fact that they had left behind those things which were specifically Anna's militated in favour of the victim being Maria. Someone after Maria would not have known the significance of those particular possessions. On the other hand, if Maria had been the chosen victim, then why bother packing any of the stuff?

And more stupid still, why pack if you didn't want to take things away? Even if the killer had been scared... Marris imagined whoever it was waiting in the bedroom, seeing Rob come into the room and then take off in such a fright. Then the down-stairs neighbour coming on the scene. Even had the person in the bedroom panicked and run, it would have been no effort to take a couple of bags with them.

There was another option, of course, one he had almost dismissed when he'd noted the odd order in which the bags had been packed, but one which could make perfect sense. Maria herself had packed her bags, had swept everything into the holdall with no notice taken of order or requirement. She'd been packing to leave then and there, in a hurry, and whoever had killed her had arrived before she'd done. That would fit with Rob Carr's claim that he'd had a phone call from Maria/Anna, telling him she was afraid of someone threatening to come round.

He took out his mobile and found Geordie Willets' number. Give the lad something to get his teeth into.

'Geordie, something new for you. I want you to ring round all the taxi firms local to the crime scene, see if any of them took a call for a cab to pick up from there on the night Maria Warner was killed.'

She might have taken a chance and tried to hail a black cab, of course, but he didn't think so. Had she actually got around to leaving, she'd have had two cases and a holdall, she wouldn't have wanted to carry them far or be on the streets laden down at that time of the morning.

'When you find the company,' Marris added, 'they should have made a note of the destination, when you've got that, give me a call.'

Rob let Marris in then went back to the window and pressed his head close to the glass. That way, he could just glimpse those standing below on the pavement with their cameras and microphones and outside broadcast vans.

He felt besieged and not a little scared.

'Can't you get rid of them?' he demanded. 'They were here, waiting for me when I got back yesterday. I managed to get in and close the door but they've not gone away. There are even more of them today. They're like sharks, smelling blood in the water. Circling till I give up and drown.'

He could feel Marris examining him curiously. 'You think I'm making a fuss over nothing, don't you?'

'Back from where?' Marris asked. 'My officers didn't report any media interest

195

when your solicitor dropped you home.'

'You had someone watching me?' Rob turned angrily.

Marris shrugged. 'You're a suspect, Mr Carr. But you're not under surveillance, if that's what you mean. Frankly, until you become more of a suspect, I can't justify the man power. So, where did you go yesterday?'

'More of a suspect. You think I killed her? You still think that.'

Marris shrugged again. 'You're on my list, Mr Carr, nothing more. Nothing less. Now, where did you go?'

'Mind your own damned business.' Rob turned back to the window, craning his neck to try and get a better view.

Marris waited.

After a while, Rob grew tired of straining his eyes and cricking the muscles of his neck and shoulders. He sighed and sat down on the broad windowsill, leaned back against the frame.

'I went to see Lyn Chapel,' he said. 'I tried to see Pete and Jenny, but when I got there I couldn't remember their new address. You have my books,' he accused. 'When do I get them back?'

'When I've done with them.'

Rob frowned. 'I'm sure you can't do that,' he said petulantly. 'They're my property and unless you've charged me with something I don't see you've any right to take my stuff.'

Marris perched on the layout table and Rob was reminded both of Simon sitting there, in that same position, and of Marris two nights before. Had he been there or had Rob dreamed it?

'You're probably right,' Marris said. 'But I'm sure you want the killer caught as much as I do and would instruct your brief that you plan to fully cooperate with the police efforts to find Maria Warner's murderer.'

Marris paused. He had expected a response but Rob just looked at him with dead man's eyes.

'I talked to Lyn, she told me it wasn't Anna, that Simon had arranged the whole thing. I called him. I wanted him to tell me I was wrong, that Lyn was wrong, that she was lying, but he couldn't tell me that, could he, because it wouldn't have been true.'

Marris considered. 'So far,' he considered, 'I've not noticed that Simon Roper worries too much about truth. So, what did Lyn Chapel have to say?'

Rob closed his eyes and laid his head back against the cold glass. He recounted his conversation with Lyn as closely as he could remember it. He left out the details of his walk beside the river. Somehow that was too personal, too painful to share with Marris. 'I didn't know,' he said. 'I can't believe I didn't know.'

'I find it pretty hard to believe, too,'

Marris confirmed. 'Mr Carr, you knew Anna; when you met this girl did you not once suspect she might not be genuine?'

Rob didn't reply, he was thinking deeply. Had he suspected? Had he, in his heart of hearts, so wanted this to be Anna, so wanted to have done with all the hassle and the overweening interest, that he had given in and gone along with things just to have the easy life? That, he was honest enough to admit, had been a trait of his of late. 'I don't know,' he said at last. 'I really don't know.'

He opened his eyes and regarded Marris mournfully. Marris nodded and Rob suspected that the Inspector thought more of that reply than he'd thought of most Rob had given him. He wondered at it.

A shout from the street caused his hackles to rise and he swivelled round, resumed his watch. 'Can't you make them go away?'

'Probably not.'

'Doesn't it bother you?'

'It should bother me? Why?'

'They're out there. Waiting. And now they know she wasn't Anna. They won't believe me, will they? They're going to tear my life into little pieces and flush it down the pan.'

Marris didn't think there was an answer to that, at least, not one that Robert Carr would want to hear. 'Do you have to go out anywhere?'

'No.'

'Do you need groceries? Anything bringing in?'

'No, I don't think so.'

'Then my advice is to sit tight, get on with some work and try to forget about the media circus downstairs. You're two floors up, you can barely even hear them. You have to practically break your neck even to see them. I'll get an officer posted to keep order, that's the best I can do.'

'You're enjoying this,' Rob accused.

Marris shook his head. 'No, but, frankly, I'm more concerned with justice for the dead than the convenience of the living.'

Chapter Twenty-Five

There were eight notebooks covering around twelve years, so far as Marris could tell. The first had been started a year or so before Anna became so central to Robert Carr's life and it seemed obvious that this one, at least, had started life as a common or garden sketch book. The first pages were filled with notes on colour, scribbles, outlines, small scenes, portraits and sample textures worked in pen, pencil or a combination of both.

The transformation seemed to have come about around a third of the way in, when

Rob had noted down a name and telephone number and drawn a little picture of a girl beside it. Two pages later and there was an address, followed by lines from a poem that Marris didn't recognise and a truncated and subverted proverb. 'Too many cooks ... (but who cares about the spag bol?)'

From that point, the book transformed from sketchbook to notebook come ... what was it his father used to call such things, yes, that was it – a Commonplace Book. Vic Marris had not heard the expression for years, but it fitted perfectly. A book in which day to day observations and notes kept company with snatches of poems, song lyrics, dreams and desires and, in Rob Carr's case, even shopping lists and notes reminding himself not to wear his blue tie to job interviews any more.

Marris wondered why. What was wrong with the blue tie? Had it met with a spag bol accident?

On impulse, he rang the first number in the book and found himself talking to an answer machine. The message informed him that he was through to an employment agency and advising him to call back in office hours.

Marris had just dropped the phone back onto its cradle, when it rang. It was Gina.

'Joe Sykes has done a runner,' she said.

'Joe Sykes? What are you doing out there?'

'Oh, you know, thought I'd do a follow up visit. He went off somewhere at about three this morning, so his neighbour reckons. The car that picked him up sat with its engine running and woke them up. His neighbour said he took a bag with him.'

'Reg number?' Marris asked with more hope than conviction.

'We should be so lucky. No, but Sykes had been boasting about this story he'd been paid for and they reckon the paper he sold it to came to pick him up.'

'At three in the morning? But then, who the hell understands the world of tabloid journalism,' Marris observed. 'I always suspected the buggers were nocturnal or at least crepuscular.'

'Nice word. Sounds insulting but classy. So, what now?'

Marris thought. 'Sunday tomorrow. So, we wait and see. Any joy with Lyn Chapel?'

'Lights on, no one home.'

'Lights?'

'Porch light,' Gina clarified. 'She must have forgotten to switch it off this morning. I'll call back.'

'Do that. Our man went to see her yesterday.'

'Carr?'

'She told him she wasn't fooled by Maria Warner's act, persuaded him to phone Roper and confront him with the lie.'

'And Roper?'

'Had no option, did he? He confirmed it.'

'Do you believe, I mean, can you believe Rob Carr wasn't in on the whole thing? I find it hard, Guv.'

Marris hesitated. 'I'm not so sure,' he said. 'I think that Robert Carr lives in his own little world and doesn't think too closely about what goes on outside. Still, time will tell. Have another try at Lyn Chapel. I want to know what she told our artist friend. I've had his version, now I'd like hers.

Gina gone, Marris went back to the books, flicking through the pages now to try and get an overview of the contents, noting down addresses and phone numbers as he came to them. He recognised Lyn Chapel's address, the Walters and Joe Sykes (two entries for him, two books apart). The Walters had three moves recorded and two changes of phone number. There were others he had not heard about, some he suspected might be ex girl-friends, some banal notes such as takeaways and the dentist. Marris noted them anyway adding them to a now growing list against which he had attempted to add some kind of time scale and sense of worth in Rob's eyes. He guessed that the most significant entries were those which had received the greatest number of drawings and jokes. On some pages, a single phone number had been surrounded by such depth and layering of words and images that the fibres of the page, blackly textured from edge to edge, seemed ready to part beneath the onslaught. Sometimes, the fierceness with which Rob had defined this territory on behalf of a particular contact had worn holes through the paper and scratched through to the sheet below.

Rob either resented this, or signified it in some way Marris could not guess at, but he had circled these intrusions in broad strokes of his pen, decorated the edges of those barriers with barbs and arrows and left the surrounding page blank and stark.

It disturbed Marris, though he couldn't define why or how.

His thoughts were interrupted twice in quick succession by the ringing phone. The first was Geordie Willets and he had a result.

Marty's Cabs, a little two-horse – well two-car set up – had agreed to the pick up.

'They sent the car but she didn't show,' he told Marris. 'She wanted it for half past three. She phoned them just after two but here's the thing: she said she didn't want to wake everyone in the house so she'd wait on the corner. They recognised the road and remembered because it was a bit unusual, but she didn't give the house number.'

'What name did she use?'

'Ah, well, y' see, I tried both names on them,' he paused, waiting for approval.

Marris grunted something which might pass.

'She ordered the taxi under the name of Maria Warner, asked the price and said she wanted to pay in cash. She could have done it by card over the phone seeing as it was a big job. An hour or more each way even at that time of night.'

'And are you going to put me out of my misery and tell me where she wanted to go?'

'Oh sure, yes Guv. It's on that list of Anna Freeman's contacts. The address she gave is Joe Sykes's place.'

'Well, give the man a biscuit. Hang on, the mobile's going.' He flipped it open and lowered the land line receiver so he could hear. It was Gina again, sounding out of breath.

'I went back to Lyn Chapel's place. Light was still on and, I don't know, didn't seem right. I got the next door neighbour to let me through, it's a terraced house. So I climbed into her yard and looked through the window. Guv, Lyn Chapel's dead.'

Chapter Twenty-Six

In chasing after Lyn Chapel, Gina had been fishing in someone else's pond, albeit with their knowledge and consent. By the time Marris arrived, local uniformed officers had taken over, established their perimeter and were waiting for SOCO to do their bit before the scene could be released to CID.

Gina perched on the bonnet of her car, supping coffee and chatting to one of the locals.

'Guv this is DI Parks, this is his patch.'

Marris extended a hand, aware of Parks' scrutiny. Those who worked most closely with Marris no longer took notice of his old suits and shabby coat, but newcomers to the world of Victor Marris could be relied upon to do a double take. Parks, to his credit, only took the one.

'DS Lees has filled me in,' he said.

'Good. Cause of death?'

'On the face of it, single stab wound. The next door neighbour saw her yesterday afternoon and reckoned she had a visitor, a man. He returned about five thirty, six o'clock, went off again a half hour later.'

'Description?'

'Five ten, maybe, average build, she says. Brown hair and wearing a dark grey jacket. He arrived by taxi about lunchtime, stayed for a while, and then left alone mid afternoon. She was working in the garden and spoke to him. She noticed he'd come back later, heard him ringing the bell and went to look to see who it was.' Parks grinned, 'She admits to being a nosy bugger.'

'Thank the Lord for nosy neighbours,' Marris said.

'Sounds like Robert Carr,' Gina commented, 'but would he have come by taxi? It's a bloody long way.'

'I reckon he's good for it, not short of a bob or two,' Marris observed. 'And he doesn't have his car, remember. He dumped it in a no parking zone and it got towed. Then we impounded it, so...' He paused. 'He told me he'd been here. Time of death?' he asked Parks.

'Not as yet, the medical examiner's in there now. It's a bit lacking in space, best we stay out here for the interim, then I'll show you the sights.'

Marris nodded. He joined Gina in her bonnet perch and looked back down the street. Georgian houses on one side, Victorian on the other. Terraced, but not of the most basic kind. They had gable-ended roofs and fancy bits of egg and tongue moulding above the windows and a patch of garden behind the palisade wall. Down the road he could see the open space he had passed on his drive, grass and trees stretched out on either side of the river. A pleasant place to stroll in the spring sunshine, he supposed, though, this late in the afternoon, a light mist was rising and the air was chill.

'First Anna, or should I say Maria Warner, and now Lyn Chapel. Not to mention the disappearance of our friend Joe Sykes. Does this put another complexion on that?'

'We've checked the cottage,' Parks told him. 'No bodies, nothing suspicious and gaps in his wardrobe and drawers that look like he packed clothes. Let's assume for the moment that he's just done a flit. Though it's still moot if he's run because he killed this Lyn Chapel, or he's been taken into, shall we say, protective custody by his tabloid pals.'

Marris nodded approval. 'Anyone contacted the Walters?'

'Jenny and Pete? Yes. They've got a police liaison officer with them now,' Gina said. 'Jenny's devastated, not to mention scared witless. She wants to go to her mother's place for a few days but Pete's resisting. So, do we bring Rob Carr in for questioning?'

'In good time,' Marris told her. 'He's not going anywhere and I want to get a feel for the scene before we make a move.'

'How do you know he won't flit too?' Gina objected.

'I know, because when I left his place was heavily guarded by representatives of our beloved free press. I can't see him wanting to run the gauntlet and, if he does, I've got a crew on obs. I think we should have another little chat to our Mr Roper too. See if Lyn was the one that coached Anna for the role. Oh, and I gave Geordie Willets a little job and he came up trumps.' Marris elucidated for the benefit of Gina and DI Parks, explaining about the taxi and his conclusion about the half packed suitcases. 'It occurred to me that Maria herself might have been the one bundling everything into the bags. It made no sense for someone to leave the journals and pictures behind, unless they were after Maria, of course.'

'Seems less likely now,' Parks was confident of that.

Marris nodded. 'Less likely, but not ruled out,' he said. 'Most interesting, though, is the fact that she was going over to Joe Sykes' place. I wonder, now, if the story was meant to be a joint affair.' He shrugged. 'Sunday tomorrow, at any rate. That should cast some light. Next move then will to bring in our friend Joe, get him to tell his tale for free this time.'

It had taken three phone calls for Simon to persuade Rob to see him. Finally he gave in and at five thirty-five, half an hour or so

208

after Marris had stood playing shuffle the pros and cons with Gina and DI Parks, the officer on watch outside Rob's flat reported the arrival of Simon Roper.

'Should I let him through?'

Marris, phone to his ear and his thoughts still fixed on the prone form of Lyn Chapel, hesitated for a mere instant. 'No reason not to,' he said. 'Make sure he's the only one gets inside.'

Simon took the stairs two at a time and arrived breathless on Rob's landing. The door was ajar and he peered inside, not totally sure of his welcome.

Rob glanced up but didn't speak. He was drawing, working on the layout table with pens and charcoal. An open box of water-colours lay beside the pad. It was years since Rob had used that particular medium. They were St Petersburg pigments, Simon noted, the same tin he'd had when Simon first knew him. He just replaced the semi-moist cakes from time to time. Simon had tried to switch him on to tubes, but Rob had resisted. This was his lucky tin, he said. He'd been given it as a teenager and it had been the first proper colour box he'd ever owned.

Rob could be oddly superstitious. Same brand of charcoal, same fine nibbed technical pens, same knife used to put just the right point on his pencils.

Simon came closer and looked at the work spread out on the desk. It was mostly a pen and wash technique that encouraged fast handling of the subject; simple, spontaneous sketches rather than the more complex multi layered work that Rob was famed for. He had filled page after page with restless drawings, added colour washes to give the impression of light and shadow, delivered an emotional intensity by using short sharp strokes of the pen and an impatience in the subsequent wash that showed clearly in the finished work. The result was stark and powerful and it was the power of the drawing that first caught Simon's eye, then, after a split second lapse, the subject matter.

'What the hell are you doing?'

'What I always do, fixing it down. If I don't fix it down it'll be there,' he gestured a point a few inches from his eyes. 'There, playing like some damned film I can't turn off. I'm fixing it down.'

Simon stared in horrified fascination at the strewn pictures. They depicted the crime scene, Anna, lying on the floor, wedged awkwardly between the table and the sofa. The viewpoint changed from image to image, as though Rob had stopped the film he accused of playing in front of him and grabbed stills at ten or fifteen second intervals. Put together, Simon could have walked the scene it was mapped out so clearly. He could see the room, the starkness of it, the threadbare furnishings and scruffy carpet.

He recognised it, of course, from when he'd been there to visit Maria, but the clarity with which Rob had conveyed the emotional impact of the setting shook him to the core. He lifted one of the pictures to examine it more closely and saw that his hand was shaking.

He felt sick, light-headed ... afraid.

'Rob, you've got to let me burn these. God, what do you think Marris will say? Rob, this has got to stop. Now.'

Simon began to gather the still damp work into a pile. He'd take it away, get rid of it, no one would know. No one else would see. He reached for the final image, the one Rob still worked on and over which his brush was poised, laden and dripping with Prussian blue, ready to lay a deeper shadow across the face of his precious Anna. The Anna that wasn't Anna.

Simon froze. Rob had painted this from the perspective of the killer; the woman in his drawing was already falling backward, her eyes dead, head lolling, hair swept up by the movement as her body turned. It had been drawn as though the killer stood or sat lower than his victim and struck upward, then thrust the body away from him as the knife was withdrawn.

'Rob?'

'What if I killed her?'

'Don't be stupid, you know you didn't.'

'But what if I did? Simon, when I close my eyes, I see her like that. She's falling, moving away so fast it seems like I'm dreaming or I'm watching it from a great distance and all the time a little piece of me is there. What if I killed her, Simon, what if I did? I see things, I'm painting things that shouldn't be there. I shouldn't be able to see it like this. And there are these memories, Simon, things that keep coming into my head like ... suddenly, they're there. Wham and I'm remembering things I didn't know had happened.' He paused, stared hard at the drawing, rinsed his brush and then reloaded it with the same paint. 'That policeman, Marris, he's convinced I did it, he's just looking for a way to prove it.'

'You know you didn't do it. Rob, have you been taking your meds?'

'If you mean my happy pills, I don't see the point.'

'Rob, you need help. You can't just take yourself off your meds. Remember last time?'

'This isn't like last time.'

'What is it like?'

'It's like ... being there.'

Simon took the brush from his hand and laid it down, pausing, through habit – Rob's, not his – to wash it through in the water jar. He took the final picture and placed it with the rest, then led Rob through to his bedroom and rummaged in the bedside drawer. Rob kept sleeping pills; Simon knew that, though Rob didn't take them often now.

He left him alone while he fetched a glass of water, then fed Rob two pills, made him drink.

'Now, go to sleep and when you wake up I'll have taken those damn pictures away and got rid of them. OK, Rob, this is not a time for self-doubt. You've got to be strong and you've got to believe.'

'Believe in what?' Rob asked him. 'Even you lied to me. Anna's gone. I can't see her any more.'

He closed his eyes and, as Simon watched, he fell asleep. Too fast for the pills to act, Simon thought. He must be exhausted. Though they would work soon and they'd keep him asleep for long enough to give him a break from the anguish. At least, Simon hoped they would. Rob's dreams were intense and often more terrifying than anything he had to face when waking.

He went back into the studio and found a folder in one of the drawers, slipped the drawings inside, then scanned the space for more of the same. He knew Rob when he was like this, he'd paint and paint until he couldn't see what he was doing, reprising the same subject over and over again. Truthfully, that's what he'd been doing and doing profitably for the past decade, reprising his image of Anna.

He found a further stack of pictures, less precise but of the same subject. Rob had stacked them on the windowsill. Some must have still been damp because they had glued themselves together with that same blue pigment he had used in the heaviest shadows.

He went back to check on Rob. He seemed to be sleeping though Simon knew you could never really tell. Rob's body dealt oddly with medication.

Retrieving the drawings, he left the studio and retraced his steps down the stairs. Marris stood just inside the lobby.

'Mr Roper, I was hoping to have a word.'

'Rob's asleep. I gave him sleeping pills.'

Marris raised a slender black eyebrow. 'You're his nurse now, too? You know, I didn't expect to find you still here. When I last spoke to Robert Carr he was pretty annoyed with you. I'd even say he felt he'd been betrayed.'

'He's upset. He's bound to be upset.' Simon looked over Marris's shoulder. The door had a glass panel in the upper section and their conversation was attracting attention from the waiting crowd. In the lighted hallway, Simon felt exposed, targeted. 'Look,' he said. 'I have to go. Rob's sleeping. Come back tomorrow.'

'Turn around and go back up the stairs, Mr Roper, I'll see you now anyway and

214

maybe we can wake sleeping beauty while we're about it.'

'You've no right to detain me, Inspector.' Simon made a move towards the door. Intent on his goal, he missed Marris's hand as it reached for the folder he carried and gripped tight.

'What's this, Mr Roper?'

'It's nothing, just some drawings Rob wanted me to look at.'

'Really. I know you said you collected the odd discard for your portfolio but I didn't think you collected whole portfolios.'

Angrily, Simon tugged the folder out of Marris's grip. Marris let go with a suddenness that sent Simon staggering back. The drawings flew from the folder and fell onto the floor.

Marris looked down and then back up at Simon. 'Pick them up,' he said, 'and go back upstairs. I came to tell Rob the latest news. But you'll be interested too, I don't doubt.'

'Latest news?'

Marris pointed at the floor and Simon, almost without thinking, bent to obey the imperious gesture. He gathered the drawings, slid them back into the folder and then placed them, numbly, in Marris's outstretched hand.

'Lyn Chapel was murdered,' Marris said. 'Rob visited her yesterday and our best guess for time of death is yesterday evening. Now,

215

shall we go back upstairs?'

Marris spread the pictures on the layout table and examined them. His lips thinned, eyes narrowed, even his cheekbones seemed to have sharpened, Simon thought. The fingers that moved the drawings, ordered and reordered, were bone held in place by translucent skin. There was nothing spare on the man, nothing extra, just bone and skin and sinew and too large eyes. Simon, uncomfortable on the stool he'd chosen, wishing he didn't feel so high and so exposed, with his feet on the cross bar and his behind growing numb on the hard blonde wood. He wished he could move. But if he moved Marris would look at him. Marris would turn those too large, too dark eyes upon him and the lips would thin even further as he smiled that death's head smile and got ready to deliver the words that might feel like a *coup de grâce* after all that waiting but which would still cut like wire through flesh.

'What did you plan to do with these?'

Simon had been thinking of an excuse since he'd met Marris in the lobby, but now he decided that only the truth would do. 'I planned to burn them,' he said. 'I knew what you'd think. Rob ... works out his problems by pinning them to the page, but I couldn't expect you to understand that.' He ended defiantly, then quailed as Marris looked at him.

'I'm not the artistic type, I suppose,' Marris said. 'Personally, I prefer to walk the dog or run. Something physical.'

'You have a dog?' It was an irrelevance, Simon knew, but the idea of this cold, skeletal man owning something warm and furry and fleshy and dog like was just impossible to envisage.

'No,' Marris told him, 'but I expect I'd walk it if I did.' He paused and scrutinised Simon. Simon writhed beneath the harsh gaze. 'You said Robert Carr seemed distressed. How distressed. What did he say about these?'

'Nothing sensible. He said he saw these pictures in his mind. The only way to get rid of them was to pin them down, like this.'

Marris nodded. 'They're good,' he said. 'The foreshortening on this leg, difficult to get right, I'd imagine, especially as the foot is pointing directly at the viewer. This final picture, at least, I'm assuming it was the last, all the others seem to be leading up to that moment, is extraordinarily intense. Quite ironic really seeing as this should be the first in the sequence and, yet, I know it's not. You want to know how I know?'

Numbly, Simon looked at the drawing Marris held. It depicted the woman, falling, dead eyes turning back in her head, body losing its control and rigidity.

'It's the shadow across the face. See, here

and here,' he stabbed the bony finger at two of the other pictures. 'He's trying to place it, the way the light falls through the curtain. It slices across her body, as it would have done, you see, with the streetlamp through the window. There was a gap in between the curtains. In this last picture. He's placed it perfectly. That harsh line between light and shadow. See?'

Simon glared at him, utterly bewildered. 'What game are you playing?' he asked. 'What you're saying, it doesn't mean a thing. It's all...'

'You've not asked me how she died – Lyn Chapel.'

'I did, I...'

'No, you didn't and I find that interesting. She died from a single stab wound, same as Maria Warner. Whoever the killer is, he, or she, is either very lucky or very accurate.'

A sound behind them made both men turn. Rob staggered from the bedroom, bleary eyed and unsteady on his legs. He came over to where they were, swept the pictures from the table and then picked up the pen he'd been using. Desperately, he looked around for the paper and Simon realised he'd used all that was in the pad on the desk.

'Rob, it's all right, there's more.' He ran over to the plan chest and found a new sketchbook, returned with it to the table.

'Mr Carr?' Marris took his arm and tried

to turn Rob to face him. Rob seemed oblivious.

'Mr Carr. Mr Roper, how many pills did you give him?'

'Just the two,' Simon was alarmed now. Rob seemed entranced, his eyes blank and empty. He didn't see them, didn't seem to hear. Suddenly, he turned his head and stared across the room at something neither of the other two could see.

'Rob? What is it Rob?' Simon took his arm and shook him hard.

'Rob, come on man, snap out of it.'

Robert crumpled, his legs giving way he slid from Simon's grasp onto the floor.

Marris frowned, then crouched beside him, laying his fingers at Rob's throat and then at his wrist. Rob's breathing was laboured, his skin clammy and cold.

'Are you certain he'd not taken any other pills?'

'I ... I don't know.'

'Check the bedroom while I call an ambulance,' Marris ordered. 'Fetch whatever you gave him. The doctors will need to know.'

Simon stared at him, shocked and momentarily stunned as he watched Marris make the call.

'Will he be all right?'

'I hope so, Mr Roper, Marris said. 'There are still a great many things I'd like to know.'

Chapter Twenty-Seven

Sunday, and the papers were full of speculation. The arrival of the ambulance at Rob's flat had fuelled the notion that he had attempted suicide and that, in turn, poured accelerant on the idea that he might really be responsible for Maria Warner's death.

More interesting though, so far as Marris was concerned, was that Joe Sykes was not the only one with an Anna related story in the Sunday Nationals. The ever-faithful *News of the World* had come up trumps with a three page special entitled 'My Life With Anna' and which claimed to be the account of six months living with Anna Freeman only three years before. In it, her boyfriend – alleged boyfriend, Marris corrected – painted a lurid account of their time together, complete with an encyclopaedic list of sexual gymnastics that had Marris feeling he should be consulting the Kama Sutra.

He had handed on to his superiors the task of putting pressure on their two papers to deliver their star witnesses, on to his superiors having found in the past that chief constables are more suited to that species of task. Then he retired with Gina and Willets to the nearest pub for lunch.

'I'm tending,' Marris said, 'towards the conclusion that Rob Carr is playing the "I'm nuts, I didn't mean to kill them" game, but...'

'I'm not so sure,' Willets offered nervously. Only six months out of his probation, he wasn't sure why he'd been allowed to dine in such illustrious company, but he was glad he had been and didn't want to screw things up.

Marris took another mouthful of pie and gestured him to go on.

'I read the reports, Guv. He called the same taxi firm to take him home as took him out to Kingston. He hung around outside Lyn Chapel's place for a good half hour, according to the neighbour, waiting for it to arrive. It sounds, too cool, too ... well, just plain wrong.'

'Unless he wants to play the insanity card,' Gina said. 'Then it would make perfect sense.'

'No blood on his sleeves,' Marris noted. 'Our people bagged and tagged everything in his studio that wasn't pinned down. The jacket he was probably wearing, going on the fact it had his phone and wallet in the pockets and was hanging by the door, and matches the description given by both the neighbour and the taxi driver. There was no blood on the sleeves.'

'He might have got rid of the one he wore, changed everything over,' Gina objected.

'Of course he might, but I don't think he did. Simon said something about him buying two or three of anything he liked. I thought he was joking until I took a look in his cupboards. The jacket we took from the studio last night was identical to the one he wore the night he went to Anna/Maria's flat. Jacket three is still in his wardrobe. The man gave a new meaning to the word habit.

'We know he had Maria's blood on his clothes, there was nothing from Lyn Chapel apart from a few pink fibres from the cushions on the sofa.'

'Simon Roper has an alibi,' Gina ticked off the other suspects on her fingers. 'Business lunch, afternoon meeting and then dinner. All with multiple witnesses. Joe Sykes we don't know about but we do know he'd taken the day off work.'

'A day he'd booked two weeks ago,' Marris reminded her, 'so unless he was very organised or very far thinking... It's more likely he booked the time to get ready for his little trip to tabloid heaven.'

'Um, strictly speaking, it's a broadsheet, sir,' Willets pointed out.

'Actually, Geordie, it's a Sunday supplement.'

'Which takes a longer run in time to prepare than the paper,' Gina added thoughtfully. 'Joe must have given them his story around the time of the television show. Maybe a few days before.'

Marris shovelled more pie and then reached for the supplement. It was open at the relevant article. A photograph of Joe Sykes, taken in his cottage – Gina had recognised the location – dominated the first page. He was described as old friend and ex-lover, the insinuation being that Rob Carr had broken up their relationship eleven years before and that his attentions, unwanted and obsessive, had driven Anna away.

Page two displayed a selection of Rob's artwork. It looked like a studio shot, probably lifted from an archive. Rob, perched uncomfortably on that same stool Simon had occupied the night before, surrounded by his work. The picture looked staged and awkward, Rob Carr clearly wanting the photographer to be elsewhere and the photographer probably frustrated at his own inability to get his subject to relax.

Marris, knowing how defensive Rob felt about his space, was surprised he'd allowed the shoot.

It was interesting, he mused, seeing a half dozen or so images of Anna in one place. From picture to picture, there was a definite shift in emphasis that had nothing to do with contrasting style. In each it was clearly the same woman, but one emphasised her eyes, another seemed to capture a moment seconds before she moved. In another that transience was even more marked. Anna, blurred, like a photograph taken on a long shutter speed. Her body turning, hands reaching out towards the viewer. Her head, almost the only thing remaining still, though the impression was that, like a dancer performing a pirouette, who selects a point of focus, then turns their body before whipping the head around, Anna had begun the turn while still holding fast to the viewer's gaze.

It was a disturbing, vertiginous work, less commercial, Marris guessed, than the other pictures, three at least he remembered seeing on billboards or in magazines.

'What do you make of the so called boyfriend?' Gina asked.

Marris glanced at the other article and snorted. 'I think he has a vivid imagination,' he replied.

Chapter Twenty-Eight

Monday began with a press call and made explicit the links between the deaths of Maria Warner and Anna's old friend, Lyn Chapel.

'We have several leads,' Marris intoned,

'But no, as yet, no arrests have been made. Mr Carr is understood to be suffering from exhaustion and is being kept for observation. Yes, we will be interviewing both Mr Joe Sykes and Philip Arnott in relation to the newspaper articles, probably later today. We have been assured of full cooperation by both the papers concerned. They have emphasised that both of their informants are eager to cooperate in this matter. After all, this is now a double murder investigation. Yes, we are liaising with our colleagues in Kingston, but neither we, nor they, have anything to add at this moment in time.

'No, I was not aware that the mother of Maria Warner had been approached with a view to selling her story. Mrs Warner was offered the services of a police liaison officer which, I believe, she declined, though of course that offer still stands. No, we have nothing to say on the matter. If Mrs Warner were to decide to tell her story to the media then that is a personal matter and one for her to decide.'

He escaped, gratefully. Gina met him by the door. 'Any news on our artist?' he asked.

She shook her head. 'No change, the doctors say. He's still under sedation but Joe Sykes and Phil Arnott are on their way. Should be with us within the hour.'

'Good. It's about time. Toss you for it? No, second thoughts, you can have Sykes seeing

225

as how you're already acquainted. I'll have the boyfriend. I wouldn't want his lurid tales of sexual exploits to pollute that pure mind of yours.'

'Hoping something'll rub off, Guv?'

'One can always hope,' Marris told her.

Rob had slept, part exhaustion, part sedative induced, but it was a sleep that brought no relief and no refreshment. Time after time, he'd struggle into wakefulness in an effort to escape the dreams but each time his body proved traitor, his eyes would close and he would sink back into the abyss.

She was there, waiting for him. She was always there in that darkest of places.

Anna, running, shouting something he didn't quite hear. Anna on the bridge, her hair, dark curls, tumbling onto her shoulders, blowing in the sharp breeze, hiding her face from him. Then the cold shock of the water, the taste of earth and cold in his mouth as he swallowed, choked, clawed his way through reeds and marsh. He could feel it sucking at his feet, dragging him down, but he could see her face now, mouth open, eyes wild and staring as she struggled first against the chill water and then, as he reached for her, against his grasping hands.

She fought so hard he thought he would drown, be pulled down into the filth and silt. He could smell the decay stirred up by

226

their struggle, threatening to engulf them both, rising up around him like a miasma. He swallowed water, choked, fought for breath, choked again, her arm flailing and striking him on the mouth, the throat, feet kicking, pushing against his body, pushing away and he was losing hold.

Frantically, he tried to keep her head above the water, though each time he lifted her she forced him down, the water closing over his mouth and eyes. Lungs bursting, he was forced to let go, strike upward, at least what he hoped was upward. For a terrifying dizzying time he could no longer remember which way to go. Finally he broke surface, gasped air into lungs that burned and yet seemed filled with water. Broke surface to the vision of brooding sky and, seconds later, bitter rain falling hard upon his face.

Three times he dived, three times, feeling about in the murk in increasing desperation until, finally, desperation gave way to pure despair. He had failed and she was gone.

No, he thought, not gone, only now she waited in his dreams.

Chapter Twenty-Nine

Joe Sykes and Phil Arnott arrived within minutes of one another. Both accompanied by lawyers and representatives of the papers that had printed their stories. The declaration that 'my client is here of his own free will, not charged with any crime but of course willing to cooperate' spiel was spun out by both lawyers and permission sought and granted to tape the 'informal interview'. Gina and Marris led their respective interviewees away and got down to business.

Marris was not impressed by Phil Arnott. He was thirty-five trying to look seventeen. Skater jeans teamed with a hooded sweatshirt, bleached blond hair, roots recently attended to, Marris thought; his own darker tone attested to by the dark stubble on his chin.

Marris thanked him for attending. Arnott grinned, turning the too confident smile onto his solicitor and the PA girl who had accompanied them – with her own tape and notebook.

'You don't mind, do you?' she asked, a bright-lipped smile only partially masking her nervousness. She placed what Marris now saw was a digital recorder on the table. 'I mean, as we're taping things...' she trailed off, then giggled nervously as Marris turned his gaze upon her.

'Take a seat,' he said.

She retreated.

'Mr Arnott, where did you meet Anna Freeman?'

Arnott leaned back in his chair, balancing it on its rear legs. Marris thought, if I just shove my foot out, by accident on purpose... Resisting, he plunged his hand into the pocket of his coat and caressed the cigarette box lying there. So far, he'd not given in to that urge either, but he wasn't betting on his chances of getting through the afternoon without that changing.

'I met her in Brisbane,' Arnott smirked. 'Like it said in the article.'

'Actually, the article didn't give an exact location,' Marris reminded him. 'It stated quite specifically that you'd not disclosed the locale out of consideration for Anna's friends and neighbours.'

'Oh yeah,' Arnott sat forward thumping the chair legs back onto the concrete floor. 'Yeah, that was right.'

Marris doubted he'd read the article once printed. He'd probably just admired the pictures. He compared this lout of a man to Rob and found he just couldn't see the

Anna Freeman he knew through the eyes of Robert Carr wanting anything to do with him.

'So, how did you meet and when did you make the connection?'

'Connection? I didn't make no connection.'

Marris sighed, surely he couldn't be that stupid. 'When did you realise that the Anna Freeman you'd met in Brisbane was the Anna Freeman everyone was looking for?'

'Oh, that. Look, I'd gone out there for the surfing, like.'

Spare me, Marris thought. This idiot wouldn't know one end of a surfboard from the other, let alone actually ride one. He didn't 'get' surfing, but he did know it called for a bit of intelligence.

'So, you met...?'

'Three years ago. Yeah. At this beach party. Some mates of mine invited me and Anna's lot were hanging around too. We got chatting and, well...' he broke off, gave Marris what Marris presumed was supposed to be a man to man look. 'One thing led to another, as they say.' He grinned again. 'Good summer it was too as you know, if you read me article.'

So, Marris thought. It was his article now. As if he'd actually written it. 'And since you returned? Have you kept in touch with Miss Freeman?'

'No,' he looked momentarily discomforted. 'I thought it best, you know, holiday romances, well, they're all well and good but with her being over there and me being over here?'

Marris nodded his understanding. 'It was a long holiday romance,' Marris noted. 'If it lasted all summer.'

He waited for a response from Phil Arnott, but the man looked blank, the relevance of the comment lost on him. Blank, Marris thought, was something Phil had a talent for. Marris moved on. 'You've still not told me how you made the connection between the woman you met in Australia and Robert Carr's model.'

'Oh, oh well. One of her mates told me, see. She were drunk and having a laugh. She'd got this copy of a magazine article her mam had sent her or something. It was about Anna and that Robert Carr bloke. Some book or other coming out about a something or other obsession. I don't remember the bloody title, anyway. They were having a laugh about them not knowing Anna was here on the beach on a Sunday night in Brisbane. I thought oh, right, someone famous like, and like I said, we got close that summer. Then when all this stuff blew up about them looking for her I did some phoning round my contacts in Aussie land, but she'd moved on and no one seemed to know where.'

I wonder why, Marris thought.

'Then when I heard she was going to be on the telly, I thought good, we can meet up for a drink, maybe, rekindle the flame.'

'And then you saw the television show.'

'Dead right and I knew straight off they were pulling a fast one.'

'So you thought you might be able to make some money out of that information?'

Arnott's smile faded. 'No way. I mean, that wasn't the first thing on my mind, I mean, yes it's nice having a bit of cash from it and why not. But my first thought was, that's not my Anna, what they doing, trying to do her out of her dues are they?'

'Dues?'

'Well, she'd have got money for being on the telly, wouldn't she and she'd have maybe got money for being in all those paintings, surely.'

'I don't think being a model qualifies you for a cut of intellectual property,' Marris said, more because he wanted to see the look on Arnott's face than because he thought what he was saying made any sense.

'You what?' Arnott looked at his lawyer. 'Is he taking the piss or what? I came here out of the goodness of my...'

'Mr Arnott, can I just clarify this then. You last saw Anna when?'

'Three years ago in April. Like I said, I'd

232

been out there for the summer. Aussie summers are in the winter.'

'And you parted on good terms?'

'Well she were sorry to see me go, but yeah, we said goodbye and all that.'

'And you've had no communication with her since.'

'I told you I didn't.'

Marris nodded and thanked him for coming in. 'I'll need the address where you stayed,' he said, 'and contact names, numbers, addresses for anyone you met over there.'

'Already done that,' Arnott told him, looking pleased. 'I'm cooperating fully, see.'

The lawyer opened his briefcase and withdrew two sheets of paper, one handwritten and the other typed. He handed them to Marris. The typed version was a copy of that which had been handwritten – minus the scribbling out and the spelling errors. Marris thanked him. He felt he ought really to have been thanking the typist. He stood to let them know he was done.

'Thank you again for coming in, Mr Arnott,' Marris said. 'I'll be in touch if there's anything more.'

'You can reach me through my lawyer,' Arnott told him. 'Give him a card, mate.'

A white board was extracted from the legal pocket and presented to Marris. He watched, amused, as Arnott and his entourage trailed out and wondered how Gina was getting along.

Joe Sykes had lost his cocky self-confidence. He looked as though he'd not slept well and sat down without saying a word, his fists clenched inside the pockets of his leather jacket. Gina could see the pockets straining.

She went through the formalities of thanking him for being there, telling the lawyer she was taping the conversation and agreeing when he asked for a copy.

'Mr Sykes,' she said quietly. 'I came to see you after the death of the woman we then believed to be Anna Freeman. You knew, didn't you, that it wasn't her?'

He shook his head. 'I knew about Maria Warner,' he said. 'Lyn had wormed it out of that Simon bloke and she'd told me. But when you came to see me, when you seemed so certain it was Anna, I thought...'

He looked up, meeting her gaze for the first time since he'd come into the room. Gina remembered his reaction that day in the cottage. The near collapse, the blood draining from the face. Some reactions could be faked – she'd met with the whole gamut – but she was willing to bet her reputation that his reaction had been genuine.

'I thought she was dead,' he said. 'I thought you really meant her.'

Gina paused to collect her thoughts, then

234

asked, 'When she left, eleven years ago, did you know why or where?'

He shook his head. 'No. One day she was there and the next she was gone. I tried phoning her family.'

'Family? I understood her parents were dead.'

He nodded. 'They were ... are. Car accident when Anna was fifteen. I don't think she ever really got over it. She had an aunt, her mum's sister. They'd had a falling out but after her parents had been killed they got back in touch. I think her auntie wished she'd done it sooner.' He shrugged, 'True what they say, isn't it. You don't know what you've got until you lose it?'

'Do you have the aunt's number? An address?'

'He shook his head. No, she gave me the brush off, said Anna wanted to go away, that she needed space.' He laughed. 'Useful line that, isn't it? I was pissed off, I threw the number away.'

'But you kept Anna's stuff.'

He nodded. 'To be truthful, I didn't know I had it. I thought she'd taken everything.' He smiled, a wry lopsided smile that she liked infinitely better than the over confident smirk plastered across his face on the first occasion they had met. 'I wasn't that tidy,' he shrugged. 'First flat, no mother chasing me up to tidy my room. Her stuff was in a bag, shoved under the bed. I didn't find it 'til I moved to another place about two years after. By that time, I'd cooled down. I kept it.'

'The journals she kept, did you read them?'

He frowned. 'I never saw any others, just those two, and I read a bit of one of them just after I found them. Then I stopped.'

'Why?'

He shrugged uncomfortably. 'Because what she wrote wasn't like her. It was harder, judgmental, like the face she put on for all of us was just a face.' He shrugged again. 'For a while that helped. I told myself, she wasn't worth it. The woman that wrote the books, that wasn't the Anna I'd known. Thought I'd known. Then after a bit, I forgot about the books and just remembered her. The Anna I knew was kind. She was beautiful and she was gentle and I loved her very much.'

Once more he caught Gina's gaze and held it. 'Lyn,' he said. 'She's really dead?'

'I'm sorry, yes.'

'Fucking hell!' He broke off and stared up at the ceiling. She could see him blinking back the tears. The hands came out of the pockets, fists unballed and he wiped his eyes, then delved again to see if he could find a tissue. Gina riffled for a pack in her handbag and pushed it across the table towards him.

'Thanks. God, look at me. Bloody baby.'

'You've lost a friend,' she said. 'You're entitled.'

'Not a suspect then?' he asked wryly.

'Oh, I didn't go that far. Until I've established otherwise, you're still on the list.'

He nodded, wiped his eyes and sniffed. She wished he'd just give in and blow his nose. And you've had no contact at all since she left in the October?'

'October 5th,' he said. 'Eleven years last one. You know what's so stupid? I go down to the river every year on the day she left and I wait. Like I'm hoping she'll come back.'

'Why the river?'

He shrugged. 'Last place I saw her,' he said. 'Last place, last time I saw her and you know what's worst? We'd had a stupid fight. I don't even remember what it was about. I never got to make up, to say I was sorry. I just went off to the pub and came home too drunk to realise she'd packed up and gone.'

Chapter Thirty

'So far so inconclusive,' Marris observed, dragging up a chair and flopping down on the other side of Gina's desk. 'I have a hard time seeing Phil Arnott in the role of the shit on Anna's shoe, never mind her lover.'

'What a nice picture. But no, it doesn't ring true. According to Joe Sykes, Anna lived with her aunt in Leeds for a couple of years after her parents died. She moved out as soon as she came down to London, to art school. She was at St Martins too.'

'Too?'

'Robert Carr studied there, though he'd left by the time she went. Joe thinks they met through some mutual connection though and it was Anna that introduced Rob Carr to the rest of the group, though he was still Robert Cartwright at that point. The name change came the year Anna left. It's all in the unauthorised biography.' She pulled a copy from the in tray for Marris to see.

'Anything of interest?'

'Well, I've skimmed it. He had a rough childhood. Divorce, lived with a father who beat him black and blue, ran away from home so many times they finally took him into care. He was fostered from fourteen and that seems to have been the turning point. He discovered a talent for drawing, they encouraged it, and he finally got a scholarship and worked his way through college doing what the rest of us did.'

'Oh?'

Gina grinned. Her brief stint as a kiss-o-gram was something only Marris knew about. 'No, not that. Bar work, stuffing envelopes with glossy pages no one wants to read ... you know.'

Marris nodded. 'And the rest, as they say, is history.' He frowned. 'Does he keep in touch with the foster parents? What about the natural parents?'

'Nothing on the mother, but the father drank himself into sufficient oblivion that he failed to see the bus that killed him. The foster parents moved back to Scotland about the time Rob Carr went off to university. I spoke to them, nice people, prepared to come down and help out if he needs them.'

'He keeps in touch then?'

Gina hesitated. 'Reading between the lines, I think he helps them out financially rather than indulging in personal visits, but...' she shrugged. 'I'm not so sure he knows how to do the interpersonal relationship bit anyway.'

'Except presumably with Anna?'

She shook her head. 'Simon reckoned that

239

was the whole point. Anna was a possibility, a what-might-have-been. No one I've talked to, nothing I've found out contradicts that.'

'He married,' Marris objected.

'And it lasted a year. We've not managed to talk to the wife yet, she's been off on tour or something. I believe she's an actress.'

Marris nodded. 'Apparently.'

'Have you read the journals?'

'Only the first one.'

'And what do you make of it?'

Marris considered. 'They seem ordinary,' he said. 'A little self-centred. When she talks about other people, she seems to be dismissive, though, I don't know if you noticed, she rarely names anyone. It's all, "the blonde tart" or, what was it, "Mr Washboard". I take it she was talking about his abdominal development rather than his membership of a skiffle band. But I'd also say she was insecure.' He picked up the printouts from the desk and fingered them, skimming the pages. 'Here, for instance: "That tart walked in, all strapless bra and bright red top and I could just feel him looking at her. When I turned round and he saw me looking, he went red and made all apologetic, but I wasn't having it."'

Gina sniffed. 'What teenager isn't insecure? And she wasn't much more than that. She'd just turned twenty when she went away. She's not someone I'd have idolised though, not like Rob Carr and Joe seem to have done. 'Though,' Gina added, 'Joe reckoned the notebooks didn't sound like the Anna he knew. It was as though she'd saved her bitchier side for private and kept her best face for show.'

'Don't a lot of people do that?' Marris questioned.

'Maybe.' She looked up as someone tapped on the half open door. Willets stood in the doorway with a piece of paper clutched in his hand and an eager expression on his lightly spotty face.

'Geordie. Come along in, we won't bite,' Marris told him. 'What have you found out?'

'This, sir,' he waved the paper. 'The taxi that picked Rob Carr up from outside Lyn Chapel's house logged the pick up at five-fifteen, and Lyn Chapel made a phone call just ten minutes later. We've got the phone logs.'

'So,' Marris corrected. 'Someone made a phone call from Lyn Chapel's house just after Rob Carr left.'

'No, Guv,' Geordie looked pleased. 'I checked up. It was definitely Lyn Chapel. She phoned Jenny Walters.'

Chapter Thirty-One

Rob sat by the window looking out onto a walled garden at the rear of the clinic. He'd been transferred from the hospital on the Monday afternoon – a Simon Roper intervention – and now, ten thirty on the Tuesday morning, was receiving a visit from DI Victor Marris.

'Do you always wear the same suit?' It wasn't a question Rob knew he was going to ask. It just seemed to happen.

He watched as Marris produced that thin lipped smile. 'No, I just have several suits that look much the same. A little like you, really. A jacket you wore to go to Anna's flat, an identical one when you visited Lyn Chapel. A third in your wardrobe.'

Rob shrugged. 'You didn't come here to talk fashion.'

'No and I'm glad to see you looking better and with your sense of – I suppose it's humour – intact.' That smile again, the fine stretching of the lips, so narrow and tight they made Rob think of an elastic band pulled at both ends, ready to snap back.

Marris sat down on the edge of the single bed and smoothed the blue quilt, pinching it between his fingers and then stretching it flat. Rob watched. He had never seen anyone with such bone thin fingers. Fleshless, so that the knuckles seemed unnaturally large. The nails unreasonably flat and set too deep. His thumb and first finger, yellowed, nicotine stained.

'You smoke?'

'I try not to. I keep a pack in my pocket, just so I know it's there. Occasionally, I give in, fall off the wagon. Then I stop again. Is Anna dead, Mr Carr?'

The soft, conversational tone caught Rob off guard. He blinked, tore his gaze from the lean fingers and met Marris's too dark eyes.

Rob couldn't cope with the intensity of them. He closed his own and shook his head. 'She left, that was all. She walked away and I never saw her again.' He hesitated and then added. 'After that farce with that poor kid Simon conned into playing her part, I'm not sure I'd even know her again.'

'You wanted to be fooled,' Marris told him. 'It was easy. I think, Mr Carr, you knew from the word go that Simon's production couldn't be the real Anna Freeman. You knew because she's either dead or has another reason, a reason you know about, not to come forward.'

Rob shook his head. He got up and moved closer to the window, peered down onto the garden below. Birds flew, leaves rustled and

243

when he lifted his eyes, clouds scudded across a too blue sky. 'She left,' he said softly. 'That's all there was to it. The last time I saw her, she was...' He paused, he had been going to say she was fine, but that would not have been the truth. He remembered the river, the chill of the water as it closed over his mouth and nose and eyes and the woman's face, open-mouthed as she pushed away from him, disappeared into the murk and dark.

'She was what?' Marris asked him. 'Last time you saw her, she was...?'

Rob turned from the window and straightened sharply, pulling himself to attention. 'She was alive,' he said simply. 'Last time I saw Anna Freeman, she was very much alive.'

Chapter Thirty-Two

Crank calls were inevitable and Marris had on his desk a dozen or so yellow slips recording those that claimed to be from Anna Freeman.

Marris was thankful that he could delegate this routine checking. It irked him that so many man hours should have to be spent in the painstaking checks made for each and every one. Irked him because it took people away from the real work; irked him even more that just occasionally such sidetracks should prove fruitful and he could not, therefore, put out a blanket order to pay them no mind.

He was sitting at his desk at three in the afternoon, bringing himself up to date with the routine paperwork. His desk was as scarred and battered and skinny looking as the man himself. Quite where it had come from was something of a mystery. Someone had dragged it out of store when Marris had first arrived three years before. Its size, narrower than the norm and stretched out on skinny legs, made it ideal for the cupboard that Marris had adopted as his office. It had been partitioned from the main briefing room, a fact evidenced by the sliced, half window, offset and high up in the wall, and by the fact that nothing could even be pinned to the flimsy wall without it threatening the life and limb of anyone foolish enough to sit on the other side.

Marris liked this narrow, pokey, malnourished space. He'd packed a filing cabinet into the corner, wedged his desk close to the wall on one side, giving him just enough room to slide round between desk and cabinet. He had added a wastepaper bin and a chair – additional chairs had to be brought through from the main office as required.

He sat, facing a door which he rarely closed. The corridor beyond, he regarded as an artery flowing through the police station. Sitting there, in his lair, or broom cupboard or trap – delete adjective according to point of view – he kept an eye on the comings and goings, the gossip and the alliances made manifest as they passed his door.

The phone on his desk rang.

'Got a call for you, Guv. Says her name's Anna Freeman.'

Marris could hear the amusement in the speaker's voice.

'And I'm bloody Spartacus,' he said. 'What does that bring the total up to?'

'Fourteen, I think. But actually this one's different. She's calling from the British High Commission in Canberra, Australia. They reckon she's the real thing.'

'You sure this isn't a wind up?'

'It's all been checked out. Wouldn't have bothered you with the call otherwise.'

Marris considered. Australia? Maybe that drongo, Phil Arnott, wasn't talking out of his backside after all. 'OK, put it through.'

Moments later, he was chatting to a consular official and a minute or so after that, a woman came on the line. She had an English accent, just slightly overwritten by something else. 'I'm Anna Freeman,' she said. 'I've been talking to my cousin Tel, and he reckons all hell's broken out over there.'

Five minutes later, Marris was as convinced as he could be without the benefit of actual DNA evidence, that this was indeed the mythical Anna. The cousin, Tel, or Terry, was the son of the aunt who had looked after her after her mother's death. The address checked out and the consular officials he had spoken with assured him that they'd run background checks before getting him involved.

'Did you know a bloke by the name of Phil Arnott?' he asked, curiosity getting the better of him.

'That creep? Made my life a misery all one summer. Tel reckons he's spun some yarn about me and the *News of The World* went and printed it.'

'Play your cards right,' Marris told her, 'I'm sure you could sell your version for a whole lot more.'

She laughed. 'God, I can do without that. Now tell me, what the hell is going on. No, tell me first, what they said about Lyn. It can't be true. I won't believe it's true.'

Marris took a deep breath. 'Did your cousin tell you about that too?'

'Yeah. He recognised the name from the news. God, I thought he had to be mistaken. I tried to call her, to email, but she didn't answer. But I still don't believe it. Not Lyn.'

She was close to tears. He could hear her voice breaking. But something else made an even deeper impression.

'You stayed in touch with her?'

She hesitated. Then he could almost feel her nod on the other end of the phone. 'Lyn was about the only one worth keeping in touch with. We used to write once or twice a month, then we got email and we've been mailing regularly ever since. Who did it? Do you know?'

'Not yet, Miss Freeman, but we will. Look, if we make arrangements to fly you here...'

'Of course I'll come. God, first that poor girl and then this.'

'You know about Maria Warner?'

'Yeah, Lyn told me all about the television show.' Her voice rose slightly at the end of that, turning a statement into a question.

'Then, when she was killed ... God, I was just appalled. I couldn't believe it. I kept telling myself, that should have been me.'

'What did you do?'

'God, I faffed around a bit, panicked a lot, then did what Lyn said I ought to do, got in touch with the local police. It took me a while to persuade them I wasn't completely nuts, then they advised me to go to the consulate and organised an appointment.'

'We don't know for sure who the intended victim was,' Marris told her, but he knew she would not be convinced. Hell, he wasn't convinced. 'Look,' he said. 'Did Lyn tell anyone else about you keeping in touch?'

'No.' She was adamant. 'I wanted to get away from the lot of them. Lyn was the only one I kept in touch with and she wouldn't tell, I'm sure of it.'

'I'm assuming the one you really wanted to escape from was Robert Carr?'

'Rob?' She sounded genuinely shocked. 'Hell, no. If I'd thought he could deal with it, I'd have contacted him from time to time, but he seemed to be doing OK and I certainly didn't want to upset things.'

'Upset things?'

'Oh, God, Rob was always ... fragile and anyway, he wasn't like Lyn. Lyn had a mouth like a steel trap. Rob ... Rob speaks before he's aware he's doing it. Like it's a tick he can't control.'

'So I've noticed,' Marris told her. 'But you and Robert Carr, you parted on good terms.'

'Sure. I liked him. Not as much as he liked me, but, on the whole, when he wasn't being all artistic, Rob was one of the good guys.'

'And the others. Joe Sykes, Jenny and Peter Walters?'

There was a moment's silence on the other end of the phone that was more eloquent than any words. Finally, she said. 'Joe was a summer romance. Good while it lasted, but I wanted one thing, he wanted something else. You wouldn't think a five-year age gap could make so much difference, would you? I had just turned twenty when I went away. I didn't want to settle down. Joe, he was ready for that, I think. Not me, no way.'

'And the others?'

'Jez and Steve and the rest, they were all drifting away anyway. You know how it happens.'

'And Pete and Jenny.'

'You know,' she said slowly. 'I can't believe she actually married him. He followed her around like a little dog, all adoring eyes and ... you know I'd swear if he had a tail he'd have wagged it.'

'They've been married for a while,' Marris observed. 'They have two little girls.'

'And if I was Pete I'd be having DNA tests done!' She took a deep breath, 'Sorry, that was spiteful.'

Marris had the distinct impression the apology was for form's sake only. 'You're avoiding my question, Miss Freeman. You said Rob was one of the good guys, what about Jenny and Pete Walters?'

Again that silence. That feeling of so much unsaid, so much she really didn't want to acknowledge. To herself? To him?

'Jenny was a self-centred bitch,' she said at last. 'And that's being kind. For all I care, the pair of them could burn in hell.'

This time the silence extended across the world. Marris considered if he should pursue this line, decided not. Let her think about it on the long flight when she had nothing else to do but tolerate in-flight movies and dwell upon the past he suspected she had crossed halfway around the world to escape.

'There's a lot to talk about,' Marris said quietly. 'Two deaths, Miss Freeman, and I still don't know who or why.' He paused. 'Do you?'

'How could I know?'

The response was too quick, too glib.

'Think about it,' he said. Then, almost as an afterthought, 'You kept journals didn't you? We've got two of them covering the spring and summer before you left. Do you, by chance, have any more? They may cast some light...'

'Journals?' She sounded genuinely bewildered and Marris was reminded of Gina's comments about New Year resolutions and her failure to keep a diary. Maybe Anna had failed too, after these two books.

'I never kept a journal,' she said. 'I had a hard enough time keeping up with the sketchbooks we had to produce, never mind anything else.'

'Joe Sykes had them,' Marris prompted. 'They're nothing special to look at, just like kids' exercise books, brown covers, lined...'

'Oh.' Understanding. 'No, Inspector, they're not mine. They belong to that bitch Jenny.'

251

'Jenny Walters?'

'Well, she wasn't Walters then, she was Price. But yes. She was always bloody scribbling. Got all huffy if you caught her at it though, like it was some big secret.' She tailed off and Marris felt again the weight of unseen words.

'Would Joe have known they were hers?'

She thought about it. 'Probably not. I went to school with her, remember. She was at it even in primary school, hiding the bloody things in her desk. Making like she was keeping a record about the rest of us.'

'If you disliked her so much from such a young age, why stick around later on, when you had a choice?'

'Because,' she said, and Marris got the impression she had thought about this often, articulated it sufficiently so that she could reply at once, 'she was popular, she was powerful, she had that something that the rest of us didn't and I wanted to belong, to be popular, to be... Later, I'd just got used to being in the Jenny Price gang, I suppose. Some of us take a long time to learn sense. Some of us have to do it the hard way.'

Chapter Thirty-Three

Wednesday. It was raining when Marris looked from his window first thing that morning and still raining when he arrived at work. Anna Freeman was on her way, Rob Carr was still incarcerated behind the high, luxurious walls of that very expensive clinic and, when Marris reached his desk, two flights up, along that artery of a corridor, Marris found that the post-mortem reports for both Maria Warner and Lyn Chapel had arrived, together with the forensic on Maria Warner's, AKA the impostor Anna's flat.

Marris skimmed the post-mortem reports first, comparing the similarities and analysing the differences.

Maria Warner had, as they had suspected, been standing over her killer when he or she had struck. She must, from the angle of attack, have leaned forward and the killer taken that opportunity to strike upward, beneath the ribs and into the heart.

Maria had been dead before she hit the floor.

The knife had not been easy to withdraw and the blade had been twisted in the wound, pulled free and then wiped on Maria's shirt.

Lyn, by contrast, had been standing directly in front of her killer and the blade taken a slightly different path to the heart. The result had been the same though, Marris reflected. He pursed his lips. Maria had been heard arguing with someone, but she had let them into her flat, so, either she knew them before that point, or her killer had had a pretty convincing reason for her to allow them to come inside.

Lyn Chapel had been standing near enough to her killer that one strike had been enough. There were no defence wounds on the hands or arms of either woman. No signs of struggle. The blow that killed them had literally been a bolt from the blue. They had been shoved, brutally and suddenly from life into death without pause for preparation or, he hoped, time for fear, though he had no illusions about that being mercy on the killer's part.

He turned to the description of the weapon. The conclusions were almost identical. A kitchen knife, smooth blade, triangular cross section with a narrow, straight back and a honed blade. Something like the standard cook's knife and around six inches long.

So far, he knew, nothing had been found on scene. The killer had removed the weapon and probably disposed of it some distance away.

Either that or they'd taken it home. Odd as

that might sound, Marris found it likely. The killer had taken the trouble to remove the weapon, had, in all likelihood, used the same one for a second time, again, removed and taken it with them.

Was it identifiable? Marris wondered. If the weapon had been found, would it be so unique as to betray its owner? One of a set that would be distinguished by its absence?

Thoughtful, now, he examined the forensic report from Maria Warner's flat but there seemed little that could be of immediate help. A blonde hair that definitely wasn't Maria's. It was undyed and long, probably female, and Marris thought of Jenny Walters, though forensics did not want to speculate as to how long it had been there. Neither could they speculate about the two grey hairs and single fingernail paring found elsewhere in the flat.

The blood on Anna's shirt was hers. There was nothing that might be deemed helpful beneath her nails and tox reports revealed no alcohol in her bloodstream, no sign of drug use, nothing remarkable, beyond the ordinariness of it all.

Sighing, Marris dropped the folder back on his desk and went through to the main briefing room. Gina sat at her desk, Geordie Willets facing her. Between them, photocopies of the journals and a stack of black books Marris recognised as belonging to

Robert Carr.

'What's all this then? Our Geordie boy been busy again, has he?'

Gina grinned; Geordie blushed scarlet.

'You should take a look at this,' she told him. 'It might be nothing, but ... Geordie found these two entries, talking about a girl called Judith Allen. They're pretty bitchy, but the second one talks about her being gone, a problem out of the way.' She handed Marris the pages and he skimmed them.

The entries were bitchy, all right but... 'So?'

'So, nothing much, until Geordie spotted this in one of Rob Carr's books. It dates from the October of the same year, it's about the time Anna Freeman left, so that's about a month after this entry here. Look.'

Marris looked. The name 'Judith Allen' had been written in block capitals and ring fenced, as was Rob's habit, with a band of barbed wire ink. Unusually, in a book that routinely crammed and overlaid the inform-ation stored on each page, like some paper hard drive, it was alone on the page. Alone all but a time, a date, October 11th, and the word 'Crematorium'.

'She died? That's why she was out of the way? Why the delay for the funeral?' He closed the book and dumped it on the desk. 'It's interesting, I'll give you that, but I don't see the relevance.'

'There may be none,' Gina admitted. 'I don't know.'

Marris nodded. 'And?'

'Well,' Gina began, 'we thought, for both Anna and Rob to record it, there must be a significance.'

'Someone they know dies. I'd think it strange if they didn't record it and besides...'

'No, but it's the way she talks about it. Her being a problem out of the way. No sympathy, no...'

'Anna didn't write it.'

'What?'

'I spoke to Anna Freeman last evening. She's on her way here. From Australia, so it'll not be fast.'

Two pairs of eyes demanded explanation. Marris pulled up a chair and filled them in on the details.

'Jenny Walters wrote this?'

'She did that. And Anna's opinion of her isn't high. Seems Joe got it wrong, or he deliberately set out to mislead. We'll have to find out which.'

He paused, considered. Leads were a little thin on the ground. 'Ok, we'll include this in the morning briefing. Geordie, see what else you can turn up about this girl. It may be absolutely nothing, but we'll chase it down. Try the local papers. When we've got something concrete, we'll have a chat to Jenny Walters, see what reaction we get.'

Chapter Thirty-Four

Morning briefing over, Marris contacted the solicitor acting for the paper that had printed Joe Sykes's story and made an appointment – or rather, he insisted on knowing where Joe was and on seeing him immediately.

He met surprisingly little resistance and, an hour later, was parking his shabby green Peugeot in the car park of the kind of hotel he'd never stayed in; visited only on official business.

Joe Sykes looked out of place in such surroundings. Seated in the plush red chair, a stack of magazines and paperbacks on the table beside him, he still wore that same old leather jacket over jeans and a plain black turtleneck. Marris wondered if he slept in it. The leather was supple and well fed. It carried on its surface that dull sheen which old leather acquires when it has been a regularly recipient of saddle soap and feed. In Marris's experience, leather took more care once it was off the animal, than it ever did while still in its natural place. Only the cuffs were scuffed and worn, especially the right, where it rubbed against Joe's watch.

'Are you left-handed, Mr Sykes?'

Joe lifted his head, puzzled. 'No, no right, why?'

'Oh, no reason. I just noticed you wear your watch on the right.'

'Oh.' Joe nodded. 'I broke my left wrist a few years back. I switched to the right then and never went back. To tell the truth, I still find it uncomfortable on my left.'

'Ah, that explains it then.' Marris sat down opposite Joe in an identical chair. Barrel chairs or something they called them, didn't they? This type of singularly uncomfortable seating with their low backs and arms that crashed steeply towards the seat without being of either use, nor ornament in Marris's view. Typical hotel room furniture, in these over decorated surroundings, upholstered in somewhat plusher fabric than the norm.

'I spoke to Anna Freeman last night. She's on her way.'

'What?'

For the first time a genuine spark of interest lit Joe's eyes. 'Anna's coming here? When. Where's she been?'

'I can't tell you that, Mr Sykes. She'll be here tomorrow, but as to where she's been staying; that's her affair and if she wants you to know, that's up to her.'

'But I will get to see her.'

The eagerness in his voice and reflected in his too bright eyes caused Marris to pause.

'Do you still have feelings for Miss Freeman?'

Joe blinked and looked away. His lashes caught the light. They shone with the tears he hoped to hide.

Or was he just doing this for effect?

'I still care for her,' he said. 'Maybe even more than that. Maybe even more than I did back then.'

'It's eleven years or very nearly,' Marris observed. 'She might well have changed. You might have changed. There's no telling what either of you would feel should you get to meet.'

Joe shrugged. 'I'd like the chance to find out,' he said.

'Anna told me something very interesting during our little chat. She said that the notebooks you'd guarded so assiduously all these years weren't even hers.'

'What?'

That caught him off balance, Marris thought. 'She didn't write them, Mr Sykes. She's not yet explained to me how she came by them, but they belong to Jenny Walters – or Jenny Price as she was back then.'

Joe started at him, then he began to laugh, a small sound at first as though he merely caught his breath, but which grew in volume and lost control. Marris waited him out.

'My God,' Joe said finally, wiping the tears from his eyes with the heel of his hand. 'I've hung on to them all these years like some holy relic and all the time they belonged to that ... that...'

'Bitch?' Marris offered. 'You understand, I'm only passing on the description used by Miss Freeman, not passing a personal opinion. I don't know the lady.'

Joe slumped back and closed his eyes. Then sat forward again and stared intently at Marris. 'She was a cow,' he said and Marris wondered, not for the first time, why bovinity should be such a disparagement.

'Then why did you all put up with her? And, for that matter, didn't you notice the difference in handwriting?'

Joe shook his head. 'It looked pretty much the same,' he said. 'I'd not really taken much notice truth to tell. All I had was the notebooks and couple of letters written to Anna, not by her and the photographs. I never even thought...' he broke off and got up, stood looking out of the window with his head resting on the glass in an attitude that reminded Marris of Robert Carr. He thought about the window in Maria Warner's flat; the fingerprint expert had recovered something from the glass, but reckoned it was little more than a greasy smudge.

'Maria Warner was coming to see you the night she died, wasn't she?'

Joe hesitated and for a moment Marris thought he'd deny that. Then he shrugged.

'We were going to talk to the paper together. She was getting uncomfortable where she was and wanted to leave early. I expected her the following morning though, not that night.' He turned, puzzled, expecting answers from Marris.

'She called Rob Carr and told him someone she didn't want to see was threatening to come round. Any idea who that might have been?'

Joe shook his head. 'No. Why'd she phone him and not me?'

'Probably because he lived not more than fifteen minutes away,' Marris suggested. 'So, this was all set up with the paper? That Maria would tell her story too.'

'Yeah. I gave her extra, well, coaching I suppose you'd call it. Frankly, I thought what Simon was doing stank. I didn't see why the two of us shouldn't make some cash from it.'

Marris decided to leave that line of questioning for the moment. 'Do you remember a girl called Judith Allen,' he asked.

Joe stiffened. 'She died,' he said. 'I think she drowned. She was never really part of our crowd. And for your next question. Why did we put up with Jen? Because, Inspector, I suspect that back then, we were all in our own way as perfect wankers as she was. We really thought we were something.'

Next stop on Marris's list was Robert Carr.

Clinic bedroom made up to look like a mid-price hotel – comfortable, but nothing to encourage a sense of permanence. It was, he thought, a clever ploy. It conveyed the message: look, you're too upmarket to be treated in a regular unit, but don't think that means you can bed in and escape from the world. No luxuries, no swapping one dependency for another. Get better and get off home.

Rob was looking more alert, less exhausted and, Marris noted, he had been allowed his sketchbooks and a handful of pencils.

Marris examined his drawings. Most seemed to be studies of the view from his window. There was also, the odd portrait of members of staff and even a sketch of Rob's own hand. He was clearly running out of material. Well, enough to be bored. There were no pictures of Anna or of Maria Warner.

'Who was Judith Allen?' Marris asked him as he took a seat on the edge of Rob's bed.

'Judith?' Rob looked puzzled and then saddened by the memory. 'I've not heard anyone mention her in years.'

'Not since the October that Anna left.'

Rob nodded. 'Not since then,' he confirmed. 'Not since at least then.'

'And she was a friend of yours?'

Rob shook his head. His hands strayed to

the sketchbooks lying on the table and he opened one, picked up a pencil, held it poised but did not mark the page.

It was a classic Robert Carr stress response, Marris thought. He wanted to see how far he could press the point, but at the same time was uncertain as to how far he could stress Rob.

'You went to her funeral.'

'I felt sorry for her. She died far too soon. She drowned. Sometimes you just do what's socially right. Funerals are among those times.'

Marris let it lie. Rob made some half-hearted attempt to stroke the page with the pencil point, but he wasn't seeing the page. Marris wondered what it was he did see.

'I talked to Anna,' he said. 'She's coming back to the UK to help with our enquiries.'

Rob's head jerked up. The pencil hit the page hard enough to fracture the lead. It broke with a report that seemed loud as a pistol shot in the quiet room.

'No, no, no, you can't bring her here. She isn't safe, don't you realise that?'

He was on his feet, pencil dropped from his grip and his arms windmilling. Marris, at a disadvantage sitting on the bed, wondered if he should move. Decided against it. He said softly, 'Why is she in danger, Rob? Who would want to hurt her?'

Rob froze, arms poised but going nowhere,

body flushed with adrenaline and ready for flight but with nowhere to run. He dropped his arms back to his sides and stood, limp and exhausted by the sudden slight effort.

'They killed that girl,' he said 'and Lyn is dead. Anna will be the same if you let her come.'

'I'll see to it that she's protected,' Marris promised. 'But who would want to harm her, Mr Carr?'

Rob shook his head slowly as though trying to decide on something. A decision he didn't have all the information on which to base his choice. 'I don't know,' he said. 'Anna said things, but I don't know if they were true.'

'About?' Marris asked, but he was beginning to suspect he knew. The journals, the entry in Rob's book. Jenny Price now Jenny Walters. 'The things she said, they were about your friend Jennifer,' he said.

Rob shrugged. 'I just don't know.' He slumped back into the chair and laid his arms and head on the table, shutting Marris out from his world. His body shook as though he had a high fever, but when Marris touched his hand and said goodbye, Rob's fingers were damp and icily cold.

Chapter Thirty-Five

'Our man was a hero.' Geordie Willets, framed in Marris's office doorway, his skinny six feet two reminiscent of a third doorpost, looked extraordinarily pleased with himself.

'So, grab a chair, sit down and tell me about it.'

Geordie disappeared for a moment, came back with a chair and then dropped the folder he'd been grasping onto Marris's desk.

Marris opened it and read slowly. Geordie waited with barely suppressed impatience.

'Well,' Marris said when he'd analysed the contents. 'You're up for show and tell first thing in the morning.'

Geordie blushed.

'Try not to blush, you look like a wee girl.' Geordie blushed some more and Marris sighed. 'You've done a good job, lad, now we've just got to see how this fits into the bigger picture.'

Gina, passing along the artery corridor, paused and did a double take on seeing Marris and Geordie in conference and invited herself into the meeting. The broom cupboard office would have been pushed in its task of storing brooms and to have placed a second chair in front of the desk would probably have breached a dozen health and safety regulations. She settled, instead, for perching on the corner of Marris's desk.

'What do we have then?' Picking up the photocopies she began to read. Marris slid the paper from her fingers and set it back on the desk. 'It's after six,' he said. 'I've had a belly full of lates this week, for the sake of brevity, I suggest our expert here gives us his spiel, let him practise for his little presentation tomorrow morning.'

Gina smiled. 'Over to you, Geordie boy.'

'Oh, OK, right.' He cleared his voice once and then again, took a deep breath and began.

'Judith Allen jumped off the Kingston Bridge on the night of September 19th – that was eleven years ago last September,' he added, just in case they didn't know. 'She went into the water at about nine-fifteen. The witness who gave the time was Anna Freeman.'

'Robert Cartwright, as Robert Carr was then known, went into the water after her. According to the newspaper reports at the time, he and Anna had been together. There was another witness, a man called Brad Doyle who'd been walking home from the pub. He testified, and so did Anna, that Rob managed to pull Judith Allen to the surface a couple of times, but that she was struggling so much he couldn't keep hold. Rob almost drowned. This other witness, Doyle, he saw a boat moored downstream and he and Anna rowed it upriver and pulled Rob out. They reckoned they could see him diving for Judith, trying to find her, but he'd exhausted himself. The police underwater team found her the following day. She'd got herself wrapped up in a load of weed. They figure she couldn't have made it back to the surface even if she'd wanted and according to the witnesses, she was fighting Rob Cartwright tooth and nail to make him let go.

'She'd been drinking,' he added.

'Not a cry for help then,' Gina said sadly. 'Unless it was extremely badly judged. So, she just jumped off the bridge?'

'It looks that way. I got in touch with the investigating officer. The case records are being dragged out of storage. Erm, I used your name, sir, said you'd requested it. I didn't think they'd take much notice of me.'

Marris's eyes narrowed and Geordie paled. 'Shows initiative,' Marris granted when he thought he'd suffered for long enough. 'Well, we've moved things a bit further, I suppose. Though I'm still not sure what direction we're supposed to be heading. I can't see our bosses being altogether pleased at our dragging yet another unnatural death into the mix when we've got two perfectly good ones already. However... Clear off home, the both of you.'

Marris watched them go. Gina had been like Geordie a half dozen years back, he remembered. Keen as mustard and with a fast developing feel for the bits that didn't add up. It was promising.

But, he wondered, why hadn't Rob Carr told him any of this, or Joe Sykes, for that matter? He could hardly have been ignorant of it. Did they simply think it irrelevant or was there more to it? What didn't they want to face? When he forced them all to look back into the past, was more than a sad, dead girl, bent on finishing her life too soon, looking back at them?

Rob couldn't sleep. They'd given him a pill, but it sat in the little plastic cup it had come in, beside a carafe of warm, dead water on his bedside table. His head was full up with pictures of Judith Allen and he knew if he gave in and took the pill, she'd be waiting for him there as well. There in that void, that abyss filled with what might have beens and paths not taken, words left unsaid.

She'd been a part of the scene since primary school. The shy little kid with the plump, clammy hands, soft body and wire-framed, flesh-pink spectacles that shouted their origin as free, NHS. Her clothes, though always clean, were just that little too big, bought so she'd grow into them and get extra wear. It was a trait even the school's insistence on the unifying, supposedly socially levelling effect of having a designated uniform couldn't completely conceal.

Outside of school, her clothes more often than not bore the mark of having been worn before, by someone slimmer, darker, more in tune with the bright colours that washed out already pale skin and did nothing to balance the rather pretty, white blond hair. Her status not helped by the fact that her cousin, the donor of such brilliant, butterfly bright outfits, was only one year above them in school and had been seen wearing the self same only months before.

It was a characteristic Rob noted because he too was a member of the 'cast off clan'. In his case, it also extended to the uniform, bought 'nearly new' though in truth worn to within an inch of its life, at the start of every term from the school shop. What was intended as a discreet and tactful way of helping out the poorer parents, in fact only further stigmatised the less advantaged kids.

It wasn't just him, of course, or just Judith. There were scores of Robs and Judiths scattered through the school population and most survived perfectly well by either not caring or banding together with others of their ilk. Or did they survive OK? Or did

270

they all have their personal crises over shiny trousers and patched elbows? Shirts with frayed collars, or worse still, that faint discolouration beneath the armpits that spoke eloquently of another's sweat.

By the time they all reached the dizzy heights of 'big school', the pattern was set. For Anna and Rob, Jenny and Pete and poor little Judith. All in their group had a role to play. Rob was the philosopher, Jenny the queen bee, Anna the charmer – an essential for keeping the teachers at bay when they might otherwise have paid more attention to the rumours. Pete was the puppy dog, the gopher, obeying his mistress's command and Judith, lonely little Judith, just grateful to have any role in such exalted company, the butt of their jokes. The slightly less bright, the slightly less quick-witted. Judith, the slightly less.

Rob turned on his side and faced the wall, stared hard at the dim lit patterns on the embossed paper. There might have been some excuse for their behaviour as little kids, but the role play had continued into adulthood. Until Judith herself had, against all odds, despite all they had done collectively to prevent it, begun to blossom and to pull away from their group and find her own way. Bereft, unprepared for the loss of one that played such an essential role, they had tried to pull her back until one by one, their more adult selves began to see her in a different light. Then and only then did they let her go, until by the time Rob and Anna went off to study in London, only Jenny felt the need to cling to the Judith of the past.

Being away released them from their previous world order and it was a shock upon returning to find that Judith and Pete and Jenny still remained, in a fixed, though straining, orbit.

Jenny had changed, they told one another. She hadn't used to be this bitchy, this shallow, this self-centred. The truth was they had allowed themselves to change. Jenny and the rest had largely remained the same.

Now Judith, that little girl who'd been a little bit less able to release herself from the demands of their little, intolerant crowd, was just that little bit less alive.

Chapter Thirty-Six

Anna Freeman watched the television screen with an intensity that allowed Marris to observe her closely. He moved so that he could keep both images in view. The 'real' Anna and the one playing her role on the television show.

This Anna, this flesh and blood woman

sitting beside him, was, he now realised, what Anna should look like. Still beautiful, still essentially as Robert Carr had depicted her, but with the marks of the last decade clear upon her face, maturing her, adding to the expressivity of her features.

The girl on screen was exactly that in comparison. A girl, imitating age and experience she didn't have though, not having seen the real thing, Marris conceded that she'd done a smashing job. She'd given it her best shot and he was no longer surprised that Robert Carr accepted her for what she seemed to be.

The on screen Anna idealised the image Rob Carr produced. The on screen Anna used the pictures he had painted as her guide and, like the program they had for use in creating identikit portraits, in which the operator was able to run time forward and age the face produced, Maria Warner had done the same. Run time forward for herself, for the painted Anna, and provided what might be expected, not what really was.

Age a photograph, Marris thought and the person will still be recognisable, but there will be no depth, no character, no understanding of the experience that has transformed the one to the other.

Anna paused the recording, rewound and played again that section which showed the reaction of Robert Carr. She had seen something that Marris, not knowing the man, had not.

'He's shocked,' she said. 'He takes a split second to decide, is this really her or not. Then he decides. Oh, I don't mean consciously says, OK, she'll do. I mean, something inside of him decides that he has to play the part and once he's made that adjustment, tweaked his reality, that poor girl became me for a little while.'

'You think he can fool himself that easily?'

'Oh,' Anna said. 'I think we all can, don't you? We take the easy way out, the no confrontational behaviour. We agree to sex, not because we want it, but because it seems impolite not to do it. We vote for a politician, not because we agree with their views, but because after someone somewhere fought for the right to vote, we shouldn't waste it and yet we do, voting for the sake of it. We rewrite our past because we're uncomfortable or frightened of the reality of it. And for most of the time, we can pretend that the rewritten events are the real thing. Then someone comes along and confronts us. You know, Inspector, I think that bit of Rob that recognised Maria Warner wasn't me, was glad. It let him off the hook. It meant he didn't have to face the reality.'

'And the reality centres on Judith Allen.'

Anna nodded.

'Rob and I went to the funeral,' she said.

'I'd already left Kingston by then, gone back to Leeds, though my aunt didn't let on when Joe called her. I'd had enough and wanted just to go. I came back for the inquest and then for the funeral. No one saw me except Rob. I knew I was safe, no one would be there, not one of the others. I remember, Judith's mother was so grateful that we'd come. She sent me Christmas cards care of Aunt May and I'd send one back the same way. She was so pleased to think that Judith had friends that cared enough to be there for the service and we felt so guilty. Judith wasn't a friend, not really. At best, we felt sorry for her; most of the time we didn't even care. At worst, we used her just the same way Jenny did. To feel better about ourselves. To feed our misguided sense of superiority.'

'And the mother. Are you still in touch?'

Anna shook her head. 'No. You see, I couldn't take it any more, this guilt that she felt gratitude for us, for those of us who'd persecuted her child. Oh, not Rob, looking back, Rob was the only one that ever tried to protect Judith. Later, when I'd learnt a bit about the world, enough to give me a perspective on what I'd been doing, I'd tried to make it up to her. But it was a bit bloody late by then.'

'So, what did you do?'

'I wrote to Mrs Allen, this long and

275

rambling crap, all self-justification and self-flagellation. How I was a better person now and, how...' she trailed off and looked Marris straight in the eye. 'Whoever said confession was good for the soul probably meant us to take our petty attempts at self-healing to a priest, not direct them at the people we'd most hurt in the process. I must have opened a wound that had just scabbed over, never really had the chance to heal inside. I never heard back from her.'

'And in the letter, at whose door did you lay the blame for her daughter's death?'

'All of us except Rob, I guess. Rob didn't deserve that kind of blame. Oh, he could be a prat, a self-serving, self-centred idiot, but the only person he ever really hurt was himself. And he tried so hard that night to save her life.'

Marris paused, he reached down to pick up a dusty folder he'd placed on the floor next to his chair. 'This is the post-mortem of Judith Allen,' he said. 'We had the case files sent over to us. According to this, Judith's system was so full of pills and booze, she'd never have been able to walk to that bridge unaided.

'Was that what you confessed to Mrs Allen? That you were there? That you helped her climb onto the parapet and, just maybe, gave her a little nudge in case she changed her mind?'

Anna's eyes widened and for one surreal moment, Marris was sure he had hit right and she would break down and confess. Then her shock and disbelief turned to anger, raw and unabated by the passage of time.

'I did nothing to hurt Judith on that night,' she told him. 'I did nothing!'

'Perhaps that was the trouble,' Marris said, 'you did nothing.' His voice so soft she had to lean towards him to catch the words. He saw the flame die in her eyes and knew that this time he really had struck home. 'Anna, it seems to me you've waited eleven years and one long plane journey to tell me what happened. So, tell me now, priest and confessional. Isn't that what you wanted?'

Slowly, she shook her head. 'A priest is sworn to silence,' she informed him. 'You have to use whatever I tell you.'

'I do, yes. Isn't that what you hoped would happen when you wrote that letter to Judith's mother? That she would act on what you told her and make it all right?'

He watched as the pretty face crumpled and the tears began to fall. She cradled her face in her hands and mourned, tears squeezing between her fingers, dripping down onto the faded blue jeans, her body shaking and trembling with eleven years of pent up fury.

Marris waited patiently, ready with tissues and tea when the rage passed and the grief turned quiet, though no less potent. He watched as her eyes lost their focus on the present and, as she gripped the mug of scalding tea between her hands, she let the years slip from her and began to speak.

'The summer had been a good one, long and warm and, though we'd all had jobs of one sort or another, there'd been time in the evenings and when work finished to enjoy the weather. We'd spent most of it in the park, down by the river, close to the willow tree. I guess we'd seen that spot as our personal property. I remember, we'd do our best to intimidate anyone who got there first, oh, not by doing anything bad, just by getting up close and making our presence felt. Being loud and raucous and well, not too nice to be around. Rob would sit under the tree and watch. Rob never was much of a joiner and he'd sketch endlessly. I think having a pencil in his hand was like some people need a cigarette. He used to sit with his sketch book on his knees and the pencils all lined up, sticking out of the side of his trainers. Sometimes, just to annoy him, I'd take them out and put them back in the wrong order but he never said a word, just smiled at me and put them back the way he wanted.

'Jenny and Peter were getting so it was like they were joined at the hip and she was always bossing him about. Pete, get me this, do that, don't you think you ought ... she didn't change. She was like that in school always wanting people to wait on her. I went to her house once and she was like it with her mum, wanting all the time, demanding...

'Then there was Joe. I'd been going with Joe since before the end of term. We'd met first off at a Christmas party, then again at Easter and, thinking about it, I guess that was when I first started seeing him, though it wasn't every weekend then, I'd got exams coming up and I actually worked pretty hard.' She paused, pulled a face. 'I tried to make up for in hard work what I had in lack of talent.'

'It's a prestigious school of art,' Marris said gently. 'You can't have been all that lacking.'

'Maybe, I don't know. That was where I met Lyn, in case you wondered. But anyway, I'd decided I wanted to specialise in set design and everyone told me that was a tough gig to break into, but I didn't believe them and then as I went on working and comparing what I did to what other people were doing and looking at how many people who were better than me left college and couldn't get a job, well...'

She looked up at Marris. 'I'm not telling you what you want to know, am I.'

'Go on,' Marris said. 'How did Judith fit into all of this?'

'Well, she didn't really. Not really. She'd stayed on to do her A levels and did really well but she decided to get a job. I think her mother needed her to though she always said she'd have been happy for Judith to go to Uni if she'd wanted. I think Jude was just sick of being poor. She got a job in a solicitor's office as a junior but with training to become a legal secretary so she was prepared to put up with shit wages for a while if it meant better later on. After work every day she used to go home to get changed and have dinner with her mum then come down to the river in the hope we'd be there. Sometimes we used to hide from her. You know, like infant school kids playing a trick. I'm not going to make excuses, Inspector, we were grown up enough to know better, we just enjoyed the power it gave us.' She laughed derisively. 'Power, over someone like Judith. God, what little shits we must have been.'

'And Rob?'

She shook her head. 'No, Rob didn't play games. Rob sat and waited regardless, he sketched her too, you know. Then afterward ... after she was gone, he burned them all, his pictures of her. He said he couldn't bear the sight of them.'

'Did she love Rob?' It seemed such an obvious question that he was surprised to see the startled look cross Anna's face as though she'd not considered this before.

'I don't know,' she said. 'Rob always said she'd grow out of the ugly duckling phase and you could see she was beginning to. Guys were actually looking at her, though she was too shy and insecure to notice. I guess that wound Jenny up as well. And, if I'm truly honest, I resented it when Rob paid her attention, even though I was going out with Joe. I'd wanted Rob, you see, but he never seemed to rise to the bait. Not like Joe.'

Marris waited as she thought about it. He supposed she was trying to be fair about everyone, but that she didn't want him to think badly of either the girl she had been or the woman she was now. Frankly, Marris didn't care what she wanted. 'And the night Judith drowned,' he said.

Anna sighed. Marris guessed he'd have got more of the same, left to her, but he had the picture now and wanted to get to the point.

'The night she died, she'd been with us by the river. Joe had to work late, I think, anyway, he wasn't there. Lyn had gone home for the weekend. There was me and Rob and Jenny and Peter and Jude. When it got dark, someone suggested we go for a drink. Rob said he would have to get off home soon, he had work to do. He always had work to do. Judith wasn't asked, but she tagged along anyway. I remember, she talked to Rob, but they'd hung back behind the rest of us and I felt resentful, out of it. You know, Jenny and Peter were all over one another and Rob was talking to Judith and ... I wasn't in the mood to be tolerant, I suppose.'

She paused, thought about what she was going to say. They were close to it now. The heart of the matter. The source of her guilt. Marris decided he had to help her out. 'You got her drunk.'

'Yes, we bought her vodka. Challenged her, after three or so, she wasn't in control any more. We sat outside on the grass and fed her another and another until she wasn't... She started to cry. You know how drink takes some people. Started to tell us how unhappy she was. Jenny thought it was funny. She pretended to be sympathetic, but it just got ... we were all of us pretty bladdered, I guess.'

'And Rob?'

'No,' she said bitterly. 'Rob had one or two then headed off home. He tried to take Judith with him, but she was having a good time with her good friends and didn't want to go. Good friends. Us. He made me promise to keep an eye on her and I said I would but before long I was too pissed to think about it.' She eyed Marris warily. 'No,' she said, 'it's not an excuse, is it.'

'I went back in to get another round but the landlord said we'd had enough. He told us to pipe down, that we were making too much noise, so we left, stopped off at the off license to get more and I remembered my promise to see Judith got home. Jenny thought that was funny. She said we'd all go. So, we did.

'By now, I was feeling pretty sick and I didn't drink any more and I figured out that Jenny wasn't nearly as drunk as the rest of us. She'd just wound us up and was watching us go, like we were little clockwork mice and she was the cat. Jude had reached that point where she didn't even know how much she'd had. She was crying saying how life wasn't worth living. How she'd be better off dead and Jen was sympathising, telling her she knew how it was to feel that way.

'We walked back across the park and ... I remember stopping to throw up. I'd had way too much. I heard Rob call out my name. So I stopped. The others were a bit up ahead. He said he'd been worried, so he'd come back out to try and find us. Was I OK?

'No, I wasn't OK, I felt rough as ... but anyway, all I wanted was my bed. Rob said we'd catch up with the others and take Judith home and then me. We looked up the path and saw that they were on the bridge.

'Jude was on the parapet, she was shouting something and Jenny and Pete stood there, applauding, telling her ... telling her that she should do it.

'Then she jumped and the rest you know.'

283

She jerked her head upward and her eyes challenged him to question her further.

'Was she pushed or did she fall?'

She held his gaze, but her lips trembled. 'I just saw her fall.'

'But you were never certain.'

She swallowed convulsively and looked away. 'No.'

'Are you lying to me, Anna?'

'I just don't know.'

'But you suspect?'

'She didn't try to stop her, that's all I know.'

Marris nodded, he got to his feet switched off the television.

'You told Mrs Allen this, in your letter to her.'

Anna nodded. 'I said it all, just like I said it to you.'

'So, she believed that her daughter's friends had killed her.' Marris paused. 'In those circumstances, Anna, what do you think you'd want to do?'

'I think I might want them dead,' Anna told him.

'And so you ran away?'

'No,' she said. 'No. I'd started running a long time before.'

Chapter Thirty-Seven

'We have to consider the possibility,' Marris postulated, 'that Mrs Allen decided upon revenge and that the television show acted as some kind of trigger. It's entirely possible, in fact, that she didn't know where to find Anna and Lyn by then ... however, that still leaves us with some interesting questions.'

'Such as,' Gina agreed, 'Why she would want to kill Lyn Chapel, seeing as she wasn't even there the night Judith died.'

'No, and Anna didn't implicate her, even obliquely. So... One more lead to chase up, though. I've got people chasing up the last known address, known contacts, and so forth. She moved from Kingston just after Judith's death. Anna had her next address, but she had the impression it was only temporary.'

'And what about Jenny Walters? Do we bring her in?'

'Not yet,' Marris said. 'She's spent eleven years not talking about this. Why would she start now? No, we need a little something to persuade her.'

They had completed the morning briefing, adding Anna's revelations to the mix and updating on other matters. In reality there was so little to add, Marris thought. Everyone they could find who'd worked with Maria Warner had been interviewed. Her friends had given statements. Her mother rang on a daily basis to know when she could arrange the funeral and how much further on they were in finding whoever murdered her child.

What could he tell her? It looked as though she was simply in the wrong place at the wrong time.

'If the mother killed Anna that would make more sense,' Gina mused. 'I mean, she'd only met Anna a few times; she'd easily believe Maria was her.'

'Whereas Jenny, presumably, would not.' Marris thought about it ... again. It had occupied his thoughts for most of the night. 'Rob accepted her,' he said. 'I see no reason why, all this time later, Jenny would be any less willing to accept the evidence of her own eyes. Unless, of course, she realised that Maria was a phoney, but by that time she'd shown her hand and it was too late. She had a witness, probably a witness who'd been threatened with a knife...'

'Except there were no defence wounds and we know from the angle of strike that she was standing very close, maybe even leaning over Jenny ... if that's who it was. Either way, it still begs the question "why kill Lyn?"'

'Anna told her about the letter she sent,' Marris reminded her. 'It's possible Lyn was of a similar mind and thought it was time all of this came out into the open. Maybe she called Jenny to tell her she knew what happened that night.'

'You think she'd be that stupid?'

'Who knows? People do stupid things all the time but, and it's a big but, we're assuming Jenny's the killer. It's one thing to get pissed out of your mind and help someone off a bridge, if that's what happened and, remember, so far, we've only Anna Freeman's word for that. Anna could well have her own axe to grind. In her original statement, taken the night Judith died, she made absolutely no mention of Pete or Jenny, neither did Rob, and the landlord of the pub couldn't swear to who had been drinking with Judith because she was sitting on the grass outside the pub. He only remembered telling Anna she'd had enough.'

'So, neither she nor Rob Carr are completely off the hook,' Gina agreed.

'So, what now, we interview Rob Carr again? Or do we try Mrs Jenny Walters and hubby?'

'Hubby! I hate that word. It reduces men to the status of a large eared cuddly toy.'

'Why large ears?'

Marris shrugged. 'Hubby is a big eared

word,' he said with a finality that Gina knew would brook no challenge. 'As to where next, the flat, I think. I want to get that totally clear before we proceed. Then we go and interview Jenny Walters, ask her about that phone call that Lyn made a half hour before she died.'

'Thought the locals had already interviewed her about that and drawn a blank,' Gina objected, knowing what the answer would be anyway.

'Then we'll ask again,' Marris said. 'And I think we'll go on asking until we get the answer we want.'

Maria's flat was still sealed but the guard had been removed. Marris had been given keys to both the flat and the outer door, achieving that which Mrs Gillis, who actually lived there, had found impossible. Mrs Gillis herself had left, earlier than planned, unable to cope with the idea that someone had been killed right above her head. Marris had pulled strings and had her placed in a hotel for the few days until her new home was ready.

The old house echoed with that silence that arrives when the inhabitants leave, which deepens, illogically, regardless of the fact that nothing else has changed. The same furnishings, carpets, curtains, fixtures and fittings, only the absence of life, that soft bodied muffler of sound, changed the mix, but it changed it utterly.

Marris fitted the key in the lock and opened the door, swinging it wide, but remaining on the threshold. But for the addition of grey powder, police tape and that indefinable smell that had little to do with death but which permeated empty rooms, the flat was as Maria had left it. She could, Marris thought, simply have walked away, or been in the midst of doing so, half-packed, already withdrawing her presence from the scene.

'We going in or what? God, this place gives me the creeps. Wouldn't want to live in a hole like this.'

'It was, I'm sure, a very handsome house,' Marris objected quickly. It was as though he did not want to offend the spirits of the place.

'Yeah, I'm sure, but it's not for me.' She crossed to the sofa and sat down where they assumed Maria's killer must have been. 'We're both taller than she was,' Gina frowned, 'but get yourself here and bend over.'

Marris drew his lips back into that thin smile. 'Nice line to throw at a superior officer,' he commented

Gina hooted her derision. 'Superior! Only for as long as it takes me to pass those exams, don't forget.' She frowned suddenly.

'She never knew what hit her, did she?'

'I hope not. I hope she knew nothing.' He walked over to the sofa and assessed the position. 'Where would you hide the knife?'

'Sleeve, or even pocket. The knife had a six inch blade and was pushed in up to the hilt. There was bruising on the skin to indicate the profile of the handle.'

'Six inches plus handle. Deep pockets,' Marris objected.

'Um, yes, but not impossible. How about a kangaroo pocket in front, you know like you'd get on a hoodie or a windcheater.'

'That would make more sense.'

'OK, so, I'm sitting here, weapon concealed. You come over. I stab upwards.' She demonstrated then shook her head. 'No, that doesn't work, the angle's wrong. You would have to be leaning over me.'

Marris rested a hand on the back of the sofa and moved round a fraction. 'Like this?'

She tried again, her fist this time coming up against his solar plexus. 'Back off a bit and kind of squat down, remember you're too tall.'

Grimacing, Marris obliged.

'Yeah, that's about right, so what was she doing to get in that position?'

Marris reached with his free hand. 'Taking something from the sofa?'

'Then why not go round?' She extended

her left arm outward, forcing Marris to reach across her body as though to wrest something from her hand.

'Taking something from the killer?'

He straightened up and picked up the folder he had with him, spread the crime scene photos on the coffee table. They studied them. Nothing. Nothing the killer might have been holding and Maria trying to reach.

'She could have grabbed her wrist, pulled her across, stabbed upward.'

'Makes sense,' Marris approved. 'But you're making the assumption that this was definitely Jenny.'

'Who else? Pete?'

'He was there that night. He married her.'

'Guilt by association?' Gina questioned.

'Why not. Or Maria's mother.'

'Not Rob? Definitely not Robert Carr?'

'The timing doesn't fit. Yes, he was here, but if we go with Mrs Gillis's evidence that Maria had an earlier visitor...'

'How reliable is that?'

Marris shrugged. 'OK, so Rob Carr is still in the frame but he's not heading my list.'

'And the agent, Simon Roper, he has a solid alibi until one forty-five. From then until two he was having a row with his wife. The neighbours testify to that. For part of that time he was standing outside asking to be let in. Apparently he was late home.'

291

'So we have a list of three plus Rob Carr.' He brightened a little. 'I suppose that's three more than we had to begin with.'

'So,' Gina asked. 'Next item on the list. Jenny Walters?'

'Jenny Walters,' Marris confirmed.

Peter Walters was at work even though it was a Saturday. 'He does overtime when it's offered,' Jenny told them. 'With two kids we need the extra cash.'

'You don't go to work?' Gina asked innocently.

Jenny frowned then set their coffee down on the kitchen table with a little thump. 'I look after the children and run the home,' she said. 'That's work, too.'

'Hard work,' Marris approved. 'I couldn't do it.'

Jenny rewarded him with a small, tight smile.

Gina tried not to choke on the very hot coffee and the image of Marris ever interacting with a child.

Jenny's children were in the garden, visible through the open door. It was a cold day, but sunny and inviting. The kids, wrapped in coats and with their feet in bright Wellingtons, seemed happy to be outside. Gina wished she'd kept her coat on though, the draught from the half open door cut across her back. She noted that Jenny had chosen a place to sit that was closest to the radiator.

'You've not said what you've come for,' she said. 'Is there news about Lyn or that girl?'

'Not exactly,' Marris told her, 'but you might be interested to know that I've been talking to Anna Freeman. The real Anna Freeman that is, she flew in yesterday.'

'What? You mean you've found her? That's wonderful.'

She recovered quickly but the initial shock of Marris's words could not be hidden, neither could the spilled coffee, slopped from the mug as her hand jerked upwards.

'Where was she?'

Mans ignored the question. Instead he asked one of his own. 'Lyn called you on the night she died. Can you tell me what you talked about?'

She set the mug back down with exaggerated care and got up to pull some kitchen towel from the roll fixed to the wall beside the door. 'Mind what you're doing with that,' she shouted at one of the children, then turned, tutting, at either the coffee or children. She wiped the spilt coffee and threw the paper towel away, then sat down. 'I told that other officer,' she said. 'We just chatted.'

'Short phone call for a chat?' Marris objected. 'Two minutes and fifteen seconds.'

'She phoned at a bad time. I was getting the children ready for bed. I said I'd call back later.'

'And did you?'

She shrugged. 'I don't remember. Does it matter?'

'And she seemed normal to you. Not stressed or afraid of anything?'

Jenny shrugged. 'She sounded fine.'

'Did she tell you Rob had been to see her?'

A nod. 'I told the other officer. I was surprised.'

'Did she also tell you that she'd stayed in touch with Anna?'

The expression of surprise was different this time. The eyes widened and she shook her head. 'With Anna? No. Since when?'

'Since Anna left in the October Judith Allen died,' Marris told her.

It was the lack of reaction that time that Marris found intriguing. The coffee returned to the table, and she got up again to check on the children in the garden. Anna left in the September,' she said mildly. 'She walked out on Joe one night.'

'She came back for the funeral,' Gina told her. 'Anna and Rob went to the funeral. No one else turned up, apparently, despite the fact you'd known her since you were what, nine years old?'

Jenny glanced back over her shoulder. 'She wasn't a close friend or anything. Anyway. I don't really approve of suicide.'

It was such an unexpected statement that

Gina felt her mouth fall open of its own accord. She snapped it shut and glared at Marris.

'An open verdict was recorded, Mrs Walters,' he said quietly. 'Judith's death is not recorded as suicide.'

'That's what they always say, isn't it? Spare the family the embarrassment?'

'And is that how you see Judith Allen's death? Just an embarrassment.' Gina couldn't hide her anger.

'Anna tells us you were there, that night.'

Jenny turned, sharply. 'Where? She's lying.'

'If you don't know where, how do you know she's lying?'

Jenny scowled and then shrugged. Bright spots of colour glowed on the pale cheeks. 'Look,' she said. 'I've got to get the kids' lunch. I'd like you to go.'

'I have more questions,' Marris said.

'I don't care about your questions.'

'No? I'd have thought, after all this time, you'd have been curious about Anna anyway. Especially about what she had to tell us.'

Jenny took a deep breath and shook her head. 'Why should I care? It's all lies. She was always the same, that one, drawing attention to herself, trying to put herself in a good light. Can't think why Lyn bothered with her. I thought she had more sense.'

'Why?' Gina couldn't help herself. 'Did she have sense not to bother with you?'

The red spots grew in size and deepened in shade. 'What's that supposed to mean?'

'Well,' Gina continued, winging it now. 'We've seen her phone records and the night she died was the first time in months the two of you had spoken on the phone. So I don't believe she called wanting a chat. I think she had a reason.'

'You can think what you like,' Jenny told her. 'Maybe she phoned me to tell me Rob had been round. How should I remember?'

'I'd have thought,' Marris said, 'as you were probably the last person to speak to her, other than the killer, of course, and we don't have a record to tell us whether they chatted or not before Lyn died, that the conversation would have burned itself into your brain. In my experience, Mrs Walters, people involved in a tragedy such as this go over those conversations time and time again, often until they're wrung quite dry.'

'What's that supposed to mean?'

'It means, Mrs Walters, that I don't believe you. That I think you recall word for word what Lyn Chapel said and I want to know why you're lying to me.'

Chapter Thirty-Eight

Mrs Allen, Judith's mother, had been dead for five years. That was the news awaiting Marris on his return, together with a phone number and the name of the officer in charge of the investigation.

'A police matter?' Marris was puzzled until he looked at the fax also lying on his desk. It was an outline only, with the promise that the records would be sent on to him, but it detailed the botched burglary that had let to Mrs Margaret Allen's death.

Marris dialled the number on the sheet and asked to be put through to Inspector Deal.

'To start with, it looked straightforward,' Deal informed him. 'Signs of an untidy search, money and cards missing from the purse and some bits of jewellery on the floor from a broken jewellery box. Entry through a broken window at the back. We supposed that Mrs Allen disturbed them, whoever it was, and that they panicked and killed her.'

'How?'

'Single stab wound, just below the ribs. They got lucky and hit the heart. The knife used, we think, was from a block in the kitchen. There was one missing and never recovered. So ... the assumption was that they came with intent to steal and not to kill.'

'You keep emphasising that this was assumption,' Marris challenged. 'Was there reason for doubt?'

Deal hesitated. 'On the face of it, no,' he said. 'You know, I particularly recall the case because, well, apart from the fact the woman died, the local papers made a big thing about personal tragedy. Her daughter had been killed in a drowning accident a few years before. The inference was that it was suicide.'

'The inquest was inconclusive,' Marris told him.

'Ah, but that's often the way, isn't it? There are still some coroners who'll go to any length to avoid the S word. It still carries too much of a stigma if you ask me. Anyway, there was this big splash in the local rag, journalists crawling all over for a while – well, a journalist and a photographer, if I'm being accurate. Just felt like a whole bloody cohort.' He paused to laugh at his own joke and Marris smiled slightly as though hoping that would be sufficient to transmit amusement by phone.

'Anyway, it stuck in the mind because of that. The usual cranks came out of the woodwork, claiming there was more to it than a simple break in.'

'Did you suspect there might be more?'

Deal fell silent for a moment as though weighing his options. 'Look,' he said finally. 'It's probably nothing and you'll see for yourself when you get the case file. But there was this old lady, an aunt or something, she was insistent that Mrs Allen had been threatened. She said the Allen woman had received a letter or something, telling her that her kid's death was not an accident and neither was it suicide. The old lady ... what was her bloody name ... she was outraged because she said the mother was just starting to get over the death and this opened it all up again.'

'Do you have this letter?'

'No, no I don't have it. That mean something to you, does it?'

'Yes, yes, it does.'

'Then the old lady wasn't completely off her rocker.' Deal sounded both pleased and impressed. 'What can I do for you?'

'Find the old lady.'

'She was in an old folks' home somewhere. I'll do some ringing round and just hope she hasn't popped her clogs.'

Amen to that, Marris thought. Judith Allen's mother, single stab wound, the letter, the threats. He curbed the rising excitement that came when he could feel the cogs and sliders falling into place.

Chapter Thirty-Nine

Rob said he was hoping to go home to his studio but Marris could see his heart wasn't in it. He felt safe in this unexposed world, four walls within a walled garden. He had neither radio nor television in his room. Music played and Marris recognized the piano piece. Rachmaninov, he thought. The second? He looked for the source. A small CD player on the bedside table, a stack of CDs beside. Marris recognised Simon's hand in that and in the art materials arranged on the wooden table beneath the window.

'It's good that you're going home,' he encouraged.

He studied the work Rob had been doing. More studies of the scrap of outside world he could see from the window, though now, there were also studies of clouds and dramatic skies. Marris found that encouraging.

'I spoke to Anna.'

'You never said how you found her.'

'No,' Marris confirmed. 'You seemed ... distracted. Last time we met. She's been living abroad,' Marris went on. 'Her cousin contacted her and told her what was going on. She thought she should make herself known.'

'Her cousin? Terry? He swore he knew nothing.' Rob laughed. 'Well I'll be! Simon offered him ... oh, I don't know how much.'

'Nice to know some people can't be bought. At least not easily.'

'Yeah,' Rob agreed. 'It is.'

'Lyn ... Lyn never lost touch with her. Did you know that?'

Rob shook his head, wondering. 'Lyn?'

'She told Lyn what happened the night Judith Allen died.'

'Judith?' he looked bewildered as though not sure what Marris meant. 'Judith,' he said again. 'She died. Drowned.'

'You tried to save her.'

'I failed.' Rob closed his eyes.

'Rob, stay with me, I need to know why you lied. You and Anna. In your statement to the police, you said you saw her on the bridge and that she was alone. That Judith jumped. And that she was alone.'

Rob nodded. He opened his eyes and studied Marris as though seeing him for the first time.

'They knew that wasn't true, Rob, the officers that investigated at the time, did you know that? Judith was too drunk to have found her way anywhere alone. They must have practically carried her across the park. No way she could have stood on that

301

parapet and jumped. Rob, there was no way she could even have stood up alone.'

Rob blinked. 'Anna told you all this?'

'Anna and the police report. They knew someone else had been on the bridge with her. Think yourselves lucky you and Anna, that you had a witness to say it wasn't you.'

Rob blinked rapidly now, as though his brain switched into overdrive. 'Did the witness see who was on the bridge then?'

'No, he came on scene in time to see you run into the water. He helped Anna bring the boat to fish you out. Do you remember that? His name was Bradley Doyle. By the time he looked to see where Judith might have jumped from, there was no one on the bridge. Your friends ran away.'

'Jenny swore it was an accident. Pete backed her up. They were so drunk... They said they panicked when she fell.'

'Rob, think about it. She couldn't fall. To fall, you have to be able to stand up. Think about it. Anna says that you followed because you were worried about Judith. That you caught up with her and the others were up ahead. Did you see them? Was Judith walking under her own steam?'

'I don't...' He closed his eyes again, but this time not in an effort to escape from Marris, but to aid his vision. 'They were swaying about all over the place,' he said at last. 'Judith was between them. They were singing

302

and shouting and I thought they'd wake everyone up right over the other side of the park. Anna was sick, throwing up in the flowerbeds, and I called out her name. She looked like hell. When I looked at them again, they were on the bridge and Jude, she was sitting on the parapet and laughing. Then, suddenly, she slipped forward and I saw her fall. The water splashed upward in kind of slow motion. You know,' he asked Marris, 'that double time you sometimes get? Everything seems to happen very slowly and yet you know you can't stop it happening because it's all going too fast. Well it was like that. I saw her let go of the parapet and lean forward and then she fell, head first. She had her hands out and I thought for one stupid moment that she'd decided to dive off the bridge. Jez had done that in the summer, but he was sober and he could dive and he could see what he was heading into.

'And then I saw the splash and I knew she was far too pissed to know which way was up. God, she was bad when I left them all at the pub; I'd no idea how much she'd had after that. So, I went in after her.'

'Anna said she was standing on the parapet.'

Rob shook his head. 'I've rerun it over and over in my head. I dream it often enough. I see her face while we were both in the water, that strange look she had in her eyes.

Inspector, I could have saved her if she'd let me, I'm sure I could, but she kicked and scratched and hit me in the face and tried to pull me down. I had to let go or they'd have been looking for two corpses in the river and not just one. I let go and I fought my way back to the surface, though by that time I wasn't even sure which way was up. I dived again and again until Anna and that chap with the boat arrived. I could hardly get my breath by then.' He paused and shook his head. 'It was so damn cold. I mean, warm September day and a nice evening ... who'd have thought the water could be that cold?'

'And when did you decide not to mention Jenny and Steve?'

Rob frowned. 'They took me to the hospital in an ambulance. I thought I'd never get warm again. I'd swallowed a lot of river, so they gave me a tetanus shot, kept me in overnight. The police came but I wasn't making much sense, I don't think. They told me afterwards I was crying like a baby.

'In the morning, the police came back again, this young officer in a uniform that looked too big around the neck. He read this statement out that Anna had made. It said she hadn't seen anyone else on the bridge. That Judith and the others had been drinking but then Jenny and Pete went off home and she and Jude argued. Jude ran off and Anna followed with me following

304

behind them.

'I just agreed that it was right. I couldn't understand what she was doing, but I went along with it. I suppose I thought that it was bad enough us being involved and nothing could change the fact that Judith was dead. I kept telling myself that they were drunk, that they'd never do anything deliberately and I assumed that Anna must have her reasons for letting them off the hook.'

'And did she give her reasons? Did she tell you about them?'

'No.'

'Oh. But you're going to, aren't you? Rob, not to put too fine a point on it, if you don't tell me now, I can arrange for you to tell your story formally, elsewhere.'

Rob swallowed hard and glanced around the little room. He didn't want to leave the security of it, not now. 'You can't do that. I'm a patient here.'

'You're here voluntarily. Rob, essentially you're a paying guest who's arranged for a bit of counselling and massage in with the price. That's it.'

'Oh, God.'

He turned his face towards the window and Marris wondered what he was seeing. His gaze didn't seem to penetrate the glass. It was focused on something much closer to the eye.

'Anna felt as responsible,' he said. 'She'd

bought the drinks, watched as Jenny just kept filling Jude's glass. She said, at first, that it was funny, seeing prim, proper little Judith losing control, she said she was all over Pete and Jenny encouraged it. She said she could see it was getting nasty, but she didn't know how to make it stop. She said, if she hadn't thrown up and I hadn't called her to wait for me, she'd have been on the bridge with Judith and the others and she might have been able to stop her.'

'Or,' Marris suggested, 'she might have been standing there, urging her on.'

Chapter Forty

It was late on the Saturday afternoon but Marris didn't want to lose momentum. He arranged with the local constabulary to have Pete and Jenny Walters brought in for questioning and, in response to the question did he want things kept low key, Marris suggested not.

'I want the pressure on,' he said. 'Uniform and a marked car. Apparently the next door neighbours babysit, so that might be best. I don't want the kids upset more than they have to be.'

'Fat chance of that,' Gina observed.

'Mummy and Daddy get taken off in a police car and you expect them to be sanguine about it?'

Marris considered. 'If I thought they were old enough to understand "sanguine" then I'd give the question due consideration,' he said. 'I've made arrangements to reduce the level of trauma. They'll have familiar faces around.'

'Familiar faces aren't going to help if you arrest mum or dad for killing someone,' Willets observed. He looked genuinely horrified at the thought.

'Most killers are someone's parents,' Marris told him firmly. 'Somebody's parent and someone's child. That's the way of the world. Gina, you've got Mr Walters. Happy with that?'

'Would it make a difference if I wasn't?'

'No.'

'Then I'm happy.' She paused and studied Marris, her head tilted on one side, red curls spilling onto her shoulder. 'You think they killed Judith's mother?'

Marris nodded.

'How? Why? Anna told the mother who they were? The mother tracked them down?'

'Anyway, that's problem number two. Problem number one is to get some answers on what happened to Judith Allen. Did she fall, was she pushed or might she as well have been?'

It was another hour before the Walters arrived, protesting, furious, threatening Marris with publicity and complaints to his superiors.

Marris took no notice of the threats, he expected no less; was encouraged, in fact, by just how rattled Pete, in particular, seemed. Jenny's face was congested, red, the pale skin flushed with blood. 'I want a solicitor,' she said. 'I know my rights.'

Marris nodded. 'Do you have a solicitor? If not, then we'll see a duty officer is made available. You might have to wait a little while.'

She nodded briefly. 'I'll wait,' she said. 'So will Pete. We're saying nothing until then.'

'As you like,' Marris said. He directed that the couple be taken to separate interview rooms and then arranged for a duty solicitor. Then, knowing that, as he'd told Jenny Walters, this would take some time, he went back to his cupboard of an office and brought his paperwork up to date.

He was told it would take another two hours for the solicitor to arrive. 'Tell them to take their own sweet time,' Marris said. 'I'm in no rush.'

At eight fifteen the duty solicitor arrived and Marris saw to it that he was given a cup of tea and some background and a few minutes' sit down before he went in to offer his professional advice. Then, as Jenny had been dealt with first, he joined the solicitor and his client in interview room three. He set up the tape and annotated those present. Himself, Jenny Walters, the solicitor, Calvin Andrews, and a female constable.

'Are you charging my client with anything?'

'Not yet, no. She's merely helping with enquiries.'

'Then she's not been cautioned?'

'Of course not.' Marris sounded disturbed. 'No arrest has been made. Mrs. Walters was simply invited here to answer some more of my questions.'

'Invited!' Jenny spat. 'You sent a car round, a police car. You upset my kids. My neighbours will wonder what the hell is going on, you...'

'I couldn't help but notice,' Marris interrupted her, 'that when I came to see you earlier today, you were distracted by the need to watch your children. I thought if I brought you and your husband here to a, let's say, quieter environment, you might be a little more able to give full attention to my enquiries.'

'I said all I wanted to say. I wasn't there. I don't have any more to say.'

'You weren't where when?' Marris asked innocently.

Jenny scowled at him.

Marris waited. He had a lined notepad in

front of him. He wrote on it 'where' and then 'when'. Then he riffled through the file he had brought with him as though looking for something. 'Ah,' he said finally. 'It must have been a bit of a shock when Mrs Allen came back into your life, especially making all those accusations? I can understand that you must have felt, shall we say, peeved by the whole matter. Especially as you thought you'd got away free and clear. After all, Anna Freeman lied for you, didn't she?'

'I don't know what you mean.'

'She told the local police that you were nowhere near the bridge when Judith jumped, slipped, was pushed. Whichever it was. Rob apparently backed her up. They had their reasons I know, though I happen to think that Rob, at least, was misguided. Both now confess that they lied. You and Pete, you were both there.'

'What makes you think they're telling the truth now?' Jenny was scathing.

'Because their stories tally. Detail for detail.'

'So? They got together, made it up.'

'The way you and Pete did? What did you tell Mrs Allen? That they were lying? Or that Anna was, at any rate. Did she threaten to expose you? That must have been painful. Mr and Mrs Respectable, nice house, obligatory number of kids. You must have been scared witless.'

Jenny continued to glare.

'But then,' Marris continued, 'it's not easy to have any sympathy for you on that score, not thinking how scared Judith Allen must have been once she hit the water, or Maria Warner must have been when she saw the knife, or Lyn Chapel must have been when she saw an old friend turn into something far less pleasant. Or Mrs Allen must have been the night you broke into her house, coming downstairs and finding you there? Shock enough. What happened, Jenny, did she try to call the police? Back you into a corner? It must have been a relief to find yourself in the kitchen, see the knife block, grab the knife. I can imagine the feeling of power that must have given you. You being armed and Mrs Allen being...'

'Are you accusing my client of all or any of these crimes?'

Jenny's legal eagle seemed to have remembered he had a job to do. Marris was amazed he'd been able to go so far.

'I'm inviting your client to speculate,' he said mildly.

He picked up the folder and notepad, tapped them together on the desk, arranging the pages so they all levelled up satisfactorily, then he pushed back his chair and stood up.

'I suggest we get on to your next client,' he told the solicitor. 'I'll see Mrs Walters has a cup of tea while she's waiting.'

'What?' Jenny exchanged a look with her legal advisor. 'That's it?'

'Unless you've anything more to say,' Marris told her. 'I'm going to have a chat with your husband now, I'm sure he'll be interested to know what we've been discussing.'

'We've discussed nothing,' Jenny objected.

'No? I thought we'd come to something of an understanding.'

Jenny looked baffled.

'Look,' Marris said, laying his documents back on the table and leaning towards Jenny Walters, 'it'll be a relief for him, after all this time. It isn't nice, having to live with a lie. Especially a deceit of that magnitude. It must play on the mind, don't you think?'

Then he left. Behind him, as he closed the door, he could hear Jenny Walters demanding to see her husband; the solicitor trying to calm her down.

Marris retreated to his office once again, confident that it would take a while for the situation to cool. More time for Pete Walters to sweat and Jenny to fume.

Chapter Forty-One

Marris had never kept normal hours. It was after two when he finally left work, having seen the Walters off home. Jenny's temper had not improved but she had subsided into a sullen silence that Marris made bets would end as soon as she got Pete alone.

The idea of going home didn't enter his head. He wanted to talk to Anna Freeman and the fact that it was well after two a.m. was no deterrent to that.

Marris liked to drive at night. He'd learnt to drive in the evenings, his father taking him out after work. The idea of paying for lessons not occurring to either of them ... not that they could have afforded them anyway. Marris enjoyed the peace of near empty roads, shadows and dirty sodium vying for control of the pavement. Shift workers driving home or scurrying along, eager for their beds. No clubbers here; he was several streets away from the nearest nightlife. He wondered if the hotel had a night porter, decided on basis of size it probably did, drove into the car park, the only thing in motion; the only thing stupid enough still to be awake.

Or not? The fox paused, one light foot

raised, frozen motion as it stared at him. Well fed, fat bodied, sleek, long tail streaming behind as it moved on again. A last look at the man in black and then a dive into the bushes as though deciding he might not be as innocent after all.

Marris smiled.

'Have you any idea what time it is?' Anna had taken time to brush her hair but her face was still flushed from sleep.

'It's a little after three,' Marris told her.

She opened her mouth to make further protest and then decided she couldn't be bothered. Instead, she seated herself in one of the two chairs and indicated to Marris that he should do the same. 'OK, what is it you want?'

'I've been talking to Jenny and Pete,' he said.

'What? At this time of night? I hope you get decent overtime rates.'

Marris considered. He actually applied for payment on about half of his overtime. For the rest, he was lucky if he got time off in lieu; time he rarely ever took. 'I had them brought in for questioning,' he elaborated.

'What? About Judith?'

'There's something of a list, isn't there?' Marris reminded her. 'Judith Allen, Maria Warner, Lyn and, of course, Mrs Margaret Allen.'

'What?' She stared at him. 'I don't under-stand.'

Marris brought her up to speed. Anna was leaning forward in her seat, staring hard. She had, Marris understood, come here because of Judith. No matter what had happened since, it was that night when Judith Allen had died that dominated her thoughts, had driven every decision she had made in her life for the past decade. He doubted she had looked at the bigger picture until now. She had of course known that it was there, that there would be ripples, but, even after she had been told about Maria Warner and then Lyn Chapel, she still hadn't made the full connection. Until now.

Marris watched her face pale and her eyes fill with tears. She leaned back in her chair and gnawed at her lower lip. Had she been alone, he guessed she would have drawn up her knees and hugged them to her, curled up in the too small chair. Only his presence and the thin nightdress with equally flimsy gown prevented her now.

'The letter I sent, it killed her, didn't it?'

'That's a massive leap,' Marris told her.

'Is it? You made it. You've guessed that the letter prompted her to find them, challenge Jenny.'

And we don't know for sure that Jenny killed her. It is one possibility. One of many.'

'Oh? And what others do you have?'

'These may be unrelated crimes.'

Anna's laugh was harsh and derisive. 'Oh sure. Look, they were there that night. I might have lied to the police back then and, yes, Rob was right about my reasons. I'm not proud of it. I'll have to live with it and I'm going to have to take the consequences now, aren't I? But I swear, I'm not lying to you now.'

'Rob tells me Judith was sitting on the parapet, not standing.'

She frowned and shook her head. 'No, I'm sure ... I saw her, she was on the parapet, she tipped forward, she...'

'Since you're swearing to things, would you swear to that?' The look of resentment that crossed her face said 'you're not taking me seriously enough. I'm suffering here' but Marris was unconcerned. The living, so far as he was concerned, still had the chance to work things out for themselves, to retry and to get it right second time around. The dead no longer had that option.

'I don't know,' she said finally. 'I've been sure all these years, but now...'

'And what makes you less certain?'

'Well, what Rob said. I ... he was always good at remembering.'

'And, maybe the idea you've held onto all these years, that it's easier to push someone, to nudge them off balance when they're standing on a narrow ledge than it is if they're sitting down.'

Again, she opened her mouth to deliver a swift retort, then shut it again. She shook her head. 'She was on the bridge; she fell forward into the water, that's all I know. I don't believe she jumped. I've never believed she jumped.'

Marris nodded. 'We've got to put belief aside and see what we can prove. The courts are not interested in what you might believe.'

Chapter Forty-Two

Marris drove home via a little café he knew that opened all night. The usual clientele being delivery drivers and those whose shifts started when the daytime world was napping. It was a regular haunt, first discovered when Marris himself had been an incumbent of that world, working his way through university to supplement his basic grant.

He shuddered to think how many years had passed since then.

Gina, who swore she never saw him eat enough and who worried about him when he tightened his belt yet another notch, would have been astonished to view Marris partaking of the full English – with extra bacon and black pudding.

Jim, proprietor since Marris first became a customer, eyed him with interest.

'Late night or early morning, mate?'

'Bit of both.'

'No change there then. I saw you on the telly. Funny, you know, we've got one of that bloke's pictures hanging in our lounge and I said to the wife, when we saw that thing on the telly, that doesn't look like her.'

Marris nodded, but made no comment. None was expected. Jim, once set in motion could talk for both of them. This morning, however, Jimmy's Café was busy and Marris retreated with his breakfast and pot of tea, sitting where he could watch both the counter and the door.

From time to time, Jim would point him out to the passing trade collecting bacon cobs or the breakfast band descending for a sit down and a cup of tea. Marris was used to being a local point of interest and it no longer bothered him. Jimmy reckoned his custom kept trouble away and Marris could be certain that, however many times they looked, the clientele would leave him well alone.

As an arrangement, it worked just fine.

So, what was he to make of things now? He'd have appreciated the opportunity to talk things through. Gina, Willets, one of the others on his team, but in lieu of reality, he thought he could predict anyway what Gina might say.

'He did it, or she did. Maybe both. He can't not know. He covered for her.'

'Why not the other way around? He committed the murder and Jenny covered for him.'

No.' Gina would emphatically disagree. 'She wears the trousers. He'd cover for her but he'd never have the backbone to do it himself.'

He figured she'd be right. He imagined Gina, tucked up in bed with her off and on partner. Maybe. Maybe she'd just crashed alone, exhausted enough to fall, as he knew she had before, still into her clothes, pull the duvet round her and sleep. Then wake later, shower and crawl back into bed.

He thought about phoning her, suggest they meet for lunch and discuss ... but no. People had lives, he reminded himself. What more was there to say? The investigation was in motion now, the chief suspects upset and off balance, the chief witnesses the same – Marris didn't believe in letting anyone get too comfortable. He'd do best to go home, pick up the morning papers on the way and then catch up on some sleep himself. About a week's worth.

Marris wandered back to his car. No market today. No early crowds. No noise. He picked up a selection of the early editions on his way and dumped the papers on the front passenger seat of the car. The top one caught his eye.

Tragic Anna Returns followed by the story that Anna was back in the country, in a police safe house being kept apart from her one time friends such as Joe Sykes.

Marris wasn't surprised to find that the paper was the same as had carried Joe's story the week before.

Neither was he entirely surprised to find that, according to the same paper, he had reopened an investigation into the tragic – they seemed fond of that particular adjective – death of young Judith Allen, a suspected suicide.

Joe had brought them up to speed on that then. Marris smiled. He wondered what Sunday paper the Walters read and if he should have a copy sent round.

Chapter Forty-Three

Monday rolled around, but by mid morning a fax arrived that gave the day a sense of direction. Mrs Allen's elderly relative had been found and Milly Havers had agreed to see Marris that morning. The residential home she lived in was an hour's drive away. Marris grabbed Gina Lees and set out.

Oakfield Park was a purpose built, concrete lump of a building, unprepossessing at first glance. Inside though, Marris was surprised to find that it had been built around three sides of a square, enclosing a large and attractive courtyard garden onto which all the rooms opened. The fourth side led out onto a lawn, safely fenced and surrounded by trees.

Milly Havers waited for them in the residents' lounge, television in one corner, residents chatting and playing cards settled in small groups. She sat in a high-backed chair looking out of the window, watching the birds encouraged by strings of nuts and fat-filled coconut shells. A Zimmer frame stood within easy reach and her swollen feet rested on a bright red stool.

'I hope you don't mind if I don't get up?'

'Of course not,' Gina told her.

Marris was watching the birds. 'Coal tits,' he said.

Milly Havers smiled. 'That's right. We get a nice selection. I love to watch them.' She leaned forward slightly and told him confidentially. 'It's often more interesting than the television.'

Gina fetched chairs and they sat down close to the old lady. 'Pass me that, will you, dear?' She pointed to a straw bag on a nearby table from which knitting needles protruded.

'Thank you.' She rummaged. Brought forth a much creased envelope from which she withdrew an equally creased letter, three or four sheets long. 'This is what you came to see,' she said. 'Do you know how long I've waited for someone to take this seriously?'

Marris opened the letter and read, Gina leaning in to share, close enough for him to smell her shower gel and the lick of perfume she wore. Anna's account had been almost word perfect. He wondered how many times she had written this in her head before committing it to paper; how many times since she had reviewed the words, telling herself it was for the best.

'Tell me what happened,' he said. 'When your niece got this letter, what did she do?'

Milly Havers sighed. 'You never think you'll outlive your children, do you? Margaret never thought she'd outlive hers. She just couldn't cope with it. The father left when Judith was a little thing and, so far as I know, he never came back, never got in touch either. It was just the two of them and a right struggle it was too. Margaret worked all hours and Judith often had to let herself in and start the dinner. But they made out well enough. We helped out all we could.

'I knew Judith was bullied at school, but

Margaret couldn't seem to get her to talk about it. She was just glad, as the girl got older, that she seemed to be making friends at last. She started to go out of a night to see them and I think Margaret felt she could begin to get a bit of her own life back.

'I was there the night the police came and told her Judith had died. She just fell apart. I went with her when they found the body and needed her to say it was poor Judith. She stood and looked at Judith's face as if she couldn't bear to say yes, that's her. In the end I said it for her. Yes, I said, that's our girl.

'Then the funeral. Those two that came to the funeral, that boy that grew into the artist and changed his name and that girl, Anna,' she spat the second name; the taste of the words bitter on her tongue. 'Margaret was grateful! Grateful! Oh, I don't blame the lad, the police said he nearly drowned trying to save our girl, but her!

'Margaret were just getting over it when that letter arrived. We never believed our girl killed herself, but we could accept that she'd slipped. An accident, we could just about deal with. We've all been young, all been stupid; the shame of it is that Judith didn't have long enough to grow out of her stupidity. That's what's hard. And to have that girl claiming someone pushed her to her death. That was the hardest of all.'

'What did she do? When the letter arrived, what did Margaret do?'

Milly nodded, thinking about it all. 'I'd given up my house and moved into a care home. It was a nice place, not as nice as this, but small and clean. I was having trouble walking, you see, and then I fell and broke me leg in three places. It's not been right since. They said I had osteo ... osteoporosis and that another break could be right serious so I sold up and got somewhere where I could be looked after. She came to see me that day the letter came. Frantic, she was, and I told her, go to the police. Mebbe there's nothing in it, mebbe there is but you got to find out. I think that's what did it. Me saying she'd got to find out but I never thought she'd do it the way she did. Somehow, she found out where that pair were living and she went to see them.'

'Jenny and Pete Walters?'

'They'd got married. Got a little girl and another on the way. Margaret said she showed them the letter, well, a copy of it anyway. I asked the office at the old home if they'd copy it for her. Told them it was something official, not that they minded, they were good sorts. I kept the original.'

'What made you do that?'

'Oh,' Milly shrugged, 'I don't think it was a decision I made, it just got left in the photocopier. Margaret was in a right state and didn't notice.'

'Did she tell you how they reacted, the Walters?'

'She phoned me. Said he was scared and they'd started arguing with one another, made the baby cry. Jenny threw her out and told her if she came near again she'd be sorry.' Millie paused and pursed her lips, compressing them until they blued. 'She'd said Judith was better off dead. That losers like that didn't have a future.'

She fell silent. Remembering.

'What did Margaret do after that?' Gina asked softly.

'Exactly what she did she's taken to the grave with her, but I know she wouldn't let up. On one day she stood outside their place, shouting that they'd killed her daughter. The police came and took her away. She knocked on doors and told anyone who'd listen. She wrote to the papers, I know that, but...' she shrugged. 'It never got her anywhere. I remember reading in the local paper after she was dead something about tragedy striking twice, but that were all.'

'You showed this letter to the police?'

She nodded. 'They knew all about it anyway, from the complaints they'd had. They said they wanted to talk to this Anna about it but no one knew where she'd gone. I knew she'd said something to Margaret about relatives in Leeds, but I didn't know no more and when I suggested they try and talk to Rob Cartwright, or Carr or whatever he started calling himself, they didn't seem that interested.'

'Did Margaret feel threatened? You said Jenny threatened her, did she take it seriously?'

'I think she was beyond feeling scared,' Milly told him. 'She had one thing in her head and that was finding out the truth.' She paused thoughtfully. 'No, it wasn't even that. It was getting them to admit they'd killed Judith. You know, I think, bitter as the pill might be, the idea that Judith had been murdered, once she'd swallowed it, it poisoned her and there was no cure anywhere but getting them to admit to it.'

Chapter Forty-Four

'What have we got?' Marris asked, though the question was rhetorical. 'We have the suspicions of an elderly lady. We have circumstantial evidence which any good lawyer would dispose off in two seconds flat and we have nothing to connect either of them to any of the crime scene apart from a possible blonde hair.'

'You could get a warrant, search the premises, take DNA samples,' Gina suggested.

Marris nodded. 'I spoke to the super-intendent this morning, he thinks we've got just cause, but he'd like more. I told him I was going out to talk to Milly. He's sympathetic; I'm hoping the letter will make our case.'

'And there are witnesses to the death of Judith Allen.'

'Which location we can't even classify as a crime scene and which witnesses can't agree on a pretty crucial point. Again, any half way decent lawyer...'

'So,' Gina asked, 'what now?' She added, 'I wish you'd let me drive.'

'And why is that then?'

'You know why. You drive slower than my grandma. It is still seventy on the motorway, you know.'

'And I like to think when I drive.'

'You can't think and drive?'

'No. I can't think and drive.'

'Another reason you should let me do it.'

'I'm a terrible passenger, remember that.'

'How could I forget? You brake sooner than I do. I always expect to find your hand on the stick first when I'm changing gear.

'So, better that I drive then?'

Gina didn't answer, she was nagging at their problem. 'You think she's worried enough yet?'

'Worried enough for what?'

'To give herself away somehow. She ain't going to confess, no way no how.'

'Ain't? Where did you scrape up your English.' He sighed. They were stuck behind a car driving even more slowly than Marris. Reluctantly, he checked his mirrors, indicated, checked his mirrors again and pulled out. Gina, peering over at the speedometer, noted that he just topped seventy in order to overtake. She waited until he'd pulled back across before asking another question, taking to heart his statement that he couldn't think and drive.

'Wouldn't you like to bring her face to face with Anna Freeman?' she said.

'And that would achieve?'

'I don't know. Put them in a room, watch them fight it out.'

'It could be entertaining. Could also be a tad messy. But I'll tell you what I would like to do. I want to get them all together, Hercule Poirot style.'

'Who? What? Oh, the Agatha Christie guy.' She laughed, 'But aren't you supposed to be able to point the finger and say, "Jennifer Walters, you are the killer. Take her away constable!"'

'I think it might add to the pressure,' he argued. All these years, since Judith's death, the Walters have been allowed to live quietly and get on with their lives. To pretend nothing bad ever happened. Except when

328

Margaret Allen appeared and carried out her one woman campaign. And now, with the reappearance of Anna Freeman, first the substitute Anna and now the genuine article, all that's changed.

'If we're right, each time something happened to threaten them, Jenny, or possibly Pete, though, like you I'm inclined towards Jenny, was forced into action. Or, should we say, reaction. My guess is, we keep the pressure on, she'll feel compelled to act again.'

'Surely she wouldn't be that blatant?'

'I don't know. I suspect she might. Or that we might apply so much pressure that Pete breaks on her. He's the weak link in this chain, I'm sure of it.'

'If Jenny was forced to take action, that could be dangerous.'

'It could, yes. Especially for Anna. We discussed that when I saw her on Saturday night. Well, Sunday morning as it was by then.'

'You what? You never said.'

'I didn't think you'd appreciate the phone call at four in the morning.'

'Well, no. But you've had all today.'

'And I'm mentioning it now. I wanted to see what Milly had to say first. What did you think of her?'

'Um, genuine, sharp, reminded me of my Aunt May. I'm surprised no one took more notice at the time. After all, the death must still be unsolved and no one likes dead bodies cluttering up their statistics.'

She broke off and looked sideways at her boss. His sensibilities when it came to discussing the deceased could be unpredictable and thin skinned. She'd never heard him share in the black humour most of her colleagues employed to keep reality at bay. He didn't comment. Maybe he really couldn't think and drive. She played around with that as a slogan. 'Don't think and Drive. Think Kills'.

'Anna suggested she set up a meeting with Jenny. She offered to wear a wire.'

'She what?'

'She watches too many films.'

Gina laughed, glad to be off the hook. She relaxed too soon.

'I told her no.' Marris said. 'I told her we'd break this safely and that it was just a matter of time. I don't want any more dead people in my statistics either. Solved or unsolved.'

Chapter Forty-Five

It was a very public and deeply uncomfortable meeting, the park, by the bridge, all of those present who had been there on that night, even the man who'd helped Anna with the boat, Brad Doyle, who, by some strange quirk, still lived at the same address, worked at the same shop and drank at the pub he'd been leaving on that night.

This wasn't a public reconstruction of the crime and Marris had invited no media though the interest of passers by, stimulated by the strange goings-on in this most public of places, was inevitable.

The only major change was that this reconstruction was happening in broad daylight and not in the dead of night.

And the other difference was that the role of Judith had been taken by the red-haired DS Gina Lees.

Rob looked fragile. He pulled his coat close to his body and shivered, though the day was not especially cold. Simon danced attendance and Marris was, on balance, glad he was there. Rob looked ready to bolt.

Anna stood apart beside the female police constable he had appointed as her minder. The Walters were as far away as they could decently get without falling in the river. Pete Walters complained loudly about having to take the day off work; Jenny was silent. From time to time her gaze flicked across at Anna or at Rob. She resolutely kept her back turned away from the bridge.

Only the impartial witness, Brad Doyle, looked at ease, chatting amiably to Willets and examining the assembled company with ill concealed curiosity.

As well he might, Marris thought.

He stepped out onto the path and gestured everyone to gather round, which they did, though still maintaining as much personal space as they could decently acquire.

'Thank you for coming,' he said.

'You mean we had a choice?' Jenny snapped.

Marris ignored her.

'I'd like to reconstruct the events which led to Judith Allen's death almost eleven years ago. To help me, I have this letter. Some of you may recognise it.'

Anna looked away. Jenny's eyes were daggers. Pete seemed to have something stuck in his throat and his nervous cough was irritating Marris as much as it was getting to his wife. She nudged him in the ribs. That made it worse.

Rob ... well Rob was somewhere else, Marris thought.

He began to read. Not the whole letter, just those parts pertaining to the night in question. He paused. 'If you could take your positions, please?'

No one moved. Then Rob sighed and seemed to haul himself back into the present. 'I must have been down the path a little way.' He laughed uneasily. 'I hope this doesn't mean I have to take another dip?

No, all right. I was...' he walked a few paces back down the path, '...somewhere about here when I called to Anna to wait for me.'

Anna uncrossed her arms and stepped over to the flowerbed bordering the path. 'I,' she said laconically, 'was busy throwing my guts up about here.'

'We'd gone home,' Jenny protested. 'We weren't even around.'

Marris ignored her. 'Mr Doyle, can you give me some idea where you were when you first noticed something was wrong?'

'Um. Back that way, where the path bends. Only, I was walking across the grass.'

'Across the grass? Then,' Marris calculated, 'you would have had the bridge in view?'

Brad Doyle shrugged. 'I suppose I should have. To be honest, I'd had a few. I told the police at the time I'd had a row with my wife and stormed off out. While I was walking home I was a bit more concerned with how to apologise without actually saying sorry,' he grinned sheepishly and earned himself a telling laugh from Pete.

'When did you first realise something was wrong?'

'When I heard the young lady scream.' He pointed at Anna. 'She was running across here, the grass in front of me. He,' indicating Rob, 'was already in the water. Then I realised I'd heard a splash just before, but

I'd not taken much notice.' He frowned. 'No, it might have been I heard the splash first and then ... No, I heard the scream. You know, I might even have imagined I heard the splash.'

'If Anna screamed when Judith fell from the bridge,' Simon commented, 'then that would likely have masked the sound of her hitting the water.'

It was a sensible suggestion, Marris thought. He nodded.

'We weren't even here,' Jenny was insistent now. She plucked at Pete's arm and made to pull him away. 'We had gone before any of this happened. That's what they said in their statements at the time.'

'They lied,' Marris began, but Brad Doyle was shaking his head. 'No, you were there.'

'What, on the bridge?' Marris turned to look at him. Doyle's face was a picture of confusion and utter disbelief. 'It's only seeing everything again ... look. I didn't see you on the bridge, but you were on the path on the other side. Running.'

'Oh, this is stupid!'

Jenny grabbed Pete's arm this time and turned away from the others. She stormed off down the path towards where they'd parked their car, dragging her husband with her.

'Shall I go after them?' Willets asked.

'No, let them go. I've got someone waiting

by their car. Gina, I still want to take a look at that bridge.'

She nodded and headed away from them onto the bridge. Marris watched as she climbed up on the parapet and, sitting, swung her legs over the side. She clung tightly to the wall.

'It's a long way down!'

'Hang on then,' Marris shouted back. 'Is she in the right place?'

Anna nodded, so did Rob. He seemed fixated by the sight of the woman on the bridge. Fixated and disturbed.

'Was she standing, Anna?'

'I ... I'm not sure.'

'Gina.' Marris shouted, 'Any chance of you standing up?'

'No way,' she shouted back. 'You'd need to be a bloody gymnast.'

Marris signed to her to come down. He turned back to the assembly that remained.

'If you've anything to add, I'd like to know.'

Silence. Rob was staring at the water seeing the ghost of Judith's fall. Anna, hands plunged deep in the pockets of her coat, was staring at the ground. Bradley Doyle seemed even more confused.

'Bloody funny the way you remember things,' he said. 'If I think of anything else I'll let you know.'

Marris nodded and, having checked Doyle

had been given his number, he thanked him and shook his hand. 'You've been a great help,' he said. He turned his attention back to Rob. 'Best get him home,' he told Simon.

He reflected upon the fact, as Simon led Rob away, that the artist and his amanuensis, or muse, or whatever she had been, had not exchanged a single word.

'So, what happens now?' Anna questioned as she watched Rob go.

'You go back to the hotel. I've arranged an escort. I'll come and see you later but right now I've got a property to search.'

'Pete and Jenny's?'

Marris nodded

Anna sighed. 'Will this be over soon?'

Marris nodded. As over as it can be,' he promised.

Only Jenny had returned to the car. The officers detaining her had not seen Pete and she insisted he had simply gone on to work. 'We can't afford for him to miss a whole day when a half day is all this farce needed,' she told Marris icily. 'We have a mortgage to pay and children to care for. Now, why the hell are you detaining me?'

'One of my officers will take your car,' Marris told her. 'You can ride with me.' He reached into the grimy faded pocket inside his waxed coat and produced a document. 'This is a warrant,' he said. 'To search your

336

house and your car. You have the right to be there if you wish.'

'Damned right I'll be there. You'll pay for this, Inspector. Don't think you won't.'

Marris had put out a call that Pete Walters should be detained. At work should he actually be going there, or anywhere else he might turn up. He was angry with himself for not having thought of the couple separating; now an obvious misjudgment based on the impression that Peter Walters would make no move without permission from his wife. Presumably that permission had been given for him to leave.

Of course, he told himself, she might be simply telling the truth about where Pete had gone.

Jenny had fallen silent in the car, her expression dour and sullen. She said nothing on the drive, surrendered her keys without comment and, once at the house, turned on the television, took a seat on the plum-coloured sofa and doggedly ignored Marris and the eight officers who had entered her home behind him.

Marris posted a female officer on watch and then left her to it.

She made no move when they removed knives from her kitchen, jackets from the understair cupboard, letters from a drawer in her desk upstairs. Rooted through the boxes of children's toys. Took hair from the hairbrush to compare to that found in Maria Warner's flat.

'I'm going to want a DNA sample,' Marris told her, 'from both yourself and your husband. It would be helpful, also, to have samples from the children for the process of elimination. A mouth swab, that's all, nothing that will hurt them.'

He'd anticipated her response and was not surprised when she looked daggers at him and snarled. 'You leave my kids out of it. This is nothing to do with them.'

Marris sat down beside her on the sofa and stared at the television. Yet another house makeover programme. Someone was painting a wall the exact shade of fuchsia pink Lyn Chapel had used in the small front room. 'You see,' he said very softly, knowing she was clinging to his every word, even while she feigned indifference, 'that's where you're wrong. You've had to live with the death of Judith Allen all these years and, I do believe, it's affected everything you've done or thought or said. It has ruled your life one way or another. And I'm prepared to believe that Judith's death was a tragic accident or, at worst, a stupid prank that went too far. Manslaughter, at the very, very worst. Can you imagine how much of an effect it's going to have on your children if their mother turns out to be a murderer?'

He hadn't been prepared for her response. All self-control, all tight restraint vanished in a split second. She was on him with her hands clawed, nails biting into his face. She was fury itself, spitting like a cat, then howling with such a mix of despair and rage that it was terrible to hear.

So swift was her attack, so unexpected, that before he could respond he was on the floor, beneath her, curling into a defensive, foetal ball. Hands up to protect his face, he kicked out at her and tried to turn away from the clawing hands and biting teeth.

Then, relief and release. He opened his eyes and struggled to sit. Two officers held her. One had a pair of quick cuffs and had pinioned one wrist, then the second.

'Bloody hell, sir, you all right?'

Marris wasn't sure. He struggled to his feet and then felt behind him to locate the sofa, dropped down onto the soft velvet cushions. Blood ran into his eyes and a sudden awareness dawned, shut out by the rush of adrenalin until the moment had passed, of a pain in his left ear.

Willets appeared in the doorway, assessed the scene, disappeared and came back moments later with a first aid kit taken from one of the cars.

'Keep still,' he commanded. Marris felt him wipe the blood away from around his eyes. At least he could still see. The way she'd clawed at him, he was certain she'd been aiming for the eyes.

'What's she done?' He reached up a hand towards the source of the pain. Willets batted it down. 'Keep your fingers out, Guv, let me clean you up. I hope your tetanus shots are up to date.'

'Why, what's she bloody done?'

Willets grinned at him and continued to wield the antiseptic swabs. The smell of it invaded Marris's nasal passages and made him want to sneeze.

'She thinks she's Mike Tyson,' Willets grinned. 'She's bitten a chunk out of your flipping ear.'

Chapter Forty-Six

Marris was adamant he wasn't going to the hospital. He instructed Willets to patch him up and had Jenny Walters taken away.

At least we can get her for assaulting a police officer,' Willets said, trying to keep a straight face as he plastered Marris's ear and asked if he should put the missing bit on ice in case it could be reattached.

'Just clear it up off the floor and find me some aspirin,' Marris instructed sourly. He could imagine how he looked. A quick feel of the offending and offended ear advised him of just how unsuave he must appear. Half of it seemed to have been replaced by angular sticking plaster and it hurt like hell. He could feel that it was still bleeding beneath the dressing. The flesh around his eye was swelling, he could feel the pounding blood in his cheek and the tightening of his skin when he tried to blink.

'You really should see a doctor,' Willets said anxiously.

'What's up? Afraid I might sue you for malpractice?' Marris growled.

'It crossed my mind.'

Marris grimaced. 'Any sign of Pete Walters?'

'No. Not at work and no one's picked him up en route. Here, take these. They melt on your tongue.' Willets dug in his pocket and produced a pack of ibuprofen. It looked as battered from carrying as Marris's pack of cigarettes. Marris felt in his own pocket. 'Oh, look what she's gone and done.' He withdrew the flattened pack. Only one remained intact and that was bent almost double. He tried, unsuccessfully, to straighten it out but it broke along the crease, sprinkling shredded tobacco onto the floor.

'Bad for you anyway.'

'They are now.' He eyed the painkillers with suspicion then popped two into his mouth. They dissolved, leaving a powdery residue. Marris grimaced again. 'Check on Rob and Anna,' he instructed. 'Then drive me back to the station. I want to continue my chat with Mrs Walters.' He eased himself painfully off the sofa. His head was throbbing and his calf felt tender enough to have been kicked by something twice Jenny Walters' size. 'Better check up on Brad Doyle, too,' he said.

'Any particular reason?'

Marris thought about it. 'No,' he said. 'Just the way the bloody day is going.'

Jenny Walters had been processed and shut in a cell by the time Marris arrived. She was shouting and screaming, demonstrating a knowledge of obscenities that Marris would not have credited her with. 'Broad vocabulary,' he said. 'Her solicitor on his way?'

The duty sergeant shrugged. 'She didn't state a preference so we've summoned whoever's on the duty roster.'

Marris nodded. He'd stayed at the Walters' house long enough to sort out that the kids could stay with the neighbour who'd cared for them during the search until other arrangements were made. The youngest seemed oblivious to the fuss and circumstance but the elder one asked for her mother. She looked close to tears and Marris, not *au fait* with children anyway, didn't know what to tell her. One more casualty, he thought and suddenly could comprehend the level of Jenny Walters' anger.

Not that it made his ear and face any less painful.

He closed his baggy eyes for a moment, listening to Jenny's string of obscenities and wondering how much more complicated it was going to get.

'You OK?' The duty sergeant was scrutinising him.

'I'm OK.'

'Who patched you up?'

'Oh, this is Geordie Willets's handiwork.'

'You seen yourself?'

'Not yet.' Marris tried to smile but found it hurt too much. 'I'm saving that treat. Let me know when the legal eagle arrives.'

Anna felt flat. That was the word for it. Flat. Squished like a swatted fly. Only difference being that a fly would have been long past pain and she still hurt so much. It didn't help, she thought, that it was partly self-inflicted pain.

Pain was pain.

Seeing the bridge again brought memories back into such sharp focus. Demanded a payment in gilt-edged guilt over and above that which she had already made. And she hadn't even begun to mourn for Lyn, had been forced to put that loss aside for the moment even though Lyn had been the

most constant, faithful and loving of friends
– on occasion the bluntest too, Anna
reminded herself. She had never been one to
spare the – verbal – rod, to spoil this particular child. It struck Anna, not for the first
time, just how much older than herself Lyn
had always seemed. Lyn had mothered her,
organised, persuaded and cajoled as was
necessary for all of Anna's adult life. She felt
the loss now, like she had not felt loss since
her parents died.

She lay on the bed and thought about Rob.
He'd barely looked at her. Though Marris
had warned her that he'd been ill and he
might not feel up to talking, the keenness of
his silence seemed more than personal.

Why the hell had she come? It had seemed
to make perfect sense at the time but now...
She could have left well alone. Marris would
have fixed things up eventually or, if not
Marris, someone else. So far as she could
see, Anna herself had just complicated
matters. Once more looking for absolution,
she had created yet another mess.

Her passport was in the drawer beside the
bed and there was only one bag to pack. She
could be up and away from here in no time
flat. Lose herself again but, this time, keep
no contacts. Neither family nor friends.

Her reverie was interrupted by a knocking
at the door. Puzzled, she got up and opened
it.

Pete Walters stood on the threshold.

She stepped back, startled, and he came inside. Closed the door behind him.

'What the hell are you doing here?'

'I wanted to talk.'

'How did you find my room?'

'I told them at the desk that I was a police officer, waved my railcard at them. They didn't look. People never really look at things, do they?'

Anna took another step back. There was a phone on the bedside table. Could she reach it?

Pete stepped around her, blocking her way.

'I want you to leave,' she said, trying to keep her voice from shaking.

'We never wanted you to come back. Just shows, we can't always get what we wanted. It was all right when we thought you'd done your disappearing act. Left the scene. Rob Carr never did more than send us bloody Christmas cards anyway, so he was no bother.' He laughed. 'Half the time he's off his head anyway. But you, little Miss Self Righteous.'

'I lied for you,' Anna reminded him. 'On the original police statement, Rob and I both lied.'

'So why change things now? That's what we can't understand. Why get all self-righteous and want to change things again?'

345

'Did you kill her? That kid pretending to be me?'

Pete shrugged. 'Not me,' he said. 'Though I was there. We knew it wasn't you but we couldn't be sure what Rob might have told her. What she might have known or at least, thought she knew.'

'Nothing!' Anna yelled at him. 'She was an actress. What could she possibly have known? Rob and I were never sure. Rob is still convinced that Judith fell, that's why he went along with the lie. He didn't want anyone blamed for what was just a tragedy.'

'But you, you believed it was Jen and me?'

'I. Didn't. Know.' She punctuated her words between gritted teeth. 'I saw her fall. I saw the two of you there. I knew what we'd all done. She was blind drunk, Pete, and we behaved like... You kill me, they'll know who did it.'

'It doesn't matter.'

'The police are with Jenny now, they've gone to search your place.'

'Even better. They'll be with her so they'll know she couldn't have got to you. Once you're dead, they won't look for anyone else.'

Anna backed away. 'I don't understand. You'll take the rap for her? Did you kill Lyn too?'

'Lyn! All these years making out like she was a friend. Then she calls that night, says

346

she knows what happened to Judith and it's time we all came clean. Like it was for her to decide. Jen went to talk to her but she wouldn't change her mind.'

'So Jenny killed her too?' Anna couldn't believe what she was hearing. 'But why, even if it did come out about Judith, about you being there, we were all kids, stupid bloody kids who'd had too much to drink and taken a joke too far. We didn't murder anyone!'

Pete just looked at her as though her words made no real sense. 'You have to protect those you love,' he said simply. 'We decided the kids need their mother more, so, I'm doing this to protect what's mine. I'll leave her and disappear for a while. We both know how possible that is. Later, Jenny will bring the kids and we'll get on with our lives again.'

'You're off your heads, the pair of you.'

Pete was advancing slowly across the room and Anna, backing up towards the wall, was running out of places to run. In some half frozen slow motion time she watched as he drew the knife from the kangaroo pocket of his windcheater, pointing it towards her as he continued to advance. And then her back touched the wall and she knew she couldn't retreat any further. She closed her eyes, waiting for the knife to pierce her skin.

Then it was all over. Pete was pinioned between two officers, the knife was on the floor and DS Gina Lees was cradling Anna in her arms.

'You OK?'

'Where were you?' Anna yelled at her. She had begun to cry. Reaction and pure relief. 'I thought you'd forgotten me. I thought I was going to die.'

Epilogue

Anna stood in Robert Carr's studio examining the triptych. It was finished now, the figures he had painted in the shadows, watching, but at first unidentified, now had faces. Pete and Jenny and Judith stared back at her, watched as she walked away from the painted image of Rob himself. In the distance, at the end of the road, standing on a bridge behind which was mist and even greater shadow, was Lyn. He had captured them all, pinned them down and, Anna hoped, for the moment at least, been able to switch off that screen that flickered before his eyes and obscured this world, the real, living breathing world, from view.

'It's wonderful,' she said. 'But Rob, it'll never sell. I can't imagine anyone wanting to live with it.' Or maybe, she thought, that was exactly the point.

'I can't believe Marris set you up like that. You could have been killed.'

'I told him I'd do anything. I pestered him, not the other way around. And there were police officers waiting in the next room. Gina was in contact with the front desk. They knew who they were looking for.'

'So why not arrest him then?'

'On what charge? Visiting an old friend?'

'He had the knife on him.'

'True, but we didn't know for sure. That way...'

Rob signed. 'You're really leaving?'

She looked down at the holdall lying on the floor between them. 'Yeah, but I'll be back. We've got to have our day in court, remember.' She grinned suddenly. 'Have you seen Marris's ear? He looks like an old tomcat.'

'An emaciated old tomcat,' Rob agreed.

'Look, I'd better go. I didn't want to fly out of here without seeing you, but I've got a taxi waiting.'

He nodded. 'Thanks for dropping by.'

She picked up the bag and then, standing on tiptoe to exaggerate their difference in height, she kissed him, first on the cheek and then on the mouth.

Rob watched as she walked away, opening and then closing his heavy studio door.

Dreamtime, he thought. He was always kissing Anna goodbye.

The publishers hope that this book has given you enjoyable reading. Large Print Books are especially designed to be as easy to see and hold as possible. If you wish a complete list of our books please ask at your local library or write directly to:

Magna Large Print Books
Magna House, Long Preston,
Skipton, North Yorkshire.
BD23 4ND

This Large Print Book, for people
who cannot read normal print,
is published under the auspices of

THE ULVERSCROFT FOUNDATION